# MURDA IN MY EYES

# MURDA IN MY EYES

## BOOK 1

### HAVOK

**Murda in My Eyes, Book 1**
**ISBN:** 979-8-9911412-0-8
**Imprint:** Havok with the Pen Productions



This novel is a work of fiction. Any resemblances to real people,
living or dead, actual events, establishments, organizations,
or locales are intended to give the fiction a sense of reality.
Other names, characters, places, and incidents are either products
of the author's imagination or are used fictitiously.

**Author:** Havok
Havok with the Pen Productions
PO Box 904
Bronx, NY 10455
Email: havokwiththepen@gmail.com
havokwiththepenproductions.com

**Publishing Services by:** Al-Saadiq Banks
**Edited by:** True 2 Life Media Conglomerate LLC  c/o Shaun Sinclair
**Email:** alsaadiqbanks@aol.com
P.O. Box 8722
Newark, New Jersey 07108
**For Editing and Typesetting Services**

*This book is dedicated to one person,*
*the only person to ever completely*
*capture my heart and soul,*
*and even more valuable, my mind.*
*My wife Iisha.*
*You are everything to me,*
*and words cannot express the love,*
*admiration and respect I have for you.*
*This book is just the beginning*
*of me keeping my word to you.*
*I love you Queen*

# CHAPTER 1

Darkness had finally descended on a cloudless NYC sky, and accompanying the stark blackness like evil twins were the all too familiar factors plaguing and thriving in most ghettos across America: violence and crime. If there was one neighborhood in the Bronx where these ingredients of chaos seemed especially embedded in the soil, it was the Soundview Housing projects, better known as "The View". Lifelong resident, Naseem Royal, could attest to this fact in ways most couldn't.

As the undisputed leader of a ruthless clique called M.B.A.M, Naseem was thoroughly acquainted with violence and crime on a level most would classify as psychotic. His lack of fear in abusing either of the two to elevate financially or otherwise, was the main reason an O.G. from "The View" named Killa T, had given him the nickname, Menace. On this humid summer night, it also happened to be the reason he found himself dressed in all black, posted up in the backyard of an abandoned Bronx tenement. Standing at an even 6'1" with a muscular build, and a chocolate complexion defaced by numerous scars, his overall demeanor oozed sinister intent. His eyes were glued to a property across the street, and for the past two hours he'd been awaiting the arrival of its owner, a man named, Lotto.

If Lotto's name by itself didn't indicate his probable financial status, then the home allegedly belonging to him should have, but it didn't. On the contrary, the modest looking 3-story home appeared better suited to accommodate a middle-class family rather than a man of Lotto's stature. There was even a forest green minivan parked in the driveway and swing set out front. Menace knew from an associate of his having previously visited the premises, the setup was an illusion of sorts, intended to deter people from paying too close attention. Still, he couldn't deny the unsettling pang developing in his gut as he glanced at his black g-shock for what seemed like the tenth time in the past hour. The neon digits glowed 3:17 am, and once again, he considered calling it a night. If it had been anybody else, he would've done just that long ago. Something though told him Lotto was different

Supposedly, Lotto was a major trick, well-known throughout NYC strip clubs for his multicolored fleet of Range Rovers, and lavish spending habits. This was evidenced not only by the money he blew in the club, but the extravagant gifts he bestowed on the strippers lucky enough to occupy his bed.

Rosez had been one of them. She was the associate who'd supplied the intel on Lotto, and after a week of surveillance with nothing to show for it, Menace was eager to reap the fruits of his labor. The sentiment was shared by his right-hand man, Crisis, seated on a crate a few feet away.

From a physical standpoint, Crisis was the opposite of Menace. At 5'7" with a slim, almost effeminate build, he was anything but intimidating. One glimpse into his hazel eyes, though, revealed a reality a few individuals had discovered far too late. Crisis was a demon, a straight serial killer. To his friends, he was known for being a ladies' man. One of his most distinguishing features were his braids, which reached the middle of his back. Chicks were always asking to do his hair, and usually, Crisis ended up doing *them.* Menace had witnessed the scenario more times than he could count, being that they were childhood friends. Their father's had been best friends too, which seemed to solidify their bond almost from the start.

Presently, there was nothing even remotely friendly about the expression Crisis wore. His eyes were actually closed, and he was tightly gripping the cross on his rosary beads, while muttering in Spanish. He looked to be in some sort of trance, but in all actuality, he was just praying, a routine of his he stuck to for every robbery. As an ardent practitioner of Santeria, he believed in spirits and the ability to connect with the unliving. He even had an alter in his bedroom decorated with dead chicken heads, candles, and other mementos he claimed protected him from danger. Whether they did or didn't, Menace had no clue. He didn't subscribe to any particular religion, and the only higher power he believed in was his pistol. Overall, it just didn't make sense to him how someone could be asking God or whoever for protection while doing wrong. Menace and Crisis had argued about this very subject in the past and Menace wasn't looking for a repeat.

Maneuvering to the edge of the building, Menace surveyed the area again. The neighborhood reflected the typical ghetto landscape. Bodega on the corner, Chinese store beside it, laundromat, and a liquor store further down the block. Tenement buildings lined one side of the street, while two- and three-story houses occupied the other. Aside from the handful of people waiting in line to purchase goods through the bulletproof bodega window, the block was deserted.

Menace felt frustration bubble up inside his gut like hot lava. Another glance at his watch revealed it was now 3:30, and he decided right then and there if Lotto didn't show up in the next half an hour, he was calling it a night.

Patience had never been one of Menace's strong suits, and it was the main reason why robbery was turning into more of a headache than a benefit. Between that, the snitches, and the cameras that seemed to be everywhere these days, the stick-up trade was becoming extremely hazardous. Jail or the grave seemed the likely outcome, and neither of those options appealed to Menace. He might've only been 20, but somehow, he had already begun to discern his life was destined for something far greater than he could imagine. He felt it in his heart, just like he felt his robbing days were coming to an end. Juxing niggas just wasn't cutting it anymore, and with a team of hungry wolves to feed, there was only one vice he knew of that would put hefty portions on all their plates. Narcotics. "The View" however wasn't the type of environment where one just decided to start hustling. *If only things were that simple,* Menace thought.

Suddenly, a pair of headlights glided into the block. In the blink of an eye, all ruminations not pertaining to Lotto instantly evaporated. Menace gave a sharp, distinct whistle, and seconds later, Crisis was at his side, 10-shot, .45 Ruger in hand.

"Is that him?" Crisis wondered, squinting. His eyesight was the worse.

Menace held his tongue as he watched the vehicle creep closer. Only after it drove under one of the remaining streetlights, was he able to confirm it was indeed a Range Rover, cocaine white in color. At this time of night, what were the chances of it being random? Slim to none!

Menace yanked a chrome .357 from his waist. Smiling deviously, he looked at Crisis. "It's him; it's Lotto," he announced with glee.

# CHAPTER 2

"**A**ll we want is the money," Menace announced as he grabbed Lotto by the shirt and slammed him up against the driver's side door of the Range. At 5'7", weighing no more than 150 lbs., he wasn't the fragile old man Rosez had portrayed him to be. Judging from the deep wrinkles creasing his brown face, and the sharply trimmed, all grey goatee, he was probably somewhere in his late 60's. His athletic build, however, indicated age hadn't stopped him from keeping in shape. Menace could feel the muscles in his lithe frame through the fitted crimson-colored collar shirt he wore. Black slacks, ostrich skin loafers, and a black Louis Vuitton *murse* strapped across his chest completed the ensemble. Wanting to immediately set the tone, Menace delivered a vicious gunbutt to the back of his head, causing him to groan in pain.

"That's just in case you was thinking about doing some dumb shit," he cautioned, tightening the grip on his shirt. "Now this is how it's going down – "

"You mu'fuckas obviously don't know who I am!" Lotto interrupted with his lips smushed against the glass window. He tried to turn, only to have Menace press him against the door with his forearm.

"Stay still," Menace warned.

"Fuck you!" Lotto spat without fear. "I'm telling you fools right now, you better kill me, because if I ever find out who you suckers is, it's a wrap for y'all."

Menace was slightly taken aback by the threats. He hadn't expected Lotto to respond so aggressively, especially with a gun pointed at his head. Neither had Crisis. His surprise however quickly turned to anger, and he jabbed his pistol against Lotto's cheek like he was stabbing him. "Keep running ya mouth, and see if I don't blow ya face all ova this truck."

"Do it," Lotto urged, pressing his face against the barrel. "You pulled ya pistol, so you might as well use it. Matter fact, let me see who you niggas is. You talking all that gangsta shit but you scared to show ya face."

Menace knew it was some obvious reverse psychology shit, but his pride wouldn't let him resist. When Lotto tried to spin around again, he let him, while keeping his hammer leveled at his head.

Scowling, Lotto gave them the once over. "Who the fuck sent you two punks? Flawless? Do you know who the fuck I am?"

"Fuck who you are! All we want is the money," Menace repeated, realizing they were doing way too much talking. At any moment, somebody could glance out their apartment window, see what was going on, and call the cops. He grabbed Lotto by the bicep, and tried to pull him towards the house.

"Nigga, I ain't going nowhere with you," Lotto said, wresting his arm free. "So, if you gone kill me, let's get this shit over with. If its money you want…" Lotto unsnapped the Louis Vuitton *murse*, and tossed it to the ground. Next, he unhooked the Range Rover key fob from the ring of keys he was holding, and chucked it beside the bag. "Its ten-thousand in there," he revealed. "Take it and the truck, and consider it a gift for catching me slipping. Make no mistake about it, that's all you getting."

Crisis retrieved the items from the pavement, unzipped the bag, and tilted it to display a brick of rolled up cash mixed in with some papers. The money looked appealing enough, but for the first time during a caper, Menace found himself indecisive on how to proceed. On one hand, he was infuriated by Lotto's defiance, and tempted to slump him based on that alone. On the other hand, he couldn't help but grudgingly respect his gangsta. One thing was certainly clear. Financially, Lotto was playing on a different level. The fact that he could throw ten racks at them like it was nothing, plus an eighty-thousand-dollar truck, meant money wasn't an issue. At least that's how Menace saw it. Now more than ever, he was eager to gain access to Lotto's pad. He could only imagine what treasures awaited him.

Before he could act, a pair of headlights appeared at one end of the street.

Lotto had his back to the approaching vehicle but he obviously heard it based on the smug grin that materialized on his face. "I'm guessing we're done here, right?" He said and attempted to walk off.

Menace snatched him back, tempted to shoot the smirk off his face. After all the preparation he'd gone through, he would only be leaving with a measly ten bands. The truck would fetch another twenty bands or so, bringing the total to thirty, all of which he would then have to split with Crisis and Rosez. It wasn't enough, and in that instant, Menace decided nothing was going to stop him from getting inside Lotto's crib. If he had to leave the old nigga stinking right there, so be it.

Menace grinned right back at Lotto. "Naw, we ain't done yet."

"Fuck you mean, we ain't done yet?" Lotto barked, but his words were drowned out by the music blasting from the advancing car, a black Honda civic.

Menace sidestepped to avoid getting sideswiped, and at the same time lifted his arm to shield his eyes from the blinding glare.

And that's when Lotto struck. He delivered a hard hook, then swatted at the gun, before taking off in the opposite direction.

The force of the punch knocked Menace backwards into Crisis, and his revolver clattered off the pavement. Furious, Menace scooped the pistol up, stumbled in between two parked cars to the sidewalk, and let the cannon roar.

# CHAPTER 3

Boom! Boom! Boom! The deafening shots shattered the silence of the night, causing car alarms to blare. And for a split second, the flash from the barrel illuminated Lotto sprinting up the block. He was fast for an old head, and when he saw he was being pursued, he began zigzagging from the street to the sidewalk.

Menace followed his movements, methodically unloading shots. Eventually, he came to a complete stop, steadied himself, aimed, and squeezed, only to be greeted by the clicking sound of an empty chamber.

"Fuck!!!" He yelled, fuming. He went to fling the gun, thought better of it, and ran into the street just as Crisis was pulling up in the Range. "Take off!" He barked the moment he hopped in.

In the distance, sirens could be heard. Crisis didn't seem to be too concerned. "Mo, that old nigga almost knocked ya head off," he joked, cackling. "Wait until I tell niggas about this."

Menace glared at him. "You serious right now, bruh! You think this shit is funny? Matter fact, why you ain't shoot that nigga?"

Crisis shrugged as if the answer was obvious. "He ran, Mo! What you expected me to chase him with you? Who would've got the whip?"

"Yeah, you right," Menace reluctantly agreed, rubbing his jaw.

Crisis peeped what he was doing, locked eyes with him, and the two friends burst out laughing. Just as fast as the laughter began, it came to an abrupt halt when out of nowhere, a figure darted into the middle of the street. The headlights revealed it to be none other than Lotto, standing there in a wide stance, with both arms raised.

"Oh shit!" Crisis said when he realized who and what he was staring at. He jerked the steering wheel to the left, causing the Range to veer sideways at the same time the crack of gunfire split the air.

"Run that nigga over!" Menace yelled, ducking down. "Run him the fuck over!" Out of reflex, he lifted the *tre-pound* to fire, only to once again hear the clicking noise. He tossed the revolver to the floorboard as slugs pinged off the truck's exterior. Crisis continued to swerve back and forth, however no amount of weaving could prevent the inevitable. Eventually, bullets slammed into the windshield, sending shards of glass flying everywhere.

Crisis lifted an arm to guard his face as he tried to keep from crashing. At the same time, Menace frantically attempted to grasp the .45 off Crisis waist. The moment he tugged it free, more shots obliterated the passenger's side headrest. Seconds later, the back windshield exploded from gunfire.

"Shoot that nigga, Mo," Crisis yelled, his eyes watering from the rush of incoming wind.

Still crouched down, Menace threw his arm out the space where the windshield should've been and started dumping. After emptying the clip, he cautiously peeked over the dash board, just in time to see Lotto dive in between two parked cars as they sped past. At the corner, Crisis made a hard right, sending the Range careening around the bend full speed. And just like that it was over.

For a minute or so, both men remained silent, too stunned to speak. It wasn't their first time being involved in gunplay, and probably wouldn't be their last, considering their lifestyle. Nonetheless, the near-death experience had them a bit unnerved. Menace still felt his adrenaline pumping as he looked himself over for injuries. Seeing and feeling nothing, he turned to Crisis.

"You good bro, you ain't hit or nothing right?"

Crisis kissed his rosary beads with gratitude "I'm good Mo, what about you?"

"I'm good too," Menace assured, sweeping glass from the seat. "How the fuck I forget to search that nigga," he wondered aloud.

Crisis shook his head in disbelief, not fully comprehending such a mishap. His heart was still thumping erratically, and he silently vowed he was done doing stickups. For a punk ass ten thousand dollars, he'd almost met his doom.

"Slow down, slow down, police on the right!" Menace suddenly blurted out. Crisis saw them at the last second but he was going way too fast too slow down.

"Damn Mo, it's just not our day," he said, watching the squad car screech to a halt. He took a right at the next corner, and when the cruiser appeared in the distance behind them moments later, he knew they were in trouble. "We gotta ditch this whip, Mo."

Menace nodded in agreement as he peered out the back window to discover several more cop cars had joined the pursuit. Spinning back around in his seat, he searched for a place to hop out. He spotted a housing complex a block away and pointed it out to Crisis . Seconds later, the SUV jumped the curb by the entrance.

"I love you, bro," Menace said readying himself.

"Love you more, Mo," Crisis replied, pushing his door open.

The Range hadn't even come to a full stop before both friends hopped out, and took off in different directions.

# CHAPTER 4

**M**aleka didn't know whether to hug her son, Naseem, or smack the shit out of him. She was definitely relieved he was safe, but the urge to put hands on him became almost irresistible when she thought about how she'd spent the last 48 hours, anxiety ridden, and unable to sleep because her only son hadn't called or come home in two days. And just when she'd been on the verge of finally falling asleep, he called to say he was in "the bookings."

Central booking, or "the bookings" as it was commonly known, was actually a detention facility under the criminal courthouse where people were taken after being arrested and processed at the police station. After days of relocating from one filthy cell to another, detainees were then arraigned before a judge, and remanded with or without bail or released on their own recognizance. Fortunately for Naseem he'd been granted bail in the amount of $75K.

Maleka had given 10% of that in cash to a bondsman to secure his freedom, and they were now in a Uber on their way home from the courthouse. Although she was far from rich, the money really wasn't the issue for Maleka, especially knowing Naseem would pay her back. The issue was him getting arrested for grand larceny, evading arrest, resisting arrest, and an assortment of other charges she couldn't even remember. If that wasn't bad enough, the presiding judge had seen fit to single her out, and in so many words, question her parenting in front of a packed courtroom. Even now, hours later, the recollection of snickers and comments from some of the spectators caused Maleka to blush with embarrassment. Never in her life had she felt so humiliated.

She glanced at Naseem once again tempted to backhand him. Sucking her teeth in disgust, she averted her gaze. One thing was certain: she definitely planned on having a serious talk with him once they got home. Before anything, though, he needed to take a shower. Words couldn't begin to accurately describe how foul he smelled. All Maleka could think of was spoiled milk. Scrunching her nose, she leaned closer to the partially closed window, and inhaled some fresh air. She was all too happy when the Uber finally pulled up in front their building.

Menace exited the car first. He sensed his mother's anger like a dog senses fear, and was already preparing for the tongue lashing he just knew was coming. He was eager to get it over with, but not so eager he forgot the dangers of the neighborhood he lived in. Not being on point in a place like "The View" could be costly, and Menace never forgot that. He paused in the doorway of the cab, shielding his mother as he surveyed the surroundings. Other than the crowd gathered in front of the building, and some junkies on the prowl for a late-night hit, nothing out of the ordinary caught his attention. Sighing in relief, he slid to the side so Maleka could exit, and they headed for the building.

In the distance, the faint sound of Spanish music could be heard, provoking Menace to grin as he pictured Gigi salsa dancing. She lived a few buildings down, and was the only person living in "The View" that could get away with blasting music in the wee hours of the morning. She was also Maleka's best friend, and Crisis's aunt. Menace viewed her as a second mother, and so did a lot of other people. Gigi was the one person in the hood everybody loved and respected. And boy could she cook! After barely eating for the past two days, Menace would've given anything for a plate of her food. Then his eyes settled on the crowd in front of the building and his appetite vanished.

Despite it being close to four in the morning, there were at least 20 individuals loitering in front of the building, smoking, drinking, or hustling. Then, there was Rosez, the lone female present. Menace heard her distinct squeaky voice before he actually saw her. When he finally did lay eyes on her, he shook his head in amusement, not at all surprised to see Rosez twerking and rapping to the Spanish music, while the crowd egged her on. Quiet as kept, Rosez was super nice at spitting. She was a Cardi-B and Lil Durk fanatic, and her style was tinged with influences from both super stars. Menace was constantly telling her to take her craft serious, but Rosez loved the streets more than anything. Her outfit – plum-colored Burberry sweats with a purple KAUSE KARMA V-neck – did little to restrain her juicy ass, and cantaloupe-sized breast. Black Gucci slides displayed pretty toes painted in the same shade of cotton candy pink as her fingernails.

A black Gucci scarf secured her shoulder length locs, the tips of which were dyed light brown to match her complexion. Add to that description, hazel eyes, deep dimples, and pouty lips that were rarely without lip gloss, and there was only way to describe Rosez: super bad. The term "gangstress" defined everything else. Someone not knowing any better would never suspect such a pretty face belonging to a human being so cold-hearted, devious, and capable of the brutality that made Rosez the most feared chick in all of Soundview. Her team of bitches, whom she called, "Flower Girls" were just as ruthless. Each of them had been named after a flower or plant by none other than Rosez, the undisputed leader. She was also the only female M.B.A.M. member and Menace was glad she played for his team.

Maleka though, couldn't stand Rosez for whatever reason, and she never missed an opportunity to let it be known. "Damn hood rat," she muttered, sucking her teeth. "Its damn near 4 in the morning and this bitch out here shaking her stink ass like she at the strip club. Who does that?" Maleka spat in disgust.

*Rosez does that,* Menace wanted to say, but he held his tongue. For a reason he'd yet to figure out, his moms couldn't stand Rosez.

"Somebody need to drag her ass upstairs with that fake ass of hers," she muttered.

"It's real, ma, stop hating," Menace joked.

"Naseem, shut the fuck up!" Maleka snapped. "What I look like hating on that little girl. She need to stop hating on me. Next time I hear she got my name in her mouth, imma step to her. She might have all these other bitches around her shook up, but I'm a grown woman."

"So, why is you stressing it then?" Menace asked, confused by her hostility.

"I'm not stressing shit," Maleka replied. "It's the principal; bitches need to stay in their lane. Now hurry up and holla at your peoples, and come inside. You know we need to talk, because if you think..." She stopped mid-sentence, and jabbed a finger into his forehead. "Got me out here at 4 in the morning," she angrily huffed, speed walking ahead.

Menace watched her go, still somewhat taken aback by her disdain for Rosez. Maleka was almost twice her age so it wasn't like they even moved in the same circles. Yet still she'd made it seem like her and Rosez had history. *What was that about*? Menace wondered. And the crazy part was, Rosez detested Maleka just as much. She knew better then to violate, though.

Rudeboy, on the other hand, had made his name off violating people. Dressed in a multicolored net wife beater, blue jeans, and black chukkas, he stood with one foot kicked back on the building, a chew stick perched between his lips. Nearby, his right-hand man, Raw, was posted up smoking a blunt. Both men were over six feet tall, and weighing well over 300 lbs. of mostly muscle. Most of the individuals present were either their workers or associates.

Menace felt his anger stir when he peeped Rudeboy eyeing his moms as she walked past. Even more so when he realized Maleka seemed to be encouraging the attention by switching her hips. At 42, she was still an attractive woman, and could give girls half her age a run for their money. Menace was overprotective of her as most sons are when it comes to their mother. It took all his restraint to keep from saying something as he watched Rudeboy damn near break his neck to stare at his mother's ass. Only after the building door closed behind her, did Rudeboy avert his gaze, which not surprisingly fell on Menace.

Rudeboy smiled sheepishly like a kid who'd just been caught with his hand in the cookie jar. Then, had the nerve to extend his fist for dap. "Good to see you alright," he said in his thick Jamaican accent. "If you need anything, let me know."

Although his words were laced with the proper amount of sincerity, Menace knew better then to take them at face value. The moment he dapped Rudeboy and stepped off, he peeped through his peripheral and observed the Jamaican's smile transform into a grimace. The dude was a straight snake, but what made him more lethal than the average reptile, was the fact that he was indeed a bonafied gangsta. Not only did he have the entire projects on smash on the drug tip, his gun game was even more prolific. If the rumors were to be believed, Rudeboy had more "groundhogs" than people had fingers. The term, "groundhog", was hood slang for homicides, and according to what some of the O.G.'s said, he'd been killing niggas since the eighties. He was now in his late fifties, and showing no signs of slowing down. Menace knew if he ever got into any kind of drama with Rudeboy, he would have to kill him immediately. Just being in his presence made him uneasy.

Eager to remove himself from the man's circumference, Menace signaled the three individuals whom he wanted to pow wow with. Rosez, B.R, and Guntalk. The tattoo of a hundred-dollar bill on back of their right hand signified their alliance to M.B.A.M. aka Money By Any Means.

# CHAPTER 5

There were 13 M.B.A.M. members in total. Menace was the HNIC aka Head Nigga in charge and Crisis was his second in command. Three members were currently locked up. 18-year-old B.R. was considered the baby of the clique. Indications of his youth were reflected in the minor acne littering his brown-skinned face, and the few strands of hair sprouting from his chin. Make no mistake about it though, young, or not, B.R. was an extremely violent adolescent with an insane temper. He was also super talented at basketball. Menace had practically raised him as far as being in the streets were concerned, so his love for B.R. was a little more intense than what he felt for the majority of his other cohorts.

Guntalk was the quiet one, and at 19, was already well-known throughout "The View" for being a shooter. His most noticeable feature were the burn scars blanketing 80% of his body, stemming from a house fire that killed his entire family. To camouflage the disfigurement somewhat, he wore nothing but black attire.

Last, but not least, was Rosez. Menace smelled her Gucci perfume even before he embraced her. He palmed her yeeks possessively because although she wasn't his girl in the general sense, she was definitely his down-ass bitch.

Encircling her arms around his neck, Rosez muttered, "Why the fuck that nigga smiling all in your face like we don't know he praying on our downfall?" As she spoke, the razor she kept hidden in her mouth clicked against her teeth. She opened her mouth to continue then stopped. All of a sudden, she shoved Menace away. "Damn nigga, you fucking stink," she spat, scrunching her nose.

*Good ole Rosez,* Menace thought, chuckling in mock amusement. He could understand why his moms didn't like the slick talking bitch. Sometimes he didn't like her. At 23, Rosez still hadn't learned to control her mouth. She was blunt, and usually said the first thing that came to mind, which more times than not was some disrespectful shit. Despite knowing her a little over five years, Menace still found himself surprised sometimes by some of the shit that came out of her mouth. Only because he was tired, and eager to get inside did he ignore her.

He turned to BR. and Guntalk, and gave an abbreviated version of the events that had led to his arrest. His most pressing concern, however, was Crisis. None of the trio admitted to seeing him for at least the past two days.

"We thought he was with you, big bro," B.R. said, looking confused.

"He was," Menace confirmed, without going any further. He was too busy contemplating what the absence could mean. Had Crisis gotten away? Did he still have the money? Of course, the answers eluded him, but not for long, Menace concluded, ready to make his departure. Not even Rosez begging him to come home with her could change his mind. He promised to get up with her the next day so they could discuss her cut from the Lotto robbery, then uttered some final words to B.R. and Guntalk before heading inside.

# CHAPTER 6

"**N**aseem!" Lauren squealed with joy the moment he walked through the door. In a flash, she rushed from the couch and leapt into his arms knocking him backwards with her 130 lb. frame. Menace caught his baby sister, and squeezed her lovingly. At 17, she wasn't really a baby anymore, however, he would always see her as such. He wasn't surprised to see tears streaming from her eyes. They were the same shade of olive green as Maleka's eyes, and it never ceased to amaze Menace how the two woman he loved most resembled each other so closely. So much so, people sometimes mistook them for sisters. Without having to ask, he already knew the reason for Lauren's tears.

"You scared me," Lauren said, confirming his suspicions. She punched him playfully in the chest, before hugging him again. "Ma is super pissed." She whispered in his ear, "And I talked to Crisis this morning. He said he's good, he got the bread, and for you to holla at him A.S.A.P."

Her words brought Menace instant relief, and for the first time in 48 hours, he smiled. Then he peeped his moms staring angrily at him, while impatiently tapping her foot.

Maleka cleared her throat loudly. "Lauren, tell ya brother goodnight and take it on down."

"Ahhh come on, ma," Lauren whined, twisting back to look at her. "It's already like 5 something in the morning, how you expect me to go back – "

The stern look from Maleka silenced her mid-sentence. Lauren knew her pleas were useless.

She turned back to her brother. "You stink too," she told him, giggling.

"Yeah whatever," Menace said, unwrapping her arms from his neck. "Just make sure you come holla at me later. We need to talk."

Lauren raised an eyebrow curiously. "About what?" She asked, hand on her hip.

Menace shook his head, once again amazed how his sister had the body of a grown woman. "We'll talk later," he said, gently pushing her in the direction of her room. She was halfway down the hall when he mouthed the word, *Romeo*, causing Lauren's jaw to drop. Romeo was the name of the dude she was dating, and she'd done everything in her power to keep her overprotective brother from finding out about him. And yet still, he had. *How*, she wondered as she strolled into her bedroom and shut the door, eager to call her best friend, Belinda.

"Sit," Maleka immediately ordered, pointing to the one-seater to her left. She muted the TV before taking a sip of peppermint tea from the mug she was cradling. Menace observed his moms watching him over the rim of the cup and purposely avoided her gaze as he plopped down in the black leather recliner. He'd been hoping to at least hop in the shower first, but obviously that wasn't going to happen just yet. He could tell his moms was ready for bed though, based on the fact she was drinking tea, a ritual she performed every night before going to sleep. Menace hoped her exhaustion would shorten what he suspected was going be a lengthy speech.

Maleka felt her eyelids droop with fatigue as she sat the mug on the coffee table in front of her. She was, indeed, exhausted, but nothing was going to stop her from setting Naseem straight.

"Look at me," she demanded, scooting to the edge of the cushion. She waited until their eyes met, then without warning, slapped the shit out of him. The sound of the smack resembled a shot from a small caliber pistol. "You embarrassed me!" Maleka said, tempted to strike again. "You embarrassed this family. And most importantly you embarrassed – " She jabbed a finger into his forehead "Yourself!"

Menace uttered the first thing that came to mind. "Ma, I'm sorry."

"No, you not," Maleka erupted angrily. "So don't even say that shit. And even if you are, its only because you got caught." Menace opened his mouth to respond. "Don't say shit!" Maleka shouted, not letting him get a word in. "I don't want you to do nothing but sit there and listen because if you think you gone keep playing in these streets and imma run and save you every time, you got another thing coming." She took another sip of tea to calm herself, and when she felt composed, she continued. "I love you, Naseem; you're my only son, not to mention my first born. I'll always love you more than life itself. But don't think for one second, imma let you keep abusing that love. It's bad enough I already give you more leeway than the average parent. In fact, some people would probably say I'm a bad parent for the way I let you do damn near anything you want. There's a reason for that though. You're 20 years old, practically a grown man, and no matter how much I've guided you, it's you that has to ultimately choose the path you walk. It's you that has to make the decisions that will shape your future." She paused to let her words sink in.

"I've been allowing you to do that in hopes you would come to your senses and find your purpose in life. Lord knows, I've tried to steer you in the right direction, for the most part. It seems all my efforts have been in vain because you seem to only be getting deeper in the streets." Maleka shook her head with sadness. "You remind me so much of your father, Naseem, and it scares me because I see you're trying to follow in his footsteps. I don't want to lose you like I lost him," she said, her voice cracking. "I don't even know exactly what took him from us, but I'm sure it had something to do with whatever he was doing in those streets. I don't want to lose you like that," she reiterated, tears streaming down her face.

The sight of his mother crying crushed Menace. "You won't lose me, ma," he assured her, taking hold of her hand.

"You don't know that," Maleka replied sadly. She wondered if her son was so naive, he truly believed he could escape the pitfalls that had befallen so many before him.

For the next 15 minutes, she tried to convince him his actions could only have two outcomes, the cage, or the grave. She even named examples of legends who had succumbed to such a fate, people like Big Meech, John Gotti, Larry Hoover, Supreme, and of course, Soundview's most revered icon, Pistol P. Unfortunately, her words appeared to be falling on deaf ears. Maleka could tell by her son's lackluster response, his mind was already set on trying to become an even bigger gangster than the ones she named. Being the authentic woman and mother she was, she saw no option than to give him the truth straight up no chaser.

After draining the rest of the tea, she calmly sat the cup on the table. "So, you want to be a gangsta, huh?" She inquired, staring him in the eye. "You want to be some kind of kingpin? Well let me tell you something, all this petty shit you doing ain't gone cut it. You out here stealing cars, like you trying to go joy riding. Not even three months ago, it was gun possession. What you got a gun for if you ain't using it to put money in ya pocket, in our pocket." Menace was shocked. "Yeah, you heard me right," she said, seeing his look of astonishment. "In *our* pocket," she repeated. "Don't you want to get ya family out the hood? Don't you want to take care of me like I took care of you for the past 20 years and counting?"

Menace nodded vigorously. "Of course, I do, ma."

Maleka sucked her teeth. "It sure is hard to tell. You must want one of these lame motherfuckers to put a baby in ya sister, instead of her going off to college."

Menace scowled at the picture she was painting. "I'd die before I let that happen," he sneered.

"Well, you might have to," Maleka remarked. "Because with the way you moving, it's only a matter of time before you catch a bid or a bullet, and when that happens, who gone protect Lauren. Your father would be extremely disappointed with you because I know this isn't the life he wanted for you, and now that you've chosen to go this route, you're moving like a petty criminal instead of the son of a legend."

Menace felt his heart ache from her words. Disappointing his pops was the last thing he wanted to do. Ashamed, he lowered his head.

"Go hard, or don't go at all!" Maleka shouted, seeing her words were penetrating. It wasn't the typical advice a parent might give their child. Maleka, however, wasn't the typical mother. She knew what the streets were like firsthand and understood that in order for Naseem to give them up, he would have to experience his own hardships, just like she had. While he was at it, it didn't make sense for him not to generate some money for the family. To those who might view this as pimping her son, in Maleka's mind, she was simply capitalizing on his decision to traverse down a road he planned on traveling with or without her blessing. What were the alternatives? Turn him over to the police? Kick him out? Maleka loved her son way too much to do either. And now that his aspirations were clear, there was only one thing left to do: ride with him until the wheels fell off. That is exactly what she told him. She cupped his face, gazing lovingly into his eyes as she spoke.

"Even though I wish you would choose to do something else with your life, I'm going to hold you down no matter what. Stop making yourself look like a fool. Think big, son! You're a natural born leader. Check how you got all these people looking up to you, like you God or something. Some of them is grown ass man old enough to be ya father." She chuckled. "Can't even say I'm surprised. Your father had the same effect on people. He knew how to use his power, though. The question is, do you know how to use yours?"

# CHAPTER 7

Trouble! That's what Redd's real name should've been. It always seemed to find him, or rather he always seemed to find it. At 5'6" with short bleached locs, and a peanut-butter complexion, his butter ball stature wasn't one anybody would normally associate with the havoc he frequently wreaked. More times than not, the 20-year-old NYC native had no one to blame but himself for the problems he constantly encountered. The two traits that stagnated him most were his temper, and impulsive nature, a deadly combination – literally – being that Redd went nowhere without his pistol. If that wasn't enough, his gambling addiction was comparable to a fiend's thirst for crack. In fact, his swift departure from his home in the Bronx weeks earlier, and reason for currently being in Raleigh, North Carolina, stemmed from a shooting over an unpaid gambling debt.

Redd had been the triggerman, however, the incident hadn't deterred him from gambling. Not surprisingly, it was because of this exact vice he once again found himself in a predicament that would more than likely bring him the one thing he didn't need an ounce more of: trouble.

Redd felt a sense of Deja vu as the three white dice rattled around in his loosely closed fist. "I'm about to show you country boys how we do it in New York," he taunted. Although a good-natured smile accompanied his statement, he found nothing remotely amusing about his current situation. Two hours earlier, armed with close to 10 bands in cash, he dropped off his girl, Monae, with intentions of then going to cop a few pounds of bud from her brother, Serious. Redd didn't even like the nigga, nevertheless, there was no disputing his heavyweight status on the drug tip. Monae had finally convinced Serious to do business with him, and their first transaction should've occurred hours ago. Not surprisingly, Redd let his penchant for gambling get the best of him when he pulled into the gas station and peeped the dice game taking place. So extreme was his thirst, he neglected to replenish the tank. Doubling his money had been his only thought when he strolled over and asked what's in the bank.

Unfortunately, things hadn't gone as planned, and now he was down to his last thousand dollars. Make no mistake about it, Redd intended on getting the money back, one way or the other. Although he hoped to win it back fairly, a part of him was wishing the dice continued to betray him just so he could have an excuse to get crazy. Not that he needed one anyway.

*Picture me letting one of these mu'fuckas get me for my paper*, Redd thought to himself, as he surveyed the crowd of about fifteen.

"Let them things fly," one of the participants shouted, impatiently smacking a bundle of cash against his palm. His name was Jon-Jon, and Redd recalled seeing him at the Starlight's strip club a few nights after he arrived.

It was the first time him and Serious hung out, and according to what he revealed, Jon-Jon was Raleigh royalty, not to mention a stone-cold killa with a heavy bankroll. With that being so, Redd didn't understand a couple of things. Number one: why he was rolling dice at the back of a gas station. Number two: why was he dressed like a hobo in dingy blue jeans shorts, a neon green T-shirt, and a pair of yellow Adidas. The thick glasses he wore made him resemble the lame nigga, Rico, from the movie, *Belly*. The majority of those present were either Jon-Jon's flunkies, or associates. Redd didn't give a fuck about any of them. The only thing that concerned him was the thick stack of currency in Jon-Jon's possession, most of which had previously belonged to him. The sight of it made Redd beyond furious. How the fuck could he have allowed Jon-Jon to rope him for his reup? Now, the nigga had the nerve to be rushing him. Redd knew just the thing to wipe the silly smirk off his face. Vigorously shaking the dice, he eyed the crowd with a sinister smile, taking solace in the fact that in the end, he would have the last laugh.

"What's the bets?" Redd barked. A flurry of bills floated to the concrete, and without even totaling it up to ensure he could cover the amount, he shook the dice one last time, before releasing them.

"Ace hoe, ace!" Someone yelled.

"Free money!" Another shouted, and Redd couldn't help but grin. *Free money* were his sentiments exactly, as his left hand crawled along the waistline towards the back of his blue polo jeans.

Just as Redd's fingers brushed against the object he was seeking, the dice came to a stop. Redd stared at the triple ones, undecided whether to feel excited or dismayed at the instant winner. Groans of disappointment filled the air, provoking him to snicker as he scooped up all the money, along with the dice. Unable to help himself, he immediately started talking shit.

"Fuck you thought, a nigga was gone lose forever? I'm from New York," he boasted. "Even when I lose, I still win." He shook the dice heartily, suddenly feeling energized. "I'm about to really get hot, and ain't gone spend all day talking about it either. I can show you better than I can tell you. Now, what's the bets?"

"You talk a lot of shit," Jon-Jon calmly remarked, nonchalantly flicking through some bills.

Redd snorted as if amused, but he was no longer smiling. "I don't just talk; I can back it up too."

"We'll see," Jon-Jon replied, eyeing him as he bent to place a knot of cash under his sneaker. Others followed suit, littering the ground with currency, however, the cryptic verbal exchange had transformed the vibe of the game. No longer was anyone smiling, and the tension that had been simmering below the surface was now out in the open. While it made the majority of players anxious, Redd welcomed it with open arms. Not only did he just love drama, in his warped mind, there was nobody tougher than a New York nigga. Neglecting to count the money once again, he rocked the dice back and forth in his palm.

"Get this money, bitches! Make daddy proud," he demanded, releasing them.

The squares spilled from his hand, rolling, and swerving before ricocheting off the curb, and stopping on another instant winner.

"Four. Five. Six. CeeLo, Motherfucka!" Redd shouted, enunciating each word as he stared at Jon-Jon. "I told you! I told you chitlin eating, motherfuckas I was about to get hot. Even after I leave, y'all still gone be talking about the New York nigga that came through and scraped y'all." He paused to retrieve, and light a black and mild cigar. "I'm gone make all you niggas believers," he vowed, smoke billowing from his mouth. He took a long pull, exhaled, then without further ado, proceeded to do exactly as he said.

Anyone who gambles knows how in the blink of an eye, a player can go from being ice cold, to going on the type of hot streak that defies logic. For those at the dice game who had never experienced such an instance, they did that day. Whereas before Redd couldn't win a roll, now he couldn't lose if he tried. He was on fire, going through stretches where he rolled instant winners back-to-back to back. At this rate, it took him a little over an hour to win all his bread back, plus an extra three grand for his troubles. Then he rolled CeeLo, which gave him the option of cutting the bank or simply walking away. Most people with common sense would've done the latter. Common sense, however, was a trait that sometimes eluded Redd, and in other instances one he choose to disregard. Right then and there, he decided he wasn't leaving until he at least tripled his money. That way he could cop the bud from Serious, repay Monae her 10 racks, and still have some paper for his pocket.

As is the case with most chronic gamblers, all Redd could see with his skewed vision was the chance for a come up. He was already spending money in his head as he scanned the faces of the remaining players, one of whom happened to be Jon-Jon. There was a constipated look on his face that Redd found immensely amusing, and against his better judgment, he decided to rub it in. Grinning, he skimmed through a stack of bills.

"Aye Jon-Jon, don't tell me I took all ya bread. If you need a walk..." He pinched out 2 blue faces, and tossed them to the ground.

Jon-Jon didn't even glance at the money. His eyes were fixated on Redd as he wondered if the New Yorker understood the dangerous game he was playing. Either he was too stupid to realize it, or just didn't give a fuck. Then again, Jon-Jon recalled seeing Redd at the strip club with Serious, so he was relatively sure the nigga knew of his reputation. For the sake of not wanting to have one of his men catch a senseless homicide beef for blowing Redd's brains out, Jon-Jon chose to overlook the disrespect. He knew of a better way to seek retribution. With a jerk of his head, he beckoned one of his soldiers over. Throwing an arm over the young boy's shoulder, Jon-Jon issued instructions into his ear, then sent him on his way.

*These niggas is scheming on me*, Redd automatically assumed, watching the flunkie disappear inside the gas station. Pretending to fix his belt, he rested his hand on the butt of the 16 shot, 9mm Taurus, jammed in his waistband. His vision pivoted from Jon-Jon to his crew, all of whom were smirking as if they were privy to a secret. Before Redd could discover what it was, the young boy returned holding a plastic Macy's type shopping bag. Smiling deviously, Jon-Jon took possession of the bag.

"See, the problem with most of you New York cats is y'all think you the only ones that know how to get to a bag," Jon-Jon noted. "The difference between me and you is, you still trying to make money, and me, I'm looking for new ways to spend this shit."

In one swift motion, Jon-Jon overturned the bag, dumping bricks of rubber band-wrapped money on the pavement.

"Motherfucker, I own this gas station. Does it look like I need a walk, you fucking clown? Matter fact, fuck all that talking shit. Stop the bank," he barked. "And imma keep stopping that shit until I break you."

The remaining bunch of onlookers instantly erupted into a frenzy of cheers. Let them tell it, they already knew Jon-Jon would never allow some out of towner to get the best of him. Redd heard the comments, but was too mesmerized by the sight of all the money to respond. Never in his life had he seen so much bread, which if he had to guess, was at least 100 racks. Combined with his little 13 bands, he calculated he was in the presence of a small fortune. The realization a portion could be his with one roll of the dice, caused his heart to thump erratically. His eyes slid from the money to Jon-Jon.

"Check it out, I can't cover all that," Redd admitted. "So, I'm just going to empty my pockets, and that's what the bank is."

"Do that then," Jon-Jon said, and Redd did it.

Redd's thoughts were if the dice failed him, his gun wouldn't. He could feel his hands sweating profusely as he stared at all the blue faces lying mere feet away. Discreetly, he swiped his palms against his jeans before taking possession of the dice. "This is it, don't play with me bitches," he muttered into his closed fist, like the dice had ears. "This what we been waiting for all night, don't let daddy down, you heard!" He paused as if waiting for a reply, then nodded, pretending to have received one. After a final shake, he flung the dice from his grip. They careened to one side, skipping over the cracked blacktop, before colliding with the wall and bouncing backwards. A collective sigh of relief sounded when they stopped spinning.

"Three, four, six," someone announced. The numbers meant absolutely nothing, which is why they were all shocked when they spun to find Redd pointing his pistol. He'd changed his mind. Rather than depend on the dice for a hefty payday, he would just take it.

Before anybody could react, he rushed Jon-Jon, and threw him in a chokehold from behind. "Who's the clown now?" Redd taunted, pistol pressed to his temple. "I told ya bitch ass I was gone show you how New York niggas get down. You must've thought I was talking because I got lips."

"How you think you gone make it outta here alive?" Jon-Jon mumbled. On cue, several onlookers upped and aimed their own pistols.

Unfazed by the opposition, Redd tightened his grip. "Imma give you three seconds to tell ya peoples stand down, then imma start blasting.

"You know I can't do that," Jon-Jon replied, provoking Redd to smack him in the head with the hammer.

"You gone do what I tell you to do, or imma blow ya fucking head off," he barked. "One of ya niggas might get me afterwards, but as long as I take you with me, that's all I care about. Now tell them niggas to stand down. I'm starting the count," he announced, tightening the chokehold. The sound of Jon-Jon choking was music to his ears. "One. Two!"

Wincing in pain, Jon-Jon reluctantly lifted and lowered his hands signaling for his men to drop their weapons.

Redd laughed like a madman. "That's right, be a good boy, and you just might make it outta here alive." All of a sudden, he trained the gun on the young boy who retrieved the money earlier. "You, put all the guns and money in the bag," he ordered. "And I know I don't have to tell you what's gone happen if I even think you trying some funny shit."

Cautiously, the soldier stepped forward, and did as he was told. "Toss it over here," Redd ordered once the task was complete. The bag landed at his feet with a clank, but he didn't immediately pick it up. Instead, he took a moment to make eye contact with everyone present.

"Remember me. Remember what this clown nigga from New York did to you. Now, run!" He suddenly shouted, firing at their feet. In a flash, the dudes took off like they were in a track meet. "I guess that leaves just the two of us," Redd whispered to Jon-Jon. "Just the two of us," he sang patting his waist. Surprisingly, Jon-Jon wasn't armed. "Talking all that shit, and you not even gripped up!" Redd spat, shoving him forward.

Jon-Jon stumbled forward, caught himself before he could fall, and spun with his hands raised in surrender. "Take it easy New York," he implored. "You got the money, ain't no need for nobody to get hurt."

Redd laughed out loud as if he'd just heard a good joke. You must think I'm a fuckin fool, huh? I must have stupid written on my forehead. Do I?"

Jon-Jon opened his mouth to answer, only to have his words drowned out by…

*Blocka!*

The gunshot crashed into his chest, spinning him 360 degrees like a ceiling fan. Mouth wide with shock, he staggered like a drunkard, on the verge of collapsing, and Redd burned him three more times in quick succession.

*Blocka! Blocka! Blocka!*

Shoulder, stomach, chest. The bullets propelled Jon-Jon backwards before he crumpled to the ground clutching at his chest. Satisfied with his work, Redd snatched up the shopping bag and calmly strolled off.

# CHAPTER 8

Three years, and Three months. Monae couldn't believe it had been that long since she'd seen her best friend, Kameesha. Three years earlier, before relocating to NYC with her foster parents, there had only been two people she trusted and loved more than anyone else. The first was her foster brother, Serious. The second was Kameesha. Her parents were God-fearing people who had done their best to instill proper morals and principles in both of their children. For the most part they'd succeeded. Kameesha was an honor roll student all the way through high school, which is where she met Monae. The two girls couldn't have been more different.

Kameesha, the dark-skinned, shy girl, always the object of ridicule for her quirky dress code. And Monae, the pretty redbone whose unique fashion sense, and outspoken nature, enticed other girls to emulate her, and dudes to compete for her attention. Despite being in several of the same classes, the girls didn't become acquainted until Monae began dating Kameesha's 19-year-old brother, Roy. He moved out of the family home the day he turned 18, and from the beginning, Kameesha was a frequent visitor at his crib. If their parents would've known Roy was as deep into the streets as any seasoned hustler, they would've, without question, prohibited Kameesha from associating with him. And for one of the few times, she would've disobeyed them. Such was the depth of the bond she shared with her brother. He was her breath of fresh air, and only reliable link to the world her parents tried so hard to shield her from.

Monae envied, and admired their relationship at the same time. It was a perfect reflection of the bond she wished she had with her siblings. Unfortunately, they'd all been separated at a young age, and thrust into the foster care system. Seeing how much Roy loved his sister made Monae like him even more. Because of that she made it her business to really get to know Kameesha. Considering the frequency with which they ran into each other at school and at Roy's crib, it would've been plain shady to do otherwise.

Their first interactions were filled with a lot of uncomfortable silences. Not due to the girl's unwillingness to become acquainted, but because Kameesha's upbringing rendered her uneducated in the three topics girls their age found most interesting: music, fashion, and of course, boys. Monae was all too happy to be her guide for a number of reasons. The main one being, Kameesha was super smart. What she lacked in worldly knowledge, she more than made up for with book smarts. She was glad to tutor Monae, who although smart in her own respect, lacked the attention span necessary to consistently get good grades. She did, however, harbor dreams of one day starting her own clothing line, which was the only reason she even tolerated school. The girls complimented each other well, and as their relationship blossomed, it became surprising to see one without the other.

At school, the belittling stopped, not just because Monae made it so, but mainly because she began guiding Kameesha on everything from how to dress and apply makeup, to styling her own hair. Through their frequent trips to the mall, she taught her how to coordinate her clothes until eventually Kameesha began developing her own unique sense of style. After one of these shopping excursions, they usually ended up getting their hair and nails done. It was there in the salon surrounded by mirrors that Monae began to build Kameesha's self-esteem by getting her to see just how truly beautiful she was. In time, the constant encouragement caused a sense of confidence to radiate from Kameesha that was impossible not to notice. All of a sudden, the same dudes who used to tease her were asking her out. Once again, Monae was right there to advise her on what characteristics to look for in a dude. She seemed to have dirt on everybody, and because Kameesha listened, she avoided a lot of headaches. Eventually, she stopped needing Monae to pull her coat. After conversing with a dude, she could usually tell if he was a lame or deserved more attention. Most dudes never got the latter, and the few that did always showed their true colors once she revealed she wasn't having sex until she got married. Monae, who was already sexually active, tried to explain the pleasure she was missing out on, but Kameesha refused to alter her stance. She was totally focused on becoming an actress, and the fear of a pregnancy derailing her dreams was enough to make her abstain. Although Monae respected her friend's decision, she still found it amusing people were still doing the "no sex before marriage" thing. There was nothing funny, however, about the tragedy that struck the year before both girls graduated.

Roy was found riddled with bullets, stuffed in a trunk, in what police classified as a drug-related murder. They claimed to have no suspects, but Kameesha and Monae both agreed the culprit had to be someone from his inner circle, considering Roy didn't deal with strangers. The realization only served to intensify the girls' grief. Fortunately, they had each other to turn to for comfort. It was this tragedy that truly cemented their bond, and soon afterwards they began referring to each other as sisters, vowing to always be there for each other no matter what. As they say though, promises are meant to be broken.

Not even 90 days after Roy's murder, Monae was hit with a dilemma that would not only test their sisterhood, but drastically alter the course of her life. One night, her foster parents announced they were moving to NYC. Monae, the only one out of four foster kids who wouldn't be 18 by the time of the scheduled departure, had two options: either relocate with her foster parents, or run away so she could stay in N.C. The latter option is what appealed most to her. She didn't want to move to NY, which in her eyes would be like starting over. More than anything, she didn't want to leave Kameesha.

Ironically, it was Kameesha who convinced her to go for two reasons. First, so she could try and reconnect with her two sisters who she'd heard had been relocated to NY. Secondly, to enroll in one of the many fashion schools in NYC to pursue her dream of starting her own clothing line. Reluctantly, Monae took her advice, despite knowing in her heart nothing would be the same. She was right.

For the first few months, she and Kameesha communicated every day on Facebook, and IG, in addition to texting and talking on the phone. As time went on, between school and Monae familiarizing herself with the city's many amenities, the calls dwindled until weeks passed without the girls speaking. Out of the blue, Kameesha deleted her social media pages claiming the platforms were too toxic, and suddenly months started to lapse with no word from her. It was around that time Monae met Redd at a block party, and slowly he began taking up all her time.

As the years passed, the girls would Facetime each other on holidays and birthdays. Nonetheless, the distance separating them was just as much to blame for the deterioration of their relationship as the men in their lives. Coincidentally, it was because of her boyfriend, Redd, Monae now found herself back in North Carolina three years after departing. Unlike her, Kameesha had indeed turned her dreams of becoming an actress into reality. She wasn't an A lister just yet, but had already starred in a few small productions that had received a decent amount of publicity. It was her current role in a film being shot in Vegas that had prevented her from seeing Monae for the first 2 weeks after her arrival. It was only that morning the best friends finally managed to reconnect.

# CHAPTER 9

Monae held Kameesha at arm's length, in awe over the physical transformation she'd undergone. They were in the locker room of a high-end spa, after having received several hours of rejuvenating body treatments, consisting of sea weed wraps, and full body massages. It was as they dressed that Monae got her first opportunity to inspect Kameesha's new figure. Three years ago, her ass had been flat as an ironing board, now it was plump with the perfect curve. Curious to see if it was as soft as it looked, Monae squeezed her yeeks.

"Damn," she muttered in amazement discovering they were. She playfully slapped Kameesha's ass causing it to jiggle, before cupping her breast through the black lace bra she wore. "And what size is these?" She inquired.

"D cups," Kameesha answered as she pulled her hair into a ponytail. "Cost me close to ten thousand, but I'm not complaining." In all actuality the surgical alterations only enhanced Kameesha's beauty. She might've been short at 5"4, but she'd always been pretty. Her smooth skin tone was the exact shade as a cup of hot chocolate, complimenting perfectly her honey-colored eyes. She'd even gotten her teeth straightened and had a gold hope earring in her nose. Gazing into one of several floor length mirrors, Monae took a second to appraise her own figure. She slightly favored the singer Keyshia Cole, and at 5"7, her ass was just as fat and soft as Kameesha's. Nose, eyebrow, and lip piercings further expressed her bad girl vibe, as did the sleeve of tattoos on her left arm. Her man Redd said her best feature was her juicy lips. Monae liked to think it was her smile. Satisfied with the gorgeous reflection staring back at her, she began getting dressed.

Twenty minutes later, the ladies emerged from the spa looking like runway models. Monae dolled out in black Balenciaga sneakers, a grey limited edition, KAUSE KARMA V-neck, and grey skin tight Prada jeans. And Kameesha dressed in Gucci, Gucci, and more Gucci. Her designer fetish, was but another example of how she'd morphed into a diva, and Monae couldn't wait to see what else had changed about her friend. She wouldn't have to wait long. After strolling through downtown Raleigh talking, for another hour or so, the girls decided to get something to eat.

They arrived at the parking lot to retrieve Kameesha's car, and Monae's jaw dropped when she pulled out a key fob engraved with a Benz emblem.

"A Benz! You pushing a fucking Benz!" She exclaimed, eyes wide with shock. Kameesha shrugged like it was no big deal, as she deactivated the alarm to a midnight blue G-wagon. She hopped in the driver's seat, and Monae got in on the passenger side.

Once they were situated, bags in the backseat, seatbelts attached, Kameesha continued, "Like I told you earlier sis, a lot done changed. I been grinding and this acting thing is really starting to take off," she admitted humbly.

"I can see," Monae replied as she checked her phone for any missed calls, or messages from Redd. There weren't any, and she disguised her annoyance well as she spoke. "Real talk, I always knew you were going to make it. You always had that ambition, and focus."

"The same ambition you have inside of you," Kameesha shot back, as the ignition purred to life. After a quick check of her appearance in the visor, she shifted into drive, and merged into traffic, all the while continuing to speak. "Bitch, you was the flyest chick in the entire school. Don't act like you forgot."

Monae grinned sheepishly. "And now look who's the flyest," she said, giving her the once over for emphasis. "Maybe I need to get into that acting shit too."

"Or maybe you need to stop playing, and start ya own clothing line like you always talked about doing," Kameesha snapped. "Don't chase the money, sis. When you're doing something you love the money will come."

Monae rolled her eyes. "Well, I need it to come now."

Kameesha chuckled. "Girl bye, I seen you on IG styling and profiling in all that designer shit. And it definitely doesn't look like you hurting for bread right now," she joked, as she eased to a stop at a red light. She twisted slightly to face Monae, looking her up and down. "Those is some thousand-dollar sneakers you got on, and those Chanel shades cost half of that. Don't be mad either if I find a way to steal them before the day is out."

Monae laughed out loud, as a recollection suddenly came to mind. "You still ain't give me back the glasses you took from me the day we had the big fight at the mall."

Kameesha shook her head at the memory. "All because you thought that girl was staring."

"She was staring," Monae assured, getting angry all over again. "Bitch was practically grilling me."

"Yeah, whatever," Kameesha said as the light turned green and she pulled off. "Open that glove box and hand me that eye glass case."

As soon as Monae retrieved the case, the pungent aroma of weed rushed into her nostrils. "Damn girl, this shit stink. I leave you for a couple of years, and miss goody two shoes start blowing bud. When that happen? And I know ya parents don't know, or do they?"

Kameesha selected a pre-rolled blunt, lit it, and inhaled deeply. "First of all, you weren't gone a couple of years – it's actually been three years and change," she corrected, smoke spilling from her mouth. "As far as my parents are concerned, I don't really fuck with them like that. They kicked me out after I got pregnant."

Monae's eyes stretched wide with disbelief. "Pregnant? Kicked you out? Girl, please tell me you joking."

"I wish I was," Kameesha muttered. "We'll get into that some other time though. Right now, all I'm thinking about is some Jamaican food. I haven't eaten all day and..."

"And right now, all I'm thinking about is what else you not telling me," Monae interrupted. "Like how the hell you get pregnant, and by who? I thought you weren't having sex until you got married anyway. What the fuck happened?"

At that particular moment Kameesha didn't feel like reliving the past three years of her life. Doing so would awaken many painful memories, including the secret she was actually too scared to confess to Monae. She figured she might as well get it over with. Sighing with finality, she inhaled long and deep, then passed the blunt off.

"I moved to L.A. to pursue my acting career a year after you left," she began. "Do you remember when I deactivated all my social media pages?"

Monae nodded, "You said you were tired of all the fake shit."

"And I was," Kameesha confirmed. "But the real reason I did it was because I wanted a fresh start. Like most naive girls, I thought that just by being out there in Cali, my career would take off. When it happened, I didn't want anything I'd previously posted coming back to bite me in the ass. At the same time, I wasn't out there looking for handouts – you know that's never been my style. I was putting in the work, paying for acting classes, going to casting calls, networking, and basically just doing everything in my power to get noticed. Its hard though for a black girl in Hollywood. We gotta work ten times harder than these white chicks, and if you ain't giving up no ass, ten times turns to twenty times. Eventually, I just got tired of getting the runaround from directors, producers, and agents. I guess you can say I gave up. I moved back to Raleigh feeling like a failure, and when I say I was depressed, girl I was going through it. I'm talking about not eating, hardly sleeping, losing weight, the whole nine."

She shook her head, obviously distressed by the recollection, and beckoned for the spliff. After several pulls to collect her bearings, she went on.

"Somehow, God got me through it. And just when I least expected it, the blessing arrived. One day I'm in the supermarket, and out the blue, this random dude walks up and asks me if I've ever considered acting." She chuckled sarcastically at the remembrance. "Sis, I felt like spitting in his face because in L.A., that's how all the conversations start. Next thing you know, the dude is trying to fuck you, or put you in some porn movie where you're getting fucked. So naturally, I thought he was suspect."

"I bet you still took his number though," Monae joked.

"Damn right I did," Kameesha admitted as she maneuvered into a parking spot. "And I called him the next day too. Long story short, he turned out to be the real deal. Right there during that initial call, he gave me the location where they were doing a casting call. Of course, you know I killed the part, and got the role. Ever since then, my career has been taking off."

Monae smiled proudly, "Damn girl, that's some crazy shit."

"Naw, it ain't crazy," Kameesha said as she outed the blunt in the ashtray, "It's the law of attraction. What you think about, you bring about. Let me not start preaching though. I'm hungry as hell, and you know, I'm dying to hear what you been up to."

Monae certainly wasn't eager to tell her.

# CHAPTER 10

*Lee's Kitchen*

Despite living in Raleigh for the majority of her life, Monae had never been to the Jamaican restaurant. She wondered if it was new.

"This is a new spot, it's been open for like a year now," Kameesha revealed, as if reading her mind. "We shot some scenes here for a movie I was in, and now whenever I show up, they let me eat for free. Wait until you see the view," she said, leading them inside.

Almost immediately, they were greeted by a pretty brown-skinned hostess, dressed in all white. Her eyes lit up with excitement the moment she saw Kameesha.

"It's so good to see you! How have you been?" She gushed, as the two embraced. After some small talk, a male waiter escorted them past a packed dining area, up two flights of stairs to an exclusive rooftop eating section. Four tables, two of which were occupied, were positioned in each corner. A buffet style arrangement, surrounded by palm trees sat in the center of the roof with several waiters on standby. To shield patrons from the sun, a giant Jamaican flag served as a canopy of sorts, with see-through netting cascading from its side to keep out the flies. The entire Caribbean themed alignment was classy and intimate, and Monae didn't hesitate to give her girl some props once they were seated.

"Sis, this place is super nice," Monae said, twisting in her seat to look around. "And this view is amazing."

"Told you," Kameesha replied as she poured ice water in their glasses. "Wait until you taste the food though."

On cue, servers began arriving with platters of jerk and curry chicken, curry goat, rice and peas, fried dumplings, ackee and saltfish, and macaroni and cheese. And to top it off, a pitcher of rum punch. The ladies immediately dug in, neither uttering a word besides groans of pleasure for at least the first five minutes.

"Damn girl, this shit is delicious!" Monae finally exclaimed with a mouth full of curry chicken. "Can I take some of this to go?"

"Of course, you can," Kameesha said, as she wiped her mouth with a napkin. She took a drink of rum punch, sat the glass down, and looked Monae directly in the eye. "So, what's up, you ready to tell me why you came back, and why you haven't finished fashion design school yet? And what's up with this boyfriend of yours? Redd. Am I ever going to meet him?"

Just that fast, Monae lost her appetite. The answers to Kameesha's questions weren't pleasant, and although she was comfortable confiding in her friend, she had been dreading the conversation. At the same time, keeping her emotions bottled up was seriously starting to affect her well-being. She knew for her sake at least; it was imperative she talk about it. With a sigh, she pushed her plate away before taking a swig of punch to wet her palate. Then, for the first time in years, she opened up.

She began with how she met Redd at a Block party, six months after arriving in N.Y. "He was so charming, and cute, and chubby," she revealed with a giggle. "What I liked most about him, though, was his persistence. Even after I shot him down the first two times he tried to holla, he kept coming back until eventually I gave him my number. Three nights later, we went on our first date to the movies. And I know that's so cliché, but the real highlight was afterwards, he took me to this Indian restaurant he said he heard about from some show on the Food Network called Diners, Drive-ins and Dives. I can't front, girl, the food was banging. Not as good as this, though," she quickly added. "What I remember most about that day are the stories he told me about being raised in group homes. You already know I could relate to that, being I was raised in foster homes. Looking back on it now, I might've fell in love with him that night. On top of all that, this nigga is a straight gangsta, and we both know if it's one thing I can't resist, it's a gangsta." Kameesha nodded knowingly. "Red was a gangsta and a gentleman in the beginning," Monae continued. "I still made him wait almost three months for the pussy. When I finally did give him some…" Her words trailed off as her eyes rolled back like she was climaxing right there.

Kameesha leaned forward, fork midair, thirsty to hear more. "Bitch, you lying! It was that good?"

Monae licked her lips. "Girl, if I didn't love him before then, I did after that night. That nigga fucks like a pornstar, and his tongue… like a fucking tornado. I'm getting hot just thinking about this shit," she joked, fanning herself.

For a moment she lost her train of thought recalling how Redd had thoroughly sucked her pussy that morning, provoking back-to-back orgasms.

Kameesha snapped her fingers to regain her attention. "Helloooooo, so what happened?" She inquired, eager to hear the rest.

Monae shook her head sadly. "What you think happened? Bitch, I fell hard for that nigga. Next thing I know, I'm holding his guns, helping him sell drugs one day, and robbing niggas with him the next."

Kameesha was speechless. The Monae she'd known 3 years ago definitely possessed some gangsta tendencies. Never though would she have suspected her best friend of engaging in a life if a crime, let alone for a man.

The waiter suddenly materialized to inquire if they needed anything, and Kameesha instructed him to bag up the rest to go. Once he cleared the table and left, she asked, "So is that reason you dropped out of fashion school?"

Monae nodded before lowering her head in shame. "I got pregnant," she admitted after a beat. "Then I ended up losing the baby because this nigga don't know how to keep his hands to himself." The pain in her tone caused Kameesha's eyes to well up with water. She wanted to offer some words of comfort, but was too stunned. "I just don't know what to do." Monae went on, tears streaming down her cheeks. "Between this nigga always beating my ass, and cheating on me, I feel like I'm losing my mind. What am I doing wrong?"

Kameesha reached across the table to hold her hand. "You not doing nothing wrong, so don't you dare play yourself by thinking it's your fault."

Monae wasn't convinced. "I just don't know what to do," she repeated, openly sobbing. "I know I gotta leave this nigga, but I love him, sis. And even if I did leave, where would I go? I don't have nobody."

Kameesha tenderly squeezed her hand. "You got me girl, and I love you." To emphasize her point, she slid her chair around the table beside Monae and hugged her.

For the next few minutes, neither girl said anything as they held each other and cried. "I never told you this, but in high school, you saved my life," Kameesha admitted once the tears subsided. "Between the bullying, and then after Roy got killed, I seriously thought about killing myself. Its only because of you and our friendship that I couldn't go through with it." She allowed the statement to sink in. "What I'm trying to say is, you helped me then, now let me help you, Monae. That's what friends are for, and you're more than a friend. You're my sister, so let me help you."

"How?" Monae muttered miserably, dabbing at her eyes.

"Come stay with me," Kameesha suggested without hesitation. "I'm hardly ever home anyway, so you would pretty much have the house to yourself. Plus, I'm sure I could get you a job."

"I don't know," Monae said, unsure if she wanted to live in N.C. again.

There was also the issue of Redd. For all his fuckups, Monae wasn't even sure she wanted to leave him. Call her stupid, but she loved him immensely, and believed wholeheartedly she could get him to change his ways.

"Just think about it," Kameesha urged, sensing her indecision. "And no matter what, never forget I'm here for you. You're my sister, and I love you."

"Love you too," Monae replied, rising to her feet. Kameesha stood with her and they embraced again before gathering their belongings and heading downstairs.

Back in the G-wagon, Kameesha immediately sparked a blunt, and set the tone. "We not talking about ya dude for the rest of the day," she announced. "Today is supposed to be about us, and we not letting nobody spoil that, agreed?"

Monae smiled, feeling better already. "Agreed."

Even if she wanted to think about Redd, Kameesha didn't let her. After Lee's Kitchen, they spent a few hours shopping at the mall, and enjoying each other's company. It was like they were back in high school all over again, and Monae found herself getting more and more stressed as the day wound down. She didn't even remember falling asleep, but obviously she did because when she opened her eyes they were parked in front of her crib. Yawning, she glanced at Kameesha.

"How long was I asleep?"

"Not long," Kameesha answered scrolling through her phone. "I'm glad you up though 'cause I got some shit to tell you. You remember Jon-Jon, right?"

"What Jon-Jon?" Monae said, still a little disorientated.

Kameesha sucked her teeth in mock annoyance "Bitch, you ain't been gone that long to be talking about what Jon-Jon. The same Jon-Jon you had a crush on."

"Ooohhhh, that Jon-Jon," Monae said, her memory refreshed. She chuckled as an image of his face popped into her head. "Bitch that nigga had a crush on me. You know I only had eyes for Roy."

"Yeah, whatever," Kameesha said, knowing better. "Anyway, somebody shot him up real bad earlier. They saying he might die. Whether he do or don't, it's about to be some shit."

"Why you say that?" Monae said, confused. The Jon-Jon she remembered had been a small-time nigga. And yeah, she might've had the tiniest crush on him with his bowlegged self.

"Girl, that nigga big-time now", Kameesha revealed. "He got a team of young boys that be tearing shit up, and trust, they gone find out who did it." She shook her head already imaging the mayhem about to ensue.

Monae shrugged dismissively. "Oh well, sucks to be them," she muttered, not really caring. "I had a good time today though, sis. Real talk, I needed this. I needed you. Hopefully we can do this again soon."

"Ain't no hopefully about it," Kameesha reassured her. "Just let me check my schedule and I'll let you know. In the meantime, if you need anything – and I mean anything – you know I'm here."

She leaned over with open arms, and Monae returned the hug. "Thank you for not judging me," she said. "You've always been a good person, and it's good to see you haven't changed."

Kameesha blushed from the praise. "I learned from you, so thank yourself. Now get outta here before you make me cry again. And take these with you," she said handing her the eyeglasses case. "Make sure you call me later too. Love you."

"Love you too, and I will," Monae responded as she exited the Benz. She waved a final time then spun off. It was as she stood on the porch moments later, rummaging through her purse for her keys that she noticed Kameesha had indeed managed to steal her Chanel shades. Chuckling at her sneakiness, Monae retrieved her keys at the same time her phone vibrated. After such a perfect day she didn't think anything could ruin it.

Unfortunately, she was wrong.

# CHAPTER 11

"So, you mean to tell me he didn't show up, and he didn't call either?" Monae tried to disguise the alarm in her tone, but it was almost impossible, considering the text that arrived from Serious moments earlier.

'*Ya man play a lot of games,*' The text read.

Monae called him back immediately. Phone glued to her ear, she sat the grub from Lee's Kitchen on the coffee table, and plopped down on the sofa, unable to shake the feeling of unease starting to brew in her gut.

"That's exactly what I'm telling you," Serious was saying in an agitated tone. "I waited damn near two hours for him, the least he could've did was call. Now all of a sudden he not answering his phone." He sucked his teeth, obviously annoyed. "I told you from jump I didn't want to fuck with ole boy. I don't like him. Only reason I even agreed to deal with him is because of you. Look how he shows his appreciation. You already know it's a wrap for anything else."

"Okay, that's fine," Monae snapped not trying to hide her attitude. "Ain't nobody beg you to fuck with him in the first place. I asked, and you could've said no. I'm sorry he didn't show up, but I'm sure there's a good reason. It might not even be his fault. Anything could've happened, so before you jump to conclusions, at least let me find out what's what."

Serious took a calming deep breath. "You know what, sis, you absolutely right. But that still don't change the fact that something ain't right with ole boy."

"Anyways, I'm not trying to hear none of that right now," Monae interrupted, talking over him. "You obviously don't know where my man is so I'll holla at you later."

"That's your fucking problem!" Serious exploded. "You never want to hear shit when it comes to that nigga. It's like he got you brainwashed or something. I suggest you wake up, sis. Have I ever steered you wrong before?"

"This is different," Monae said, becoming more aggravated. "You don't even know him. You chilled with him that one time when we first got down here, and now all of a sudden something ain't right about him. You sound stupid."

"Sis, I don't need to know him," Serious shot back. "I know what I feel. Son got that grimey, sneaky vibe about him. I been in the streets long enough to pick up on shit like that."

"Yeah, whatever," Monae said, waving off his comment. "If you so good at picking up on shit like that, how come you couldn't tell ya right-hand man was plotting on you? Dude shot you six times, and its only because it wasn't your time to go – not your street smarts – that you still alive. Now you got the nerve to be talking about vibes. Nigga please!"

That's what Monae really wanted to say, but she held her tongue, knowing such a comment would cause a big argument. Be that as it may, she wasn't about to just listen to Serious bash her man.

She interrupted him mid rant. "Listen bro, you entitled to your opinion but how about you do me a favor, and keep it to yourself from here on out. Matter fact, I don't even want to talk about this anymore."

"I bet you don't," Serious said, sarcasm dripping from his tone. "Tell you what, since you feel like that, don't call me when that nigga fuck up."

"Motherfucker, you would be the last one I called!" Monae yelled.

Serious, however, had already hung up. It took all the restraint she could muster to keep from calling back and cursing him out. Instead, she kicked off her sneakers and called Redd.

His voicemail picked up back-to-back, and she felt her anger climbing like a roller coaster. After plugging her cell into the charger, she headed to the kitchen with the Jamaican food. As she placed the containers of food in the fridge, she replayed the exchange with Serious. His assessment of Redd was accurate, and even if Monae only admitted it to herself, she knew her anger stemmed from the truth in his statement. Nonetheless, right, or wrong, she wasn't about to let Serious or anybody for that matter dog her man out. Redd might've been a piece of shit, but he was her piece of shit. Serious should've been the last to talk anyway. His wife, Sasha, was an ex-stripper he'd met at the strip club. Monae had only met her a few times when Serious brought her with him to N.Y., but in her opinion the bitch was nothing more than a gold-digging smut. Out of respect for Serious, though, she kept her thoughts to herself. Why Serious refused to afford her the same respect when it came to Redd, Monae couldn't understand. It was like he knew something she didn't. With a 3-minute phone call he'd managed to ruin what up until that point had been a spectacular day.

Frustrated, Monae slammed the fridge shut and returned to the living room where she called Redd another three times. Once again, she reached his voicemail. Where the fuck is this nigga at, she wondered as she began to pace. She was trying to restrain her mind from getting the best of her, but the more she pondered on his possible whereabouts, the stronger she felt he was with another bitch. What heightened her suspicions were the series of texts she discovered in Redd's phone several nights earlier from some broad named Vanilla. Although the messages weren't directly incriminating, they were tinged with the type of subtle flirtatious banter any girlfriend would find suspicious. Considering Redd's track record of infidelity, Monae had been more than suspicious. Out of fear of starting an unnecessary argument, she hadn't said anything. Now she was willing to bet money a female was the reason behind Redd's absence. Nothing else made sense.

"Fuck!" She screamed, enraged. The thought that Redd could once again be cheating filled her with such fury she felt her body trembling. Before she could think twice, she was flying up the stairs to the second floor.

Monae found exactly what she wanted in a purple Crown Royal pouch stashed in the master bedroom closet. Carefully she removed the chrome .380 Redd had given her for her last birthday. The present had also come with a voucher for free shooting lessons, and Monae had taken advantage. Long story short, she knew how to handle a pistol. After ejecting the clip to ensure it was indeed full, she slammed it back in, then racked the slide back to insert a bullet in the chamber. Chest heaving up and down with adrenaline, she flipped the safety lever on, and exited the closet.

If Redd was indeed cheating, it wouldn't be the first time, Monae reminded herself. She definitely planned on making it his last though. She could literally feel the anger resonating through her entire body as she changed into a black Nike Tech sweat suit, then headed to the dresser in search of a scarf to wrap her hair. It was as she ransacked the draws that she caught a glimpse of herself in the mirror. There were tears streaming down the face of the reflection staring back at her, and in that moment, a startling revelation dawned on Monae. Her life was a mess. Here she was at 20 years old, about to potentially throw away her entire life away on a no-good, cheating, lying, abusive man, whose claims of love were obviously as fraudulent as a 2-dollar bill. The realization was all it took for the murderous fog consuming her to evaporate. In its place arrived a crippling grief that made her collapse like a folding chair. Monae just didn't get it. She was the perfect girlfriend: beautiful, smart, and super loyal. Even risking her freedom for Redd on numerous occasions, one of which led to her catching a felony. Still, none of her demonstrations of love were enough to prevent Redd from treating her so foul. Sobs racked her body, causing it to convulse as she thought about the three years she'd wasted being Redd's backbone, giving up her own dreams, and goals in the process. In retrospect, she could now see her actions had been beyond foolish. Back then though, nobody could've told her she wasn't being the perfect ride or die bitch, something most dudes claimed to want. Everybody but Redd.

After years of abuse and betrayal, Monae had finally reached her breaking point. She loved Redd deeply, but love wasn't going to cause her to continue making a fool of herself. In that instant of reflection, she clearly understood if she ever wanted to experience true happiness she would need to leave Redd. After the talk with Kameesha, she was now ready to do just that. The conclusion stimulated more tears, but also a sense of peace she couldn't recall feeling in a long time. With Redd out of the picture, she could pursue her dreams of starting her own clothing line, travel, rekindle her friendship with Kameesha, and maybe even find a good man later on down the line.

The image of the beautiful future that awaited caused her to smile amidst the tears still dribbling from her eyes. Now all she wanted to do was smoke a fat spliff, and relax. As for Redd...

"Let the next bitch deal with his ass," she said out loud as she rose to her feet.

"Let the next bitch deal with who?" A voice suddenly echoed.

Startled, Monae gasped, shocked to see Redd standing in the doorway, gripping a black shopping bag.

"Damn nigga, what the fuck? You scared the hell out of me!" She confessed, hand over her thumping heart. "Where the fuck you been at anyway? I been calling you like crazy."

"Battery died," Redd answered, tossing her his iPhone. With a few strides, he closed the distance between them until he was standing directly in front of her. "The real question is why you crying, and what the fuck are you doing with that?" He gestured to the gun in her hand. "Let me find out you was about to kill yourself."

Monae shook her head as she handed him back the phone which was indeed dead. "Ain't nobody was thinking about killing myself. I was just having a moment," she admitted, embarrassed that he'd caught her at such a vulnerable point. "And this was for you," she revealed, holding up the .380. "Let's just say I was about to come looking for ya ass. Now where the fuck you been? Serious said you didn't come through and – "

"Yeah, yeah, yeah, fuck that nigga Serious," Redd rudely interrupted. "I know that's ya brother and all that, but son don't like me for whatever reason, and I definitely don't like him. Now, I don't need his ass." To illustrate his point, he emptied the bag, spilling guns and money on the carpet. "Caught a nigga sleeping today," he bragged with a sinister grin. "And you already know what happens when I catch a nigga sleeping. I can't help but wake his ass up."

Monae stared at the money unimpressed. She was more concerned with its origin. "What did you do, Redd?" She asked, not even sure she really wanted to know. "We ain't been down here a month yet, please don't tell me you did something crazy already."

"I did what I had to do," Redd replied.

Then before Monae could ask what he meant; he sat her down on the edge of the bed, and recounted his version of robbing and shooting Jon-Jon. He undressed slowly as he talked, and by the time he was naked, his story was done. Without waiting for a reply, he stuffed the soiled attire in the shopping bag, and sat it by the door on his way out.

"Start packing now, we outta here tonight," he ordered over his shoulder strolling from the room.

Moments later, Monae heard the shower come on. Dumbfounded, she sat there replaying Redd's tale in her mind. It didn't take a rocket scientist to figure out the Jon-Jon in his incident, was the same Jon-Jon Kameesha mentioned earlier as to having gotten shot. Redd was obviously telling the truth. Even the part about his car running out of gas on the highway then paying someone to drive him to the gas station and back to his car sounded true. Monae felt like she was dreaming. She couldn't believe that after being in Raleigh for less than a month, Redd had once again found a way to disrupt their lives. It was because of him they were in North Carolina to begin with. *Where would they go now*, she thought, feeling helpless. Yeah, they had money, but what good was all the money in the world if they were dead? And considering what Kameesha had said about Jon-Jon's goons, death was a very realistic possibility.

Not knowing what else to do, Monae decided to call Serious. Redd probably wouldn't like that, but she didn't care. With her life now in jeopardy, her brother was the only one she knew who could prevent them from ending up on the ten o'clock news. She needed to inform him of the situation asap. She scanned the room for her cellphone, and after a minute or so, remembered it was in the living room. As she went to walk out, she thought about returning the gun to its previous location. At the last moment, she chose to take it with her just in case. What exactly "just in case" meant, Monae didn't know. She just reasoned it was better to be safe than sorry.

Downstairs in the living room, she quickly secured her phone and called Serious. His voicemail picked up after a few rings. Two more attempts garnered the same result, and Monae figured he was probably still in his feelings over their earlier spat.

She sent a text: *Pick up the fucking phone! Its life or death.*

Five minutes later, she had yet to receive a response. Anxiety intensifying, Monae tossed the phone on the couch with intentions of calling Serious back in another few minutes.

Unfortunately, she never got the chance.

At that exact moment, the sound of screeching tires outside caught her attention. Thinking there might've been an accident, she sauntered over to the bay windows and pulled back a portion of the curtain. What she saw sent chills rippling down her spine.

Two men, both clad in green army fatigues trotted up the driveway toting assault rifles. Behind them, a black Suburban sat idling at the curb, both front doors thrown open, smoke curling from its muffler. As if sensing her gaze, both men simultaneously glanced in her direction. Without hesitation, they aimed and opened fire.

*Rat, tat, tat, tat, tat tat.*

"Redd!" Monae screamed in horror, diving to the carpet as a fusillade of bullets obliterated the window, raining shards of glass.

*Rat, tat, tat, tat, tat.*

Scurrying across the floor on hands and knees, she kept her head down as more slugs demolished the flat screen, lamps, and sofa, catapulting into the air chunks of plaster, electrical fragments, and furniture stuffing. In the midst of the gunfire, Monae heard something ram against the front door once, then again, just as she reached the bottom of the staircase. Scrambling up the steps two and three at a time, she reached the top, and glanced back just in time to see the door come flying off its hinges.

Both gunmen rushed inside, spun towards the living room, and unleashed a blast of fire power until their guns clicked empty. Both of them quickly jammed in fresh clips, all the while glancing around for Monae.

"Where the fuck is that bitch at?" One of them barked.

Seconds later they turned their attention to the staircase, and got the shock of their lives. Monae stood at the top of the stairs with her birthday present aimed at them. Without hesitation, she started squeezing.

*Pop pop pop pop pop.*

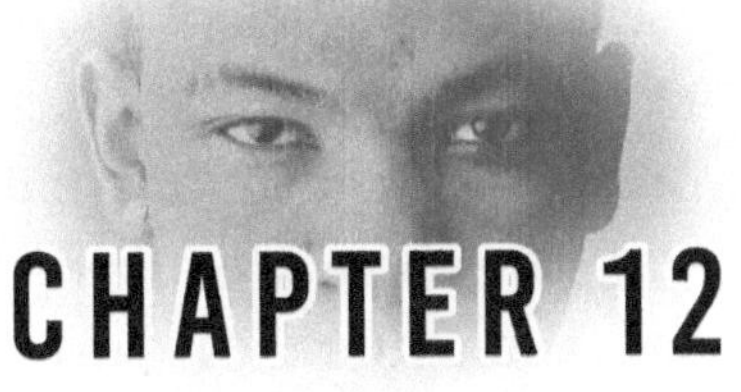

# CHAPTER 12

The first official day of summer had finally arrived, and the residents of "The View" were out in full force to greet it. Fleeing from the stuffy confines of their apartments, they convened in the "big park", located at the back of the projects to socialize while enjoying the beautiful weather. Rap music filled the air, but did little to drown out the shrieks of laughter coming from the kids frolicking in the playground sprinkler. Adding to the celebratory vibe was the mouthwatering aroma of barbecue permeating the air. Gigi was doing her thing on the grill, and everybody was eagerly awaiting the chance to purchase a plate of her delicious grub. No one was thirstier than Menace.

Dressed in a crisp white tee, polo khaki shorts, and a pair of Louis Vuitton presto's, Menace observed the gala with little interest, from a project bench. He had a lot on his mind, and despite the festive ambiance, his mood was somber. One week after the sit down with his moms, and her words were still echoing through his mind like a CD on repeat.

*'Your father would be disappointed with you!'*

Even now, seven days later, the comment still made Menace cringe. Despite his pops being M.I.A. for the entirety of his life thus far, the last thing he wanted to do was disappoint the man whom he felt so much love and admiration for. Just the thought of his father, Lunatic, provoked his heart to swell with pride. How many individuals could actually say their pops was a legend? For those fortunate enough to have even grown up with a pops, how many could say they wanted to be just like the man whose nuts they'd come from? Menace knew there weren't many, and he felt privileged to have originated from such a superior lineage. Regardless of having never met his pops, he still felt his spirit inside of him, as if even in his absence he was still guiding him. The last thing he wanted to do was tarnish his legacy. Hearing his moms utter those words had crushed him. They'd also forced him to conclude the time had now arrived for him to step his game up.

For the past week Menace had been devising a blueprint, that if executed efficiently, would remove him from the ranks of mediocrity and catapult him into the sphere of notoriety shared by other Soundview legends. Even more important than status was all the money to be gained if all went as planned. Menace saw no reason why it shouldn't, but still found it impossible not to obsess over the details once again. Concentrating, however, was proving to be a difficult task.

The "big park" resembled a fourth of July celebration, and directly in front him, a basketball game involving B.R. was taking place. Between the loud cheers, and other activity going on all around him, Menace was struggling to stay focused. On top of that he was starving. He spotted his moms assisting Gigi with the cooking, and unconsciously licked his lips, as he felt his belly growl. Much to his dislike, not even 20 feet away, Rudeboy, and Raw sat perched atop a project bench, surrounded by the usual handful of workers, associates, and dick-riders. The sight of him made Menace refocus on his blueprint to take over the entire drug trade in "The View", none of which could happen until Rudeboy was dead. There was no way around it, the nigga had to go, and Menace planned on being the triggerman. He knew it wouldn't be as hard as one might've suspected.

After controlling the drug trade in "The View" for the better part of a decade, anybody could see Rudeboy had gotten comfortable. A sentiment reflected not only in his carefree demeanor, but also in the sloppiness of his operation. In addition, the quality of his dope was subpar, and he'd been underpaying and over working his workers for years. The whispers of discord circulating within his ranks had longed since reached the ears of Menace, and it surprised even him that somebody hadn't already murdered Rudeboy, particularly the twins, Rell, and Rod. Those unaware of their track record would see the identical twins for the first time, with their light eyes, and good Indian hair, and think pretty boys. Their short stature of 5'7" also did nothing to deter people from underestimating them. There was nothing remotely soft or sweet about either of the brothers, and those foolish enough to assume otherwise based on their appearance usually found out the hard way. Rell and Rod were nothing to be fucked with. They were actually the backbone of Rudeboy's operation, and aligning himself with the brothers had been one of his wisest decisions, especially since he wasn't even from "The View". The twins had been born and raised there, and based on that alone, they received a level of respect not afforded Rudeboy. From a young age they'd developed the reputation of being violent, and unpredictable. Now in their early thirties, they controlled the entire back section of the projects with Rudeboy as their supplier. Quiet as kept they were one of the main reasons he'd lasted so long. Make no mistake about it, Rudeboy was a certified animal, and he'd definitely earned his seat on the throne. It was because of the twins though that attempts to unseat him had been unsuccessful.

Now, according to a reliable source, Menace was aware the twins had been discreetly inquiring about a connect, which in his book could only mean one thing. They were planning a takeover of their own but didn't want to groundhog Rudeboy until they secured a new plug. The Jamaican's days were truly numbered, and Menace knew he needed to move fast. He would've much rather eat with the twins than war with them. Not out of fear, but because in a sense, he fucked with them. They'd participated in a number of robberies and shootings together and although he wouldn't go as far as to label them friends, he definitely considered them comrades. Now he was trying to figure out if they should be viewed as enemies.

Menace scanned the park, his eyes probing and parting the crowd until he spotted the older, more level headed twin Rell, leaning against the chain link fence surrounding the basketball court, cheering on B.R. A few arms' lengths away, Rod stood with his back against the same fence chopping it up with members of his squad, and a handful of females. As was their norm, both siblings were draped in jewelry, and immaculately dressed in different colored Gucci linen short sets – red for Rell, and cream for Rod. It was their footwear though that literally distinguished them. Rell only rocked high end designer kicks like Gucci's, Louis Vuitton, and the red Balenciaga's he presently wore. Rod, on the other hand, was a Jordan fanatic. That day he had on a pair of black and red 11s. In fact, his entire squad of at least 15 goons were rocking the same kicks.

Menace watched the brothers socialize and mingle like seasoned politicians, and although he would never admit it to anyone else, there was no denying the slight tinge of jealousy he felt seeing them captivate the crowd so effortlessly. Anybody could see they were highly loved and respected, and he knew transgressing against either of the twins would ignite a war between both sides of the projects. The conclusion wouldn't deter him from trying to eliminate both brothers if they opposed his agenda. Before it came to that though he wanted to be absolutely sure of their intentions. He figured a face to face could establish some clarity. Then again, the fact that they hadn't reached out to him about a plug, despite their rapport, was in a way, clarity enough. Menace found himself struggling to make sense of their actions. Coincidentally, at that same moment, he spotted someone approaching that could possibly provide some insight.

Rosez would more than likely be able to shed some light on the situation, being that she had a connection with twins, specifically Rell, who she'd been romantically involved with years prior. Menace had also seen her talking to both brothers earlier, so he definitely wanted to know what that was about. Trailing behind Rosez were two of her flower girls, Ivy, and Lotus, each of them carrying a plate with a soda on top. As hungry as he was, the food didn't come close to captivating Menace like the provocative outfit Rosez wore. Lustfully licking his lips, he made no effort to disguise his appraisal as his eyes slid from her black roman styled sandals with the straps crisscrossing up her calves, to the royal blue biker shorts strangling her thighs. A matching royal blue KAUSE KARMA, V-neck displayed an ample amount of cleavage, and was knotted at the base and raised just enough to expose her toned stomach. As she sashayed towards him, her diamond rose, belly button pendant, swung slightly like the pendulum of a clock, mirroring the sway of her dreads, the tips of which were now dyed purple. Menace found himself momentarily mesmerized by her beauty and sense of style. As fast as the sensation arrived, it departed only to be replaced by a sense of annoyance that caused him to unconsciously scowl.

He had no doubt Rosez was coming to once again inquire about her cut from the Lotto jux. Usually, she got 25% off any lick she steered their way. Unfortunately, due to the outcome, Menace hadn't given her anything. On top of that, he'd been sending her calls straight to voicemail. Some real sucker shit, he knew, and he regretted treating Rosez like that. She was an asset to M.B.A.M., and more importantly, a member. Off the strength of that alone, she deserved a superior level of respect and honesty. The latter is exactly what Menace planned on giving her. It wasn't like he didn't want to pay her, things had just gone awry. Still, he felt his dick twitch as Rosez walked right between his legs, leaned over, and kissed his cheek.

"Can a bitch get a hug?" She demanded, stepping back to look at him with a smirk. "You look like you ain't too happy to see me. We letting money come between us now?"

"You tell me," Menace replied, rising to embrace her. The scent of her sweet-smelling perfume, combined with the softness of her body, made it impossible for him to resist cuffing her yeeks.

Rosez playfully smacked his hand away. "Nah nigga, don't grab that. Just a minute ago you had your face all screwed up like I threw up on ya dick. Am I lying bitches?" Both flower girls nodded, before setting the plates on the bench, then spinning off.

Menace instantly began digging in. He took a bite of BBQ chicken and felt like kissing Gigi. There were several pieces of the succulent bird, along with a slab of ribs on one plate, while the other contained Gigi's famous potato salad, and two ears of roasted corn. To say the food was good would've been disrespectful, spectacular was a more accurate description. For years, Menace had been telling Gigi she should open up her own restaurant. Maybe when he got the funds, he would do it for her. Until then he would gladly pay whatever for a plate of her food. Intent on devouring every morsel of goodness, he licked sauce from his fingers after every bite.

"Damn nigga, slow down before you choke," Rosez cautioned, laughing. "Couldn't even say thank you with ya ungrateful ass."

"Thank you," Menace mumbled with a mouthful of rib. After killing half the meal, he took a long swig of Pepsi, burped loudly, then turned to Rosez who had been texting while he ate. "So, what's up?" He asked, wiping his mouth with a napkin. "Matter fact, what's up with you and the twins? I peeped you choppin' it up with them earlier. I thought you told me you don't fuck with them like that no more."

"I don't, but damnnnn," Rosez exclaimed. "Aren't we the nosy one today. Let me find out you jealous."

Menace snorted as if the notion was preposterous. "Me, jealous? Picture that. Only thing I wanna know is why I been hearing these niggas is looking for a connect all of a sudden when they got Rudeboy?"

"You know why," Rosez warned ominously. "That was actually one of the reasons why I was calling you," she explained. "Rell reached out to me like a week ago, asking if I knew anybody selling weight on the coke tip. I told him I would get back to him because I wanted to holla at you first, just in case you wanted me to handle it a certain way. You been ducking me though. We'll get to that in a minute."

Without asking, she snagged a piece of chicken from his plate and threw it in her mouth. "Like I was saying," she continued, chomping. "You were ducking me, and I didn't want to do the wrong thing, so I didn't say shit. Today was the first time seeing each other since we spoke, so he wanted to know what was up."

"What did you tell him?" Menace inquired.

Rosez frowned as if the answer should've been obvious. "Menace, please don't fucking play with me! My loyalty is to M.B.A.M. and you know that. You should already know what I told him. I don't have a line on nothing. Them niggas is definitely plotting though," she confirmed. "They ain't say shit but I felt it."

Menace felt it too, and suddenly it dawned on him. If the twins were indeed scheming like he suspected, his own takeover plans would have to be expedited. He also wondered if it might not just be smarter to kill both brothers first, before going after Rudeboy. They were the true power behind his operation anyway, so it made more sense to crush them first, now that he thought about it.

"So, what's up with my bread?" Rosez said, breaking his train of thought. "I been calling you all week, and all of a sudden you not answering ya phone. That's what we doing now? And you be the first one to talk about how important communication is."

"Ain't no bread," Menace admitted, deciding not to beat around the bush.

"Fuck you mean, ain't no bread?" Rosez asked, scowling. "I know you not trying to play me, Menace! I know you wouldn't do me like that. I done made you thousands, done put in hella work for – "

"Something came up," Menace interrupted. "We got ten bands from ole boy but you already know I got jammed up. My moms bailed me out so I gave her back the $7500 she put up. I gave the rest to Crisis. I didn't even take shit for myself," he revealed, hoping the admission would prove he wasn't trying to sleaze her. It didn't.

Her head tilted sideways, as she squinted wickedly at him. "You gave ya moms and Crisis bread but not me? Are you fucking serious?" She yelled, enraged. "I'm the one that put y'all onto the jux in the first place. Without me, y'all wouldn't have gotten shit, right or wrong?"

She was absolutely right, and Menace knew it, which is why he was prepared to give her the rack in his pocket. Before he could say anything about it, Rosez went from zero to a hundred.

Biting her lip in anger, she stood and turned to face him. "We done, Menace. You a fucking winky dink, and this the last time I let you play me," she spat. "Take that bread and rub it on ya chest. And next time you want some pussy, or ya little dick sucked, get ya stuck up ass mother to handle that. Get that old washed-up bitch to line some niggas up for you too. Fucking busta," she added, going to walk off.

Stunned by the disrespect, Menace sat his plate down, and grabbed Rosez by the arm. Without a second thought, he smacked her once, then again with a swift backhand that sent her Chanel shades flying. Hitting a female was something he didn't condone, however after excusing Rosez and her reckless mouth for far too long, his anger finally got the best of him.

"Look like you the winky dink now," he taunted, shoving her.

Stunned, Rosez stumbled back a few steps, a look of utter disbelief on her face. She gingerly touched her cheek, then lips, before looking at her hand. Her eyes widened in shock when she saw the splotch of blood on her fingertips. Then she smiled, a cold devious expression, that should've alerted Menace of what was to come. Knowing Rosez as well as he did, he should've known better than to think she would just take it on the hop. Rosez touched her mouth again, then without warning, swung.

Menace saw the glint of metal and jumped back just in time to keep from getting his face slashed. Unfortunately, he wasn't quick enough. A stinging sensation shot through his jaw as the blade nicked his chin before slicing his shirt and cutting into the top of his chest. Menace glanced down, saw the blood spreading across his shirt, and went ballistic.

Rosez tried to run and he tripped her, sending her tumbling to the grass. Before she could put up any further resistance, he straddled her, using one knee to pin her left arm down, as he pried the razor from her right.

"No Menace, stop!" Rosez pleaded, trying to buck him off.

Her words fell on deaf ears. Menace had officially blacked out. Rage was now dictating his actions, and for Rosez, that meant her life was now in danger.

"I'm sorry," she screamed as he swung the blade, cutting her. Pain erupted in her face, and she weaved sideways in time to avoid another slash.

Menace didn't plan on missing again. He gripped her throat, squeezing, as he raised his arm preparing to strike. Before he could strike, somebody grabbed his wrist from behind.

"Fuck is you doing?" A man's voice barked. "I been waiting for you to step out of line. Now, imma beat your ass."

Next thing Menace knew, he was being yanked to his feet.

Menace wrenched his arm free and spun to find Rudeboy standing there with his face all screwed up. Raw stood beside him, and behind them a huge crowd watched in astonishment. The twins were right in front, and Menace spotted them just before he noticed Crisis, B.R., and Guntalk hurriedly threading through the crowd.

Menace turned his attention to Rudeboy, not even thinking about speaking. *What was there to say anyway?* With the quickness of a western gunslinger, he backed out his .357, and aimed it at his head. Everybody standing behind Rudeboy instantly scattered in different directions like roaches.

Rudeboy threw his hands up in surrender. He didn't have a chance to even think about drawing his own pistol, and he definitely hadn't been expecting Menace to react by pulling his own. Now, all he could think about was disarming him.

As if reading his mind, Menace thumbed the hammer back, and walked up on him until the barrel kissed his forehead. Much to his delight, he saw fear in Rudeboy's eyes, and it made him want to kill him more.

Suddenly, Raw upped his own pistol, and from the smug grin on his face, it was obvious he thought he had the drop on Menace. That is, until he felt the hard steel poke him in the back of the head.

"Fuck is you doing, stupid?" Crisis scolded, snatching the pistol from his hand. He glanced at Menace waiting for the nod to blow Raw's brains out.

Menace laughed like a madman, amused by the irony of the situation. Only moments earlier he'd been contemplating Rudeboy's death, and now this. Using his left hand, he lifted Rudeboy's wife beater, and pulled the gun off his hip. After pocketing the pistol, he decided to make it official since the nigga already had his hands up like he was getting robbed. Staring him in the eye, he dug in his pocket and relieved him of a sizable bankroll.

Rudeboy bit his lip, seething with fury, but remained silent.

Menace took several steps back. "So, you been waiting for me to step out of line, huh? Let me hear you say that shit again. I dare you," he taunted.

"Just cool yaself, bredren. It ain't even that serious," Rudeboy claimed, trying to save face. He wore the cheesiest expression as if he couldn't decide whether to be more embarrassed or infuriated over what was taking place.

"That's what the fuck I'd thought you'd say," Menace remarked, ready to push his shit back.

Make no mistake about it, he definitely didn't plan on letting Rudeboy live. The nigga was way too dangerous for that. The only reason he hesitated was because of all the people watching, most of whom were recording the incident with their phones. *How many of those same individuals would testify against me at trial,* Menace wondered

"Fuck it," he suddenly blurted, having come to a decision. He didn't give a fuck who saw it, Rudeboy had to go. Anything else he would deal with afterwards.

Gritting his teeth, he stiffened his arm preparing for the recoil when suddenly, he felt a presence behind him, accompanied by an all too familiar scent of Liz Taylor's, *White Diamonds.*

It was his mother, Maleka.

"I know you not about to do something stupid with all these people watching," she said, laying a hand in his shoulder.

Menace snorted in disgust. "Ma, I don't give a fuck who watching. If I don't kill this nigga, they the same ones who probably gone watch him kill me down the line."

"And if you do kill him, you gone spend the rest of ya life in a cell," Maleka countered. "And if you think not, you a damn fool. Now I know for a fact I didn't raise no fools, so what you going to do is let him go. For now," she quickly added. "His time is coming, but right now I need you. Your sister needs you. Don't do this to us."

For the first time, Menace noticed Lauren in the crowd, hand covering her mouth, eyes wide with shock and fright. It was that sight, along with his mother's words that sobered him some. As bad as he didn't want to, he lowered his gun. There was no doubt in his mind, he was making a big mistake, especially when Rudeboy started to laugh as him and Raw sauntered off.

Menace knew the next time he saw either of them, someone wouldn't live to talk about it.

# CHAPTER 13

The whole hood was buzzing about the incident between Menace, and Rudeboy. Let some of them tell it, they'd always known the two would eventually bump heads. Now that they had, everybody in "The View" knew with reasonable certainty what the outcome would be: more murder and mayhem. No one had more to say about the situation then the twins, Rell and Rod.

Hours after its occurrence, the twins sat in the living room of their 3-bedroom apartment, bagging up crack as they strategized on how to proceed. Quiet as kept, Menace had put them in a precarious predicament by not groundhogging Rudeboy. Chatter was already beginning to circulate on why they hadn't intervened on his behalf, and now, all of a sudden, Rudeboy wasn't answering his phone, which in their eyes could only mean one thing. He was definitely feeling some type of way about them not coming to his aid. Knowing his handywork firsthand, the twins weren't about to take Rudeboy lightly. Presently they were trying to figure out if they should just kill him the next time he showed his face. Or maybe they would kill Menace. At the moment he was the true source of their anger, at least when it came to Rod.

"Can't believe this fuck nigga didn't shoot him," he angrily spat, as he chopped into a plum sized boulder of crack with a razor. He was especially incensed because he'd been on the verge of upping his own pistol in defense of Rudeboy when Rell stopped him, probably thinking Menace was about to do them a favor by offing Rudeboy. But he hadn't, and by not doing so, he'd forced their hand in a sense. Rell didn't seem at all bothered by the situation. He even had the nerve to chuckle at his brother's comment.

"Trust me bruh, that nigga did us a favor. This was really a blessing in disguise. You think it's a coincidence we was already planning on getting rid of son, and then this happens. Yeah, Rudeboy might be a little vexed that we ain't pop that bottle for him, but let's be real, did he expect us to smoke the nigga Menace with everybody out there? Niggas ain't never been no puppets, you feel me? If he can't respect that, then its whatever. I'm sure he not trying to go to war with Menace and us anyway. And while he concentrating on that nigga, we gone put his lights out. Keep telling you this shit ain't rocket science bruh."

Rod nodded respectfully. "I get what you saying bruh, and it definitely makes sense," he replied. "I still say we kill Menace and this is why. We already know Rudeboy don't want no static with us but his guard gonna be up now. If we groundhog Menace, we get back in his good graces, then while he thinking shit is sweet, we send him on a ride. Killing two birds with one stone type of shit."

Rell saw his point, however, killing Menace wouldn't be as easy as it sounded "You do know what comes with taking him out though," he reminded his brother.

"Of course, I do," Rod confirmed. "All them MBAM niggas gotta go, and his family too. You already know I been wanting to do that anyway."

Perceived as the more reckless of the siblings, Rod's words were anything but idle, which wasn't all that surprising considering his upbringing. Born to parents that would later die in a car accident a week before their first birthday, the brothers were then legally adopted by an aunt who brought them to live in Soundview. "Aunty B" (as they called her) and whose claim to fame included overseeing the neighborhood numbers racket, and would be the first to introduce her nephews to the criminal element. Their most notable lessons, however, came at the hands of two Soundview heavyweights named B-Mo and Bear. Under the tutelage of such certified gangstas, it didn't take long for Rell and Rod to begin exhibiting the same savage characteristics possessed by their mentors.

At the tender age of 14, Rod dropped his first body. The victim, a man accused of raping a young girl from the neighborhood. A year later almost to the day, Rell smoked a dude over a drug debt, in broad day, feet away from the smoke shop on Cozy Corner. Although the slayings strengthened the twinsrep, what cemented it were the bodies they caught out of town, at the behest of some Soundview OG's. By the time Bear died in a tragic dirt bike accident a day after the siblings turned 16, their combined body count was rumored to be in the double digits. The murder of B-Mo followed soon after, and with no one holding the leash so to speak, the twins morphed into what can only be described as rabid dogs. Bodies were still missing, and a few years earlier several corpses had been discovered in the fields in back of Soundview. All suspected victims from the twin's decade-long reign of terror. It was only in the last few years they'd eased up with their murder game, and some believed it was only because Rudeboy had them eating so lovely. Others said a brief prison bid had made them more cunning. Whatever the case, not for one second did anybody doubt they were still as volatile as an idle volcano. They were in their early thirties, and throughout the neighboring projects like Castlehill, Monroe, and Bronx Dale, both brothers garnered a level of fear, love, and respect, rivaled only by Menace. And just like him, they commanded a platoon of shooters, young, and old that moved when they said so. No wonder the twins were plotting on seizing control of the entire drug trade in "The View". They possessed the reputation, the guns, and more importantly a force capable of unseating Rudeboy.

What they didn't have was a connect.

As easy as some might've assumed it was to find a solid connect, nothing could be further from the truth these days. Taking into account all the so-called connects either working with the police, or unable to consistently supply a steady stream of narcotics, securing a distributor was actually difficult. The twins could attest this fact.

After chopping it up for a few more minutes about the Menace, Rudeboy fiasco, the conversation once again gravitated to the topic of a connect.

"So, what did Rosez say about helping us put the pieces together," Rod inquired as he inserted a chunk of rock into a purple shaded baggy. Zipping it closed, he tossed it atop a pile of already sealed sacks, worth twenty dollars apiece.

Rell snorted in disgust. "Bitch gone have the nerve to tell me she don't know nobody. Like let's be serious, you in the loop with all type of mu'fuckas. On top of that, you got all ya little flower girls networking in these strip clubs. One of them gotta know something if you don't. Its aight though," he said with a devious smirk. "In a little while she gone understand she picked the wrong team."

"That's a fact," Rod agreed. "But keep it official, bruh, you don't feel no type of way about Menace doing her like that? Cutting her in the face and all that."

Rell shrugged with indifference. "Why would I? She not my bitch no more, so it is what it is. Plus, I heard she spit in his face. She lucky it wasn't me; I would've knocked her fucking head off."

"You and me both," Rod said.

"Fuck all that though," Rell snapped before they could get off topic. "I just thought about something. Whatever happened to son you was locked up with, the one you told me was coming home this month? You said his uncle supposed to be some big time connect right?"

Rod was already shaking his head in dismay. "You talking about my son, Papito. That might be a wrap," he admitted, dropping another sack on the pile. "I actually reached out to ole boy a few days ago and we spoke, but son energy was different. He said he was gone get back to me, but as you see, we still waiting. You know I was the one keeping the wolves off his ass in the clink. I guess he figure now that he home, he don't need me. He definitely getting some type of paper though. Nigga ain't been home two weeks and he already rocking the bust down Rollie. Matter fact, check this out."

He dusted his hands together to dislodge any residue, then grabbed his phone and pulled up Papito's Instagram page.

Rell took the phone and began scrolling through the images. "Yeah, this nigga definitely into something," he enviously muttered, staring at a picture of Papito holding a brick of cash. He handed Rod back the phone.

"Try and call him right now," he ordered, as a plan began to formulate in his head.

Without hesitation, Rod dialed Papito, and put the call on speaker. After several rings, the voicemail kicked in.

"Check this out," Rell immediately said. "Give son like another week, then holla back at him. If he ain't talking our language, we gone put Rosez on his ass. Once he see her, he not gone be able to resist, and when she get him to come through, you already know what time it is." He drew a finger across his throat, as if slicing it. "Lights out."

Rod nodded in consensus, before spitting the lyrics from a 50 Cent track. "*You getting money, I can't get none with you then fuck you.*"

"Exactly," Rell agreed as he rose to his feet. "It's about time we get back on our bullshit anyway. At the same time we gotta learn from this experience, and move smarter. All these years we been putting on for the hood, all these years we been holding Rudeboy down, and what do we really got to show for it? Absolutely nothing. I mean, we not broke, but we ain't rich either, and we should be." He shook his head in disgust. "Something gotta give. Never again should we ever have to depend on nobody to eat. And if we play this right, we won't have to. This is what we're going to do, and I know you not going to like it, but this is what's best for now. Imma ask Menace to plug us in with a connect." He paused to see his brother's reaction. Rod scrunched his face in confusion but remained silent.

"When you think about it, nothing else makes sense," Rell continued. "If we kill Rudeboy now, we basically taking food out of our own mouth. If we kill Menace, we still gotta deal with Rudeboy down the line anyway. Menace already jive fuck with us, and because we didn't side with Rudeboy today, he just might believe us when I tell him we want team up. At the end of the day the only objective is to get a connect. Menace has that, I'm sure of it. He can either eat with us, or we groundhog his ass. Either way, it's a win for us."

"And what about Rudeboy?" Rod asked in a skeptical tone.

Rell smirked as if the answer was obvious. "Fuck Rudeboy! This nigga been getting money in the hood for all these years, and he not even from "The View". How you think that makes us look? On top of that, he got the nerve to be spoon feeding us that garbage ass coke like we some little niggas. Yeah, his time is definitely up. Imma let Peanut handle his stupid ass. You know them two niggas can't stand each other anyway." Rod nodded excitedly, suddenly liking the idea.

Before he could express those and other sentiments, his phone jangled. He picked it up from the table, glanced at the screen, then smiled as he turned it so his brother could see who was calling. Papito.

Rell rubbed his hands together sinisterly, like a mad scientist. "Looks like we might not even need Menace after all."

# CHAPTER 14

Through a pair of Bushnell forty-by-twenty, night vision binoculars, Menace watched Peanut stroll up the walkway towards the building where the twins lived. At 6"3, weighing close to 300 lbs. and black and ugly as ever, he wasn't hard to miss, especially considering he was the thirteenth member from the twins' squad to pull up in the last fifteen minutes.

He was also their uncle.

One year earlier, Peanut had been released from the Feds after a 23-year bid and already he had two bodies under his belt. Just the sight of him solidified the fact that the twins were definitely up to something sinister. Whatever it was, Menace knew he had to find out fast. Lowering the binoculars to his chest, he reverted his attention back to Crisis who was in the middle of divulging how he alluded capture the night they robbed Lotto.

Weeks had elapsed since then, however the opportunity to disclose the details hadn't presented itself until that moment as they stood atop the project roof. They were actually supposed to be discussing the earlier incident with Rudeboy, and Raw, but got sidetracked after Menace explained the reason why Rosez tried to blow his face off. As crazy as that story was, it didn't have shit on the tale Crisis told.

According to him, after ditching the Range he'd run through a number of side blocks until finally he spotted a 24-hour chicken spot. He'd gone inside with intentions of regrouping before summoning an Uber to transport him across town to a female's crib. All that changed ten minutes later when he emerged from the eatery just as two cop cars cruised by. Already paranoid from the earlier chase, he took off running in the opposite direction without thinking twice.

At the first intersection he darted into traffic, and the next thing he said he remembered was waking up on the pavement, gazing into the face of a black woman who kept asking if he was alright. Still somewhat dazed, he happened to glance to the left where he spotted a black Nissan Altima, with a slight dent in the hood. Putting two and two together, he assumed correctly he'd just gotten hit by a car. The lady inquiring was obviously the driver, and when she offered to take him to the hospital, Crisis agreed not because he felt any injuries, but so he could get as far from the scene as possible.

Her name was Aminah he learned during the drive, and she was 25-years-old. Originally, from Buffalo NY, she had relocated to Harlem six months earlier to attend an exclusive beauty school in lower Manhattan. She was also a licensed bartender, with no man and a three-year-old daughter. Crisis admitted to being somewhat mesmerized by her at that point. So much so that when Aminah asked where he was coming from at such an ungodly hour, he told her about the chase with the police just to see her reaction. Much to his astonishment, she smiled and shook her head in amusement, before revealing an illicit secret of her own. Her most profitable occupation was that of a computer hacker.

Crisis confessed he knew right then and there he had to have Aminah. Shortly thereafter he convinced her he didn't need any medical attention, and when she asked where he wanted to be dropped off, Crisis said he looked her dead in the eye, and told her, "Your place."

"If I take you there you might really need medical attention when I'm done with you," Aminah had shockingly replied.

Half an hour later she was performing CPR on his dick. Crisis had been staying at her crib ever since, and it was evident by the Kool-Aid smile he wore, he was seriously feeling shorty. Eventually he pulled up a private Instagram page on his iPhone for a chocolate dime with huge tits, going by the handle *@NaughtyMinathethird*. Already, there were several pictures posted of her and Crisis hugged up like old lovers. And to think, they'd only met two weeks ago. Crisis was a sucka for a pretty face. This time, however, it appeared he'd hit the jackpot.

Menace could do nothing but laugh. "You lucky you didn't tell me about shorty before I gave you that bread because you wouldn't have got shit," he joked.

"Ahhh, cut the shit, Mo," Crisis said, trying to keep a straight face. Seconds later he burst out laughing. "Yeah, you right, I did," he admitted. "I'll take my baby Aminah over that little bit paper any day."

"I bet," Menace said as he felt his phone vibrate "You ain't know this girl for a month and she already ya baby. Sucka for love ass nigga," he joked, pulling the phone from his back pocket. The playful expression evaporated the second he saw who was calling.

# CHAPTER 15

Crisis didn't like either of the twins, never had. He tolerated them only because they'd proven reliable in the past, regarding a number of schemes and capers. Overall, he trusted them about as much as he trusted a hungry lion, and a lot of that sentiment stemmed from their alliance with Rudeboy.

Rudeboy was probably the reason Rell had just called, Crisis mused as he lit a cigarette. He was halfway through smoking it when the call finally ended.

"What that nigga want, Mo?" He immediately asked, smoke pouring from his mouth.

Menace slid the phone back into his pocket with an amused expression twitching across his lips. "They wanna chop it up about Rudeboy," he replied. "Said he might have some information we could use. He wants us to come through later on tonight."

"Nah, fuck outta here," Crisis exploded. "If they wanna talk let them come to our side. How we know they ain't trying to line us up for Rudeboy?"

Menace patted the air as if saying calm down. "Fuck you getting yourself all worked up for? And think about what you saying. Why would they set us up for Rudeboy, when if they really wanted us dead, they could've flexed on us earlier?"

Crisis didn't seem totally convinced. "That might be true, but why call now, what is there to say?"

Menace threw an arm around his shoulder, pulling him close. "It's not about what they have to say, it's about why they're saying it. When you're able to understand the why behind a person's actions, figuring out their intentions becomes all the more easier. Always remember that. When it comes to the twins, Rosez was just telling me how Rell asked her to help him find a connect. Now think about it, why would they need a connect when they been getting food from Rudeboy?"

It took only seconds for Crisis to figure it out. "They must be already planning on groundhoggin Rudeboy themselves, but first they need a new connect."

"Exactly," Menace agreed grinning deviously. "And now that we beefin with Rudeboy, I'm willing to bet they probably figuring it would be better to team up. How you feel about that?"

Crisis shrugged and plucked away the cigarette. "You already know I'm with whatever, Mo. If you say this is the right course of action, you know I'm riding. At the same time, we gotta watch them niggas, Mo. I'm telling you something ain't right with them."

Menace felt the same sense of foreboding but choose to keep his thoughts to himself. "Let's at least hear what they have to say before we start jumping to any conclusions," he suggested. "Not that it really matters anyway. In a little while they gone either roll with the rush or get crushed."

"That's what the fuck I'm talking about!" Crisis exclaimed. "Let me find out you decided to finally listen to me."

"I did," Menace admitted chuckling. "You been telling me for a while now we gotta step it up, and you were right. My moms basically said the same thing."

Crisis smiled reverently. "I'm not even surprised, Aunty is all the way official. Hearing it from her must've hit hard though."

"It definitely did," Menace admitted. Now I'm just trying to figure out what role Rosez gone play in all of this."

"What's the verdict on her?" Crisis asked.

Menace shook his head regretfully. "I fucked up bro, I should've gave her some bread. She the one that put us on to the jux in the first place, so she deserved that. I didn't think she would react like that though."

Crisis looked at him in surprise. "You already know how reckless her mouth is, Mo. Shorty is a straight bug out. All I wanna know is, is she good or what."

Menace sighed, undecided. "I guess we'll find out when she gets back from the hospital. I definitely gotta make it up to her. Shorty is an asset, you feel me. Thorough ones like her don't come around everyday..."

They discussed Rosez for a few more minutes until the conversation circulated back to the reason they were on the roof to begin with. "Pebble Beach" as it was commonly known, or "The Loft" as Menace had nicknamed it, was the location he relocated to whenever he needed to clear his thoughts. Today it would be the place where they plotted Rudeboy's demise.

"We should've smoked both of them niggas," Crisis reiterated when his name came up.

Menace nodded in agreement, then without further ado, proceeded to divulge the blueprint he'd created to take over the entire drug trade in "The View".

He began by pointing out the many flaws in Rudeboy's operation, like how he only used one worker in each of his three spots, simply because he was too cheap to pay for more. Then there was the issue of him having no security, or lookouts for the spots. For the most part, Rudeboy had been surviving these last few years more off the strength of the twins rep than his own. In all actuality he didn't have a team of his own in Soundview besides the manpower the twins provided.

Menace, on the other hand, commanded a squad of soldiers ready to jeopardize their life for him, which is why he was so intent on not just feeding them, but more importantly, protecting them.

After exposing Rudeboy's operation for the circus it was, Menace explained the solutions to be integrated into their own, one of which included utilizing Gigi's housing management position to gain access to the footage from the surveillance cameras positioned all around the projects. In addition, Menace wanted armed sentries with walkie talkies and binoculars patrolling from the roof. To protect them, stronger doors would need to be installed, and Gigi could assist with that as well. Being that he planned on paying for the upgrades, as well as greasing a few palms, Menace didn't foresee any resistance.

Another element Menace planned on enacting was something called *Blazer Day*. On that particular day, all funds generated from hustling would go towards supporting the O. G.'s who had really put Soundview on the map. Pistol P was the most infamous and revered of them all. Unfortunately, he was now serving two life sentences plus an additional 200 years in federal prison. Since his arrest, the Feds had raided "The View" on a number of occasions, apprehending more of the trailblazers that had helped build and sustain the reputation Soundview now possessed. Blazer Day would pay homage to these individuals, most of whom were never coming home. Some of their families still lived in The View, and the funds would also ensure they were taken care of financially. Out of the entire takeover blueprint, Blazer Day was the one component Menace couldn't wait to implement. Not only was it the perfect way to give a little something back, it made sense being that both his and Crisis's Pops had been two of those trailblazers. It was the reason he was now serving natural life in State prison. All in all, there was nothing intricate about the ingredients for the takeover recipe. It relied more on common sense than anything else. Crisis, however, was still thoroughly impressed.

"Mo, you like a fucking mad scientist," he complimented, embracing Menace seconds after he concluded his spiel. "I can already see everything in my head, and you of all people should know Gigi gone be on board with whatever. I'll holla at her tonight, then the three of us can sit down and figure out the details." He paused to take a pull from a fresh stogie. "I guess the only question now is, when are we going to start putting things in motion?"

"ASAP!" Menace replied, gazing off into the distance. "I actually wanted to holla at you before anything, but this fuck nigga forced my hand. I'm kinda glad he did. Of course, I would've preferred to still have the element of surprise, but now we don't gotta tip toe around this shit."

Crisis exhaled a cloud of fumes. "I still say we should've ground hogged both they asses."

Once again, Menace concurred with a nod. Quiet as kept, the beef with Rudeboy had him a bit anxious. Two years earlier, he witnessed with his own eyes, 50-something-year-old Rudeboy chase down one of his workers suspected of stealing. With a barrage of headshots, he damn near decapitated the dude. Then for overkill, he reloaded and emptied the clip into his dead body. Although he'd been wearing one of those Jason hockey masks, everyone watching knew it was Rudeboy because coincidentally, he'd neglected to tuck his dreads. His message, however, had been clear. At any time, for the slightest of reasons, to whoever, he was ready to go zero to a hundred in the blink of an eye. This was the caliber of the dude they now had beef with, and although not a trace of fear existed in his body, Menace knew after humiliating Rudeboy on such a grand scale, he would be itching for revenge.

"Make sure everybody is on point," he reminded Crisis. "Both them niggas is G.H.O.S. status." The acronym was pronounced ghost, and it stood for *groundhog on sight*.

"Mo, everybody already know what time it is with them dudes," Crisis assured. "We just gotta catch them that's all. They can't hide forever."

Hiding was the last thing Menace suspected Rudeboy and Raw of doing. Regrouping, and scheming on ways to murder them sounded more plausible. Before he could correct Crisis, his phone rang. Judging from the smile that erupted on his face, it was obviously Aminah.

Cheesing dumb hard, he strolled off, and began talking in hushed tones. Less than a minute later he returned even more giddy. "So, what's up? What else we need to discuss?" He asked, obviously now eager to bounce.

That he could even be thinking of a female at such a crucial time irritated Menace beyond words, and he decided to address the issue right then and there. Crisis was one of the few people he loved, and he needed to be reminded that as many women that could be credited with helping a man succeed, a greater amount were responsible for their downfall. Menace would hate to see his closest crony fall to such a fate.

"Check this out bro, we all know how you do with the ladies," he said choosing his words carefully. "But do I really need to remind you who we got drama with? Right now, things like pussy are a distraction."

Crisis sighed with irritation. "So, what you expect me to put my life on hold for this bozo?"

Menace shook his head, disappointed his best friend wasn't seeing the bigger picture. "All I'm saying is put ya priorities in perspective. You always talking this money over bitches shit. Well, you need to start sticking to the script. Rudeboy not gone stop until we dead, and he's going to do whatever he can to make it happen. Even if it means sending a chick at you or following you to they crib. Don't think it can't happen, and don't think after all these years in the game, he don't got shooters from elsewhere, which means you might not even see that shit coming. Don't misunderstand what I'm saying," he added seeing Crisis about to protest. "Ain't nobody questioning ya gangsta, and I already know when it's time you gone let that hammer blow. Remember what Jadakiss said though: *'Everybody got a gun, why not me? You gotta keep it on you now, it's just like I.D.'*"

Crisis was already nodding in agreement before he could finish. "Mo, you absolutely right. At the same time, I'm not about to be sitting around waiting for son to show up. You know how I give it up; I'm always on point."

"I hope so," Menace snapped, cutting him off. "I really hope so."

Without another word, he headed for the exit.

On the other side of the roof door, Guntalk stood guard, a pistol in each hand. Once Menace gave him the signal, he began descending. Two floors later, Crisis lightened the mood with his usual humorous banter.

"Yo Mo, I told you shorty know how to cook her ass off right? After I put that thang on her, had her in the kitchen cooking tacos, like Taraji, in Baby Boy."

"Nigga, shut the fuck up, and stop frontin," Menace said laughing. "Ain't nobody cook you shit. Rosez already told me you got a little dick."

Guntalk chuckled. Crisis didn't.

"Mo, ain't no chick alive gone tell you I got a little dick. It ain't on no pornstar shit, but – "

Menace quickly interrupted him. "Bruh, ain't nobody wanna hear about ya tool. What's up with shorty friends though?"

"I'm not gone lie, Mo, she definitely got a few nice-looking friends," Crisis confirmed. "I had all them bitches cracking up the other day when I showed them my beat it up dance."

"Ya beat it up dance?" Menace repeated, confused. "What the fuck are you talking about?"

Crisis chuckled loudly. "Mo, stop acting like you ain't never seen Baby Boy. You don't remember after Jody killed the pussy, he started doing the dance?"

Without having to be prompted, he raised his hands, and started hopping from side to side, while thrusting his hips forward. They were on the seventh floor by then, and Menace was laughing so hard he had to pause to catch his breath.

"Let me see it again," he demanded.

This time, Crisis added the funniest face to the routine. Menace leaned against the wall, unable to move as his cackles echoed through the staircase. Every time he tried to stop laughing, Crisis would start up again. Even the usually reserved Guntalk couldn't resist snickering.

Suddenly, the staircase door banged into the wall on a lower floor, drowning out their laughter. The noise reverberated through the air like lightning, and any other time Menace might not have paid it any attention. Due to the beef with Rudeboy, however, he was extra alert. The smile vanished from his face when he didn't hear the pitter patter of descending footsteps, and without hesitation, he yanked a chrome .357 from his waist, provoking Crisis to draw his own gun. Guntalk didn't have to, as his guns were already brandished. Only seconds before, they'd been bullshitting. Now, in the blink of an eye, all that was forgotten as the trio stood silent, bodies tense, and ready for action.

Seconds elapsed and still no noise arose from the lower floors, further alarming Menace. *Was someone lying in wait to ambush them,* he wondered. If so, they were in for a deadly surprise. Gun outstretched, he took the lead, and began tip-toeing down the stairs. Anybody coming around the bend would immediately be greeted by his revolver.

*Or maybe I'm just being paranoid,* he thought, creeping forward one step at a time. In his mind, it just didn't make sense for somebody to announce their presence by allowing the door to bang into the wall if they were, indeed, trying to get the drop on them. Nonetheless, there was no denying the strange sound Menace suddenly heard coming from the next stairwell. He strained his ears trying to determine exactly what it was but couldn't. Tightening his finger on the trigger, he continued his downward trek. At the bottom stairs, he cautiously stepped over a broken bottle, took a deep breath then quickly peeked around the cement partition. What he saw made him look back at his comrades in disbelief. Crisis and Guntalk rushed forward to see what he saw.

Sitting halfway down the staircase, getting his dick sucked was a dude from the hood named, Schoolboy. The woman doing the sucking was a neighborhood dope fiend everybody called Dirty Diane.

# CHAPTER 16

Menace and Crisis were still shaking their heads in amusement over the staircase incident when they emerged from the building moments later. Guntalk instantly relapsed back to his militant demeanor, positioning himself several paces in front, with both hands stuck deep in the front pocket of his black hoodie. At 8:15 in the evening, a lot of residents were returning home from work, and although the majority were familiar faces, Guntalk eyed all of them as potential foes.

"We gotta hurry up and groundhog this dude," Menace said as he greeted a few people with head nods. "Nigga got me walking around on eggshells in my own hood." He shook his head, disturbed that somebody could have such an effect on him.

"Trust me, Mo, he gone slip before we do because he moving off emotions," Crisis said as he pulled out his phone to call a Uber.

Menace hoped his comrade was right. "Make sure you holla at me as soon as you get to shorty crib so I know you good," he instructed.

"You know I will," Crisis confirmed as they embraced. Moments later he was gone.

Menace waited until the car Crisis was riding in turned the corner before heading in the opposite direction. Just as he arrived at the walkway leading to his building, a text came through from his mother. She was checking to see if he was good, and she needed him to play her lottery numbers, plus pick up some easy wider paper.

*"I got you, and I'm good,"* Menace texted back. He needed some blunt wraps and munchies anyway. After informing Guntalk of the change in plans, the two set off in the direction of the smoke shop on "Cozy Corner".

Cozy corner was the infamous block located adjacent to the projects. Back in the day, only the official had been allowed to loiter on that particular strip. It was the one place Menace expected to find a throng of activity, if for no other reason than the abundance of shops, including a supermarket, liquor store, and a pizza parlor. The bodega on the corner was nicknamed the smoke shop.

During the walk, several residents who'd heard about the Rudeboy situation stopped him out of respect to inquire into his well-being. Menace assured them he was fine but was too busy scanning his surroundings to devote any time for conversation. His eyes missed nothing as they darted this way and that in search of anything that appeared even remotely suspicious. Not by coincidence, he too was wearing a black hoodie, and his hand was glued to the revolver in its front pocket. In the event something did pop off requiring a split-second decision, he could just shoot without having to waste precious time trying to extract the gun. Fortunately, no foes presented themselves. There were, however, a few surprised glances from some of the folks posted up on Cozy Corner, as if they couldn't believe he was out and about, at least not that soon. Chuckling to himself, Menace gave dap to the few he fucked with, offered them little conversation, and left Guntalk on guard outside before entering the smoke shop.

As usual, the smoke shop was packed, and a quick scan of the many faces revealed the presence of no threats. Satisfied, Menace approached the counter.

The Indian owner Raj greeted him with a tight smile and a handshake. "It's good to see you're at least taking precautions," he said, gesturing towards the door. "Especially being that you played with fire and didn't extinguish it." His cryptic words probably sounded like meaningless babble to the customer standing at the counter. Menace, though, understood the message clearly. He wasn't even surprised Raj knew about the Rudeboy debacle. Quiet as kept, he knew about mostly everything going on in "The View", which was to be expected considering he'd been running the smoke shop for over 20 years. For some reason, Menace had yet to figure out, Raj had taken a liking to him ever since their introduction when he was a child. Their relationship had developed into a solid bond as he got older, and now he viewed Raj like an uncle. Be that as it may, Menace was getting tired of hearing how he should've killed Rudeboy. Probably why he responded sarcastically.

"As long as I didn't get burned, that's all that matters," he snapped back.

"No, that isn't all that matters," Raj shot back, looking disappointed. He waited until the remaining customer walked off, then pushed the cash register closed, and leaned forward so his voice wouldn't travel. "You should've killed him!" He spat. "He's dangerous, and what makes him even more of a threat is the fact that's he's not a fool. You have a serious problem on your hands my friend."

Menace frowned, annoyed that Raj seemed to be giving Rudeboy way too much credit. "You making it seem like he's untouchable. He bleed just like I do."

Raj smiled disarmingly. "No need to get excited, my friend. I'm on your side. And you are right, he too bleeds like everyone else. However, that doesn't mean you and him are the same. If that were the case, you wouldn't have hesitated. Do you think he'll hesitate the next time you and him meet?"

Menace understood his point all too well. Rudeboy definitely wasn't going to hesitate if he got the drop on him.

"What about all the witnesses?" Menace still tried to argue.

"What about your life?" Raj countered angrily. "Would you rather be carried by six or judged by twelve? At least with the latter, you'd still have breath in your body. Witnesses can forget, jury members can be bribed, and there are many other options. Remember that the next time you draw your weapon, my friend."

His words trailed off as a customer approached, and Menace pivoted to retrieve a few items. In his heart he knew Raj was absolutely correct. And coming from someone who was no stranger to having blood on his hands, his words held weight.

Back in his home country of India as a young adult, Raj had been part of an insurgent force intent on overthrowing the government. He knew what it felt like to take someone's life because he'd done so a handful of times, in what he described as his quest to defeat government oppression. In the end, despite all his efforts, it would be members from his own faction that betrayed his whereabouts to authorities. All this and more Raj disclosed one night, years earlier. When he concluded the tale, he lifted his shirt to display the bullet wounds sustained at the hands of the police, who came to kill, not arrest him. Somehow, he'd managed to escape, but not before suffering life threatening injuries. Menace counted 6 wounds before Raj's shirt dropped back into place. With tears streaming down his face, he then dropped another jewel.

*"I am proud of my scars because they are a reminder of the circumstances that failed to break me. Nonetheless, I'll forever be reminded that trust cannot be given, it must be earned, and even those who've earned it mustn't be trusted entirely when the elements of money and power are involved,".*

For Menace, it was a strange sight seeing a grown man cry. Growing up, the old heads had constantly reiterated the falsehood that men weren't supposed to cry because it made them look weak. That day, Menace was reminded of another valuable lesson. Never allow someone's opinions and beliefs to shape yours. Raj was far from weak, and instead of being repulsed, Menace developed a deep respect for him. Based on that alone, he knew better than to disregard what Raj said.

Before Menace could further ponder the premonition, the chimes above the front door sounded. Grabbing a strawberry Nesquik, Menace turned in time to see a familiar face enter. Her name was Isis, and Dirty Diane – the woman he'd just caught blowing cock in the staircase – was her mother. Ironically, it was because of her that Menace even knew her daughter's name. He made it his business to be familiar with everybody living on his side of the projects, at least on a cordial level. Isis, however, seemed to want to remain an enigma. On the few occasions he tried to holla, she brushed him off as if oblivious to his ghetto superstar status. Menace couldn't fathom how that was even possible. Everybody in "The View" knew of him. Everybody, but Isis, it seemed. Her rejections only intensified Menace's attraction to her, which was bizarre being that she was nothing like the baddies he was used to. At best, he would classify her a strong six on a scale of 1 to 10. Still, he found it impossible to keep from smiling as he walked to the front of the store, analyzing Isis the entire way. Presently, her hair was fashioned in a short bob, which contrasted nicely with her peanut butter skin tone, and also bought out her facial features particularly her chinky brown eyes. Even more sexy was the fact that aside from some lip gloss, Isis wore no makeup, and she still looked like a snack. She was nowhere near as thick as Rosez, but her yeeks were definitely plump enough to be cuffed. Even her feet were pretty, Menace noticed glancing down at her flip flips. Being that he had a foot fetish, pretty toes were a must. Isis had hers painted apple red to match her fingernails. Menace was imagining sucking her toes, as he pulled up beside her at the counter.

"Long time no see, stranger," he greeted, instantly realizing how corny it sounded.

Isis must've thought so to. She sucked her teeth but didn't even bother to glance his way. "Why are you always trying to talk to me?" She snapped as she pulled a wad of crumpled bills from her blue jeans and laid them on the counter. "I told you I'm not interested, and it's like you not getting the message."

"You know why," Menace said, unfazed by her rebuff. "I told you the last time we spoke, you're going to be mines one day and I meant that. Ya money ain't no good here either; I got you." He swept her currency aside, pulled out a stack of cash, and laid a twenty down.

Isis paid the money no mind, as she turned slightly to face him. "First and foremost, stop making it sound like we had a conversation. You were the only one talking when you basically followed me to my building," she recalled.

*Even got pretty teeth*, Menace observed, chuckling. "I just wanted to make sure you got home safe. You already know this is a dangerous neighborhood."

Once again, Isis sucked her teeth, annoyed. "Boy bye, you don't even know me, so miss me with the game, alright?"

"That's only because you haven't given me the chance to get to know you," Menace countered. "And that's crazy because I'm a good dude." He looked at Raj. "Tell her, Unc!"

"Miss, my nephew is very good people," Raj said on cue.

Isis dismissed his words with a backhand swat. "Yeah whatever, that's the same thing my last ...." She caught herself before she could finish, and angrily bit her lip for almost having disclosed something personal. She took a deep breath, then said slowly, "I'm going to say this for the last time: I'm not interested, and to be honest, you not even my type." She swiped his money to the side. "I don't need ya bread either, I can pay for my own stuff. How much do I owe?" she asked Raj.

"Nothing," Raj answered with a grin. My nephew said your money is no good so you may have the item free of charge."

Before she could protest, he placed the box of tide detergent in a plastic bag and slid it to her.

"Your nephew," Isis repeated in disbelief as she took the bag. She glanced suspiciously from Raj to Menace, the back to Raj. "This dude ain't your nephew," she told him. "Y'all don't look nothing alike. Probably not even the same blood."

Raj's grin widened. "Having the same blood would only make us related, it's the loyalty that makes us family. Always remember that, my friend."

The statement touched Isis, but she didn't let it show. If she went by what Raj said, that meant she didn't have any true family beside her dying grandmother. Tears welled up in her eyes like they had a mind of their own, and before a single one could fall, she rushed from the store leaving her money on the counter.

The front door hadn't fully closed before Raj spoke. "Are you just going to let her leave like that? Are you going to give up so easily?"

"Unc, fuck that bitch," Menace said, tired of being rejected. "She not even all that anyway."

"She's all that and more," Raj corrected. "You know it too, which is why you want her so bad. Well, my friend, know this: anything worth having, is worth the effort you put into getting it. Now go after her," he ordered, shooing him away. "And remember, persistence breaks down resistance."

# CHAPTER 17

The chilly night air smacked Menace in the face like a splash of cold water, but did nothing to shake the hold Isis had on him. So strong was his thirst to track her down, he failed to notice Guntalk was nowhere to be found. Nor did he notice the SUV with tinted windows, idling at the curb halfway up the block. Seeing its make and model might've set off some alarm bells. Unfortunately, Menace wasn't paying attention. His eyes swept right over the vehicle as he searched for Isis. He spotted her already on the other side of the street, and gave chase, laughing at the irony of the situation. Not even an hour earlier, he'd G-checked Crisis on the importance of not becoming distracted by women. Yet still, here he was in pursuit of one who'd made it crystal clear she wasn't interested. The prior conversation should've wakened him up. Maybe then he wouldn't have run past a navy blue MPV minivan, without noticing its occupants. Instead, he called out to Isis as he reached the sidewalk.

"Hold up for a second," he said, jogging to catch up to her. "Got a nigga all out of breath and shit. How you gone feel if I had a heart attack and dropped dead? It's gone be your fault," he joked, closing the gap. "You know police could arrest you for that right?"

"They could arrest you for stalking too," Isis shot back, clearly not happy to see him.

"Ahhhhhh, come on ma, don't do me like that. You know I ain't no stalker. I'm harmless," Menace joked.

Isis glanced at the bulge in his front hoodie pocket. "I doubt it," she muttered.

Menace was impressed with her perceptiveness. He shrugged as if the fact he was toting heat wasn't a big deal. "Alright, I'm gripped up. What does that prove? You already know the type of environment we live in; I'd rather get caught with this shit than without it. That's beside the point though. What I'm trying to figure out is, why you be shutting me down like I'm a lame or something. It's obvious you don't know who I am, because – "

"And I'd like to keep it that way!" Isis rudely interjected.

"Damn, why you gotta be so stink?" Menace asked, getting annoyed. He wasn't used to being rejected, and definitely not by such an average looking chick like Isis.

"I'm not being stink, I'm just real," she replied. "What's the matter, you can't handle it?" She said pulling a set of keys from her pocket. They were almost to her building, and Menace realized his time was running out.

"Alright, I can dig it. You not feeling me for whatever reason," he said, talking fast. "I respect that. I respect honesty, period. I just have one question, and after that, you have my word, I'm gone."

They reached the entrance of her building, and Isis faced him. "One question," she said, holding up a finger for emphasis.

Menace raised a hand like he was swearing on an imaginary Bible. "One question," he reiterated. Isis still looked skeptical. "All I wanna know is why you won't give me the time of day,"Menace said before she could change her mind. "At least let me take you out so you can see for yourself, I'm not as bad as you might think. I don't know what it is, but for some reason, I got the biggest crush on you. Every time I see you..." He looked away, embarrassed he'd said too much.

Isis however, seemed unfazed. "I'm flattered you feel that way about me," she admitted, "But the truth is, I could never fuck with someone like you."

"What's that supposed to mean?", Menace asked, insulted.

"It means you the same as all the rest of these nigga out here," Isis replied. "I'm not trying to play you," she added, "but let's be serious... yeah you cute, and all that, but none of that superficial bullshit means anything to me. What matters is what's in here." She touched her head. "And in here." She placed a hand over her heart. "I need a man in my life that has goals and ambition. He wants better than this." She spread her arms indicating their surroundings. "Now although I don't know you like that, it ain't hard to tell what type of lifestyle you involved in. You either a hustler, or a stick-up kid. And even if you not, you still carrying a gun, which means you into some shit that ain't right. The exact type of shit I'm trying to get away from. Not because I think I'm better than you, but because

I just want more for my life, Menace. I got too many things going on in my life to be worried about if you coming home at night. So, if you really feeling me like you say, you'll just respect that."

"I do respect it," Menace responded. "And I gave you my word I would step off if you answered my question. So, even though I don't want to, I'm going to respect ya wishes, and leave you alone," he lied.

After the way she'd expressed herself, there was no way Menace could leave Isis alone, especially since he heard her slip up and say his name. Contrary to what she professed earlier, she did at least know of him, which led Menace to believe maybe she was fronting about not being interested. Only time would tell. For now, he was satisfied with having gotten her to have a conversation.

"Don't act like you can't say hi when you see me from now on," he said holding the door open for her.

"Alright, I'll say hi," Isis agreed walking into the building. She boarded the elevator, and Menace waited for the door to slide shut behind her before spinning off. Isis definitely had him intrigued. She was truly a breath of fresh air, and he vowed right then and there, he would stop at nothing to make her his.

At the corner, Menace went to turn in the direction of his building only to remember he'd left his munchies at the smoke shop and forgotten to handle his mother's request. He was also eager to tell Raj about the convo with Isis. Grinning at the sound of her voice replaying in his head, he maneuvered in the direction of the smoke shop. It was as he stood at the curb waiting for traffic to cease so he could cross, that he suddenly felt a presence behind him.

Instinctively, he reached for the pistol in his hoodie pocket, as he attempted to turn. Before he could, cold steel kissed his neck, stopping him in his tracks.

"Don't try to turn around," a deep voice said, "And if you reach for that gun again, you're going to regret it. Now walk," the voice ordered, pushing him forward.

"What's this about?" Menace asked trying to drag his feet.

"Just keep walking," the gunmen instructed with another shove. Tell your buddy to back off too."

*What buddy*? Menace was about to ask. Then he saw Guntalk crossing the street towards them with his gun drawn.

"Tell him to stay back," the voice repeated, cocking the hammer.

As much as Menace didn't want to, what other choice did he have? He waited until Guntalk locked eyes with him, then slowly shook his head. Disregarding the gesture, Guntalk continued approaching, until another more vigorous head shake caused him to stop right there in the middle of the street. Before Menace could communicate anything else, a firm tug halted him at the back door of a midnight black-colored Range Rover with tinted windows.

Someone opened the door from inside, unleashing a cloud of cigar smoke. "Get in," the voice prodded with a poke of the barrel. The fear gripping Menace was unlike anything he'd ever felt. Still, he managed to find a sliver of hope in the reasoning if they truly wanted him dead, they would've killed him already. It was a minor assumption to find solace from, but it was all he had. Another sharp jab to his ribs prompted him forward. Swallowing hard, he lifted one foot into the truck as he bent to get inside.

"I told you, you should've killed me," a familiar voice said, and Menace felt his blood run cold. Staring at him with a gun pointed at his head, was none other than Lotto.

# CHAPTER 18

**"W**hat the fuck!" Guntalk roared with rage as he watched the brake lights on the Range disappear from sight. He couldn't believe what he'd just witnessed. The incident seemed surreal, but he instantly realized the severity of the situation, and went into action. Gun still clutched in one hand, he retrieved his cell with the other while sprinting to the sidewalk. He stabbed the button to call Crisis, at the same time compiling a list of everyone else he needed to contact.

"What's up, Mo," Crisis answered after two rings.

Remaining as calm as possible, Guntalk tucked his tool, and did his best to recount the kidnapping without being too incriminating.

Crisis was even more reluctant to talk on the phone. "I'm on my way back to the hood right now, I'll see you in a little while," he said before disconnecting.

One by one, Guntalk called every available M.B.A.M member, disclosing just enough info to each of them so they understood the importance of disregarding whatever they were doing, and assembling asap. Fortunately, everybody was in the vicinity.

As was the procedure, they sent texts checking in the moment they reached the meeting spot. Guntalk responded with instructions to stay put until he arrived with Crisis. He pulled up ten minutes after their initial conversation, just as Guntalk was ending his call with Rosez, who was on her way back from the hospital. Although Menace was the cause of her trip to the E.R., she went absolutely berserk when she heard he'd been snatched.

"I should be there in the next 10 minutes," she informed him.

In the background, Guntalk could hear her yelling at the driver to speed up. "We'll be in the courtyard behind Menace building," he told her before clicking off.

"What the fuck happened?" Crisis was angrily yelling as he emerged from the Uber. "Tell me you seen who did it! Was it Rudeboy and them?"

Guntalk shook his head. "It looked like a white broad, and I've never seen her before."

"A white broad?" Crisis echoed, looking baffled.

Guntalk then proceeded to give him a play-by-play of the incident, starting with how they went to the smoke shop, to Menace chasing Isis down, and finally him being accosted by the white chick who forced him to get in a black Range Rover at gunpoint.

Crisis paid no attention to the description of the vehicle, choosing instead to focus on the girl Guntalk said Menace had been chasing before the kidnapping. "Isis, Isis," he repeated aloud in an attempt to place the name. Suddenly his eyes widened with recognition, accompanied by a distasteful frown. "You talking about that weird looking bitch that live in 1711?" He pointed to a building up the block from where they were standing.

"That's exactly who I'm talking about!" Guntalk confirmed. "I think she Dirty Diane daughter."

"That's a fact," Crisis verified, looking skeptical.

"Yo Mo, you sure that's who the bro was talking to?"

"Positive," Guntalk snapped with irritation. "What you think something wrong with my eyes? That's not the first time I seen them talking either."

Crisis pondered his words as he tried to think of the best course of action. Finally, he said, "Aight Mo, let's go check the Isis chick out, and I'm telling you right now, if I even think they had something to do with any of this, I'm groundhoggin both they ass." As the words left his mouth, he started trotting in the direction of 1711.

Guntalk took off behind him. "Hold the fuck up, you speeding," he said grabbing Crisis by the arm. "I just told everybody to meet us in the courtyard. They waiting for us now, and I think we need to put everybody on point before –"

Crisis wrested his arm free. "I don't give a fuck what you think," he snarled. Suddenly without warning, he yanked the .45 off his waist and held it at his side, grilling Guntalk. "Come to think of it, what the fuck was you thinking when you let some broad snatch my brother? A fucking cracker?" He yelled, incredulous. "I'm telling you right now, you crispy fried motherfucka, if I find out you had anything to do with this, imma –"

"You gone do what?" Guntalk barked back. In a flash he tugged one pistol from his hoodie pocket and aimed it at Crisis. "You got some fucking nerve questioning my loyalty. Everybody know I'd die for that nigga, Menace – no questions asked. You, on the other hand, supposed to be his best friend, not to mention the second in command. You were supposed to have been right here with us when this shit went down. Instead, you went to go chase some bitch you barely even know. At a time when we got major static, all you could think about was some pussy. Who's to say ya bitch ass ain't have nothing to do with this? You bounce, and all of a sudden, the big bro gets snatched. Sounds real suspect to me."

His accusations enraged Crisis, mainly because they were true. Of course, he'd played no part in the abduction, but the rest of what Guntalk said was fact. Now, he was too furious to admit it.

"Imma give you three seconds to get that gun out my face, or imma park ya stupid ass right here," he threatened.

"Do what you gotta do," Guntalk urged.

Disregarding the count, Crisis suddenly leveled his hammer at Guntalk. Pedestrians, seeing them with their guns aimed at each other, scattered in random directions, hoping to avoid a stray bullet.

"Get that gun out my face," Crisis repeated.

"You get ya gun outta my face," Guntalk insisted, tempted to squeeze. The only thing that stopped him was the realization that if he bodied, or even shot Crisis, his relationship with Menace was over. More than likely, he would have to kill him as well.

Killing Menace was the last thing Guntalk wanted to do. He loved him like a brother and for Crisis to even accuse him of having a hand in his kidnapping, not only crushed him, but made him want to blow the nigga's head off. He couldn't even understand what would possess Crisis to say something so preposterous, considering all the work he'd put in for the squad. *Weren't the numerous shootings, and murders – all for MBAM – evidence of his loyalty*, Guntalk wondered. The only reason he'd abandoned his post in front of the store in the first place, was because police had drove past once, then circled again like they were preparing to hop out. They were known for employing such tactics, and to avoid getting knocked with not one, but two guns, he breezed off into Academy Gardens, the gated housing complex directly across the street from Cozy Corner.

He was standing on the inside of the entrance gate when Menace emerged from the smoke shop and chased Isis down. At the time he'd found it amusing he was pursuing such an average looking female, considering there were much badder joints practically throwing the pussy at him. Guntalk wasn't one to judge though, and he just assumed Menace saw something special in Isis, much like he'd seen something special in him. In addition to feeling like a complete idiot for entertaining such logic, he also felt like a straight bitch for not squeezing when he had the chance. Yeah, Menace had motioned for him not to, but he'd obviously been under duress. Overall, Guntalk just regretted not doing more. Anything would've been better than how he reacted, he concluded. He wouldn't be able to forgive himself if something tragic happened to Menace. Shaking his head, he tried to dislodge from his mind images of his mentor laid up dead somewhere.

Crisis stared at Guntalk wondering what he was thinking. He felt foolish for having allowed his anger to get the best of him. His pride, however, prevented him from backing down, especially when he thought about how Guntalk pointed his pistol at him first. Then again, Crisis realized, how could he even blame him after uttering such a disrespectful accusation. In all actuality, he knew with reasonable certainty that Guntalk would never betray Menace. Not only did he love him probably more than he loved himself, his entire gangsta persona was a reflection of Menace. Furthermore, Guntalk had proven his loyalty on too many occasions to count. Just recalling some of the instances where he risked life and limb for the team, made Crisis feel low about how he'd overreacted. And when he thought about how disappointed Menace would be if he could see them, it was enough to make him swallow his pride. He was wrong, and he knew it, and the distraught look on Guntalk's face confirmed it.

Without a word, he lowered his gun. Guntalk followed suit, and for a moment, both fellows stared at each other in silence. Despite the disrespect spewed, neither really believed the other was an enemy. None of them wanted to be the first to apologize, though, so they stood there, guns at their side, grilling each other. Or maybe it was actually fate they happened to be positioned facing each other. Had the arrangement been any different, Guntalk might've never saw the MPV minivan creeping towards them.

# CHAPTER 19

Crisis saw the sudden look of alarm cross Guntalk's face and turned slightly to follow his gaze. His eyes widened with shock when he spotted the MPV minivan with its headlights off, heading their way. Instantly, he grabbed Guntalk by the shoulder, and they began backpedaling towards the safety of the projects.

"Come on, come on," he urged watching as the van sped up. It was all Guntalk needed to see. He knew if he turned and ran, he would probably end up getting shot in the back. He could take being disfigured by third-degree burns, but being disfigured and paralyzed was something he couldn't stomach. He came to an abrupt stop, pulled the other gun from his pocket, and started dumping shots with both hammers at the fast-approaching vehicle.

*Boom! Boom! Boom! Boom! Boom! Boom!*

The deafening shots from the two 40 cal Rugers ripped through the silence of the night like thunder. Screams from bystanders accompanied by the sound of stampeding feet, further added to the pandemonium. Still backpedaling, Crisis squeezed off a barrage of gunfire.

*Boc! Boc! Boc! Boc! Boc!*

Several slugs slammed into the windshield and the hood of the van as it came to a screeching halt. At least 6 men brandishing artillery spilled from its interior. One of them was Raw.

*Boom, boom, boom!*

*Boc! Boc!*

The burst of gunfire from both Crisis and Guntalk sent him and his shooters scampering behind parked cars. Seconds later, they popped back up like live jack in the boxes spraying the area with A-R 15's.

*Brrrr, brrrr, brrrr brrrr!*

Crisis and Guntalk dove for cover behind a navy-blue Navigator truck as a slew of bullets tore up the pavement where they once stood, sending chunks of concrete ricocheting through the air. The gunmen who were each equipped with 100-round drums, advanced on the Navigator, and in seconds, had it looking like it had just gone through an Afghani war zone. Crisis saw his life flash before his eyes as slugs continued to rip through the truck, projecting metal and glass into the air like snowflakes. This wasn't how it was supposed to end, and it wouldn't, he told himself as he began a silent count in his head. When he reached three, he flung his arm around the rear of the SUV and blindly let off several shots.

*Boom! Boom! Boom!*

It was an act done purely out of desperation that fortunately for him, paid off. He peeked around the truck in time to see one of the shooters standing not even ten feet away, crumple in a heap, blood pouring from the space where his nose used to be. His body twitched once, then went still. The gunmen standing next to him roared with rage as he quickly advanced, firing his machine gun back.

*Brrrr, brrrr, brrrr brrrr!*

Crisis felt the heat from a few rounds whizz past his head and squeezed off a cluster of shots just to back the dude up.

*Boom! Boom! Boom! Boom!*

Two of the shots crashed into his chest propelling him backwards, causing his feet to get tangled. He fell to the pavement, immediately jumped back up, and took off running, glad he'd worn his vest.

Crisis wasn't about to let him get away that easy. He raised up to a standing position and jerked the trigger back only for it to fire once, then click empty. Beside him, Guntalk lay sprawled on the pavement like a soldier, methodically unloading on the foes in his line of sight.

*Boc! Boc! Boc! Boc! Boc!*

Seconds later, he too ran out of ammunition. Immediately, he jumped up to a squat position and reversed his hold on both guns so he was now holding them by the barrel and could use them like a club. Before he got the chance, another volley of gunfire erupted from further up the block.

Pop! Pop! Pop!

Boom! Boom! Boom!

Bocka! Bocka!

The caliber of weapons being fired was clearly different from those of Raw and his men, which could only mean one thing: somebody else had joined the gunfight.

"Who the fuck is that?" Guntalk opened his mouth to say. Then he spotted the answer. He and Crisis watched in relief as B.R., Frillz, and the rest of the squad members he instructed to assemble in the courtyard emerged from the other side of the projects, firing furiously at Raw and his henchman. Not surprisingly, at the head of the pack was Rosez, looking like Keyshia from *New Jack City*, as she chased down one joker, unloading shots all in his back. When he fell, she rushed to stand over him, and without hesitation, caved in his dome with three head shots.

Realizing they were outnumbered and outgunned, Raw, and what remained of his hit squad took flight, barely making it back to the MPV van unscathed. Burning rubber, they sped off as B.R. stood in the middle of the street continuing to discharge slugs. Only after the van bent the corner did he cease.

An eerie silence settled over the landscape in the seconds after the shootout. In the distance, the whine of sirens could be heard by the average ear. For Guntalk, and Crisis, the sound of gunshots was still ringing in their ears as they jogged toward the rest of the squad with one thought in mind. The war had begun.

# CHAPTER 20

The shootout lasted a little more than a minute although it might've seemed like longer to those involved. Throughout the entire ordeal, Isis lay in bed, nonchalantly watching an episode of *Shark Tank*, as if what was taking place outside was nothing more than fireworks show. When the shots finally ceased, she sighed in relief, at the same time wondering whose blood would now stain the concrete? Which Soundview resident would be the cause for a candlelight vigil? Shaking her head in disgust at the senseless violence, she retrieved a comb from the dresser and began combing her hair.

Between the gunfire and moans of pleasure coming from her mother's bedroom, Isis couldn't figure out which signified more what was wrong with her life. On one hand, there was her mother Diane, a forty-three-year-old, whose entire existence could be summed up with one word: dope fiend. The hood called her "Dirty Diane" and as much as Isis hated the name, there was no denying her mother fit the moniker to a tee. She hadn't always been like that, though.

Twenty years earlier, Diane had been an R&B singer on the rise. That is, until she found herself involved in an affair with the married man who was supposed to be her manager. He promised her the world as most men do, only to eventually leave her broken hearted, with a dope habit he helped create. Sadly, Diane would never recover. The downward spiral that ensued was typical of most heroin addicts. It began with her career, which began to suffer almost immediately when she started missing studio sessions and show dates. The deterioration of her vocal cords soon followed provoking promoters to stop booking her, and with no job or high school diploma, the money soon dried up. As a last resort Diane turned to prostitution, and eventually it became her first resort whenever the monkey on her back beat its chest. Not surprisingly, she wound up overdosing a number of times, and it was during one of these hospital stints stemming from an overdose, that Diane discovered she was months pregnant. She'd been so focused on supporting her habit, she hadn't even noticed. She just assumed all the vomiting and morning sickness were due to her heroin withdrawal. If it wasn't for one of the nurses who knew Diane from the neighborhood calling her mother Betty, Isis – who was eventually born premature – would've been turned over to child welfare services. Isis had heard the story more times than she could remember, and she would never tire of hearing how Grandma Betty had taken her in, and literally saved her life.

Diane, on the other hand, seemed to forget she gave birth the minute she was discharged from the hospital. Isis could count on one hand the times she saw her mother during the ten years she lived in Brooklyn with her grandmother. If she could, she would erase each memory from her mind. The hate, and lack of respect however would always remain. Then again, hate was too strong of a word. In all actuality, Isis loved her mother. It was this mysterious yet intense love that made her foolishly believe by moving in with her, she could get Diane to kick her dope habit. Now, eight years later, Isis realized how wrong she'd been. Anger flooded her body every time she thought about all the mental and physical abuse Diane had subjected her to over the years.

"Come back and stay with me," Grandma Betty would plead after seeing the welts and bruises blanketing her body. Isis always refused, not wanting to abandon her mother. It was a decision she had come to regret, especially now as Grandma Betty lay dying from a brain tumor. The cancer had spread through her like wildfire, ravaging her mind, and transforming her body into a shell of its former self in the span of 90 days. The doctors were predicting she wouldn't last another month. Isis prayed every day they were wrong. Between the stress of potentially losing her grandmother, Diane's constant drug abuse, finals for school, and simply trying to survive in an environment as hazardous as Soundview, Isis didn't know how much longer she could cope. There were no friends to confide in because she found it hard to trust people. Not even a year earlier, she'd walked in on Diane sucking the dick of her then-boyfriend, and only confidant. The dude was someone she believed she was in love with. Apparently, the feelings hadn't been mutual. Since then,

Isis had sworn off the opposite sex. She even tried dating a female only to quickly discover that dealing with the wrong broad was worse than dealing with the wrong dude. Now, here came Menace.

Raking the comb through her hair, Isis walked over to the window, and stared out into the night. The angle prevented her from seeing the actual scene of the shooting, but she could just imagine the carnage that must've occurred based on the significant amount of flashing lights, and emergency vehicles. Isis hoped Menace was alright. Why she found herself thinking of him after the spiel she gave, perplexed even her. Nonetheless, there was no denying the slight attraction she felt for him. Contrary to what she'd told him, she knew exactly who he was. What person from Soundview didn't. His notoriety intrigued and repelled her simultaneously. There was just something about him that elicited a peachy feeling, and strangely, she found herself longing to hear his voice again. She was even more eager to gaze into his eyes if only to decipher his true intentions. Was he just another nigga looking to fuck, or was he genuinely interested in her? Far from naive, Isis suspected it was the latter, for some reason. Be that as it may, thoughts of once again having her heart shredded stopped her from entertaining any further fancies.

With a flick of her wrist, she snapped the curtains closed. "Get him out of your head, he's just like the rest," she warned herself out loud.

# CHAPTER 21

Their relationship was on the verge of collapsing. Even a blind man could see it, and Redd was far from blind. Actually, he possessed 20/20 vision, and he'd seen the signs Monae intended on leaving him when he arrived home after shooting Jon-Jon, just in time to hear her say, "Let the next bitch deal with his ass."

Even though he pretended not to be affected by the sight of her sitting there with a gun in her hand, tears staining her cheeks, he'd definitely been disturbed by it. So much so, he found himself unable to think of anything else as he showered moments later. It was then that it dawned on him the *'his ass'* Monae had been referring to was him.

Things only unraveled further after the botched home invasion. Monae wounded both invaders, but somehow, they still managed to escape. Although she was no stranger to violence, the incident severely traumatized her, precipitating a mental breakdown. In her state of her delirium, the unfiltered truth came pouring from her mouth like vomit. Not surprisingly, she directed her anger at Redd, the lone individual she held responsible for the loss of her baby, and also not being able to finish design school. The felony on her record was also Redd's fault she said, and so was Jon-Jon's henchman almost killing them. Then, just when the tirade seemed to be subsiding, Monae confronted him about Vanilla.

Redd admitted to meeting her at the strip club on the one and only occasion him and Serious hung out, shortly after he arrived in Raleigh. Yeah, he was fucking her, but no there were definitely no feelings involved. Vanilla was just a down-ass white chick who stashed his bud at her crib, and also sold it at the strip club where she worked. For some idiotic reason, Redd believed his confession would get Monae to see Vanilla meant nothing to him. It didn't. In fact, it only made her more furious, compelling her to yell out something Redd now suspected was true.

"That bitch is probably the one who told those niggas where we was staying," she spat before storming upstairs to pack.

They spent the night in a hotel, with Monae barely speaking to him. Redd, on the other hand, apologized profusely, promised to stop fucking with Vanilla, and in the end, did the one thing most niggas do when they've run out of options: professed his undying love. It was all for naught because Monae wasn't trying to hear any of it. She even refused to sleep in the same bed as Redd. He went to sleep on the pull-out couch, positive she was done with him.

Imagine his surprise the next morning when Monae informed him Serious was coming to help them relocate. It was his house Jon-Jon's men stormed, so he definitely felt some type of way. If it wasn't for

Monae intervening, him and Redd would've come to blows. Eventually, after his temper cooled, he directed them to another one of his properties, this one in an affluent section of Raleigh named Six Forks. The house itself was everything Redd could've asked for. Quiet, spacious, and most importantly, secluded. There was a porch out back, which is where he presently found himself. Due to the 90-degree weather, he was barefoot, wearing only a pair of black Calvin Klein briefs. Blunt perched between his lips, he contemplated the events of the last week while staring at the dense foliage beyond. There were a number of pressing matters swirling through his head like bees in a hive, none more important than Monae.

Despite the fact they were back on speaking terms, Redd didn't know what to think of their relationship. He was a gambling man, and a week prior, he would've been willing to wage a sizeable bet it was over between them. Now Monae was in the kitchen slaving over a hot stove as she prepared his favorite meal of steak and mashed potatoes. *Were all woman this bipolar and unpredictable,* he wondered? As amusing and confusing as Redd found the sudden turn of events, he knew better than to think he was out of the doghouse just yet, especially since Monae still wasn't giving him any pussy. Seven long days without any nookie, he calculated as he took a long toke off the blunt. It felt longer, and a few times he got so horny watching Monae prance around in thongs and boy shorts, he snuck in the bathroom to watch Pornhub and...

Just thinking about the episodes made Redd shake his head in disgust. He knew Monae was purposely teasing him, and let him tell it, she was to blame for him sneaking out to see Vanilla two days before. After some intense fucking, she tearfully admitted Jon-Jon's people had indeed tricked her into revealing his address by claiming to have an important package for him. According to Vanilla, when she asked why they didn't just call Redd, they told her he wasn't answering his phone. After verifying all calls to his cell were indeed going to voicemail, she gave them the address, thinking nothing of it. Despite not knowing her for long, Redd believed her. He prided himself on being a good judge of character, and Vanilla had never displayed any snake tendencies. Besides, even if he wanted to doubt her, it just didn't make sense for her to set him up for Jon-Jon, then still have pounds of his weed and cash stashed in her attic.

At the end of the day, Redd had only himself to blame. Vanilla might've been a naive white girl, but it was his fault for even bringing her to their crib that one time. It was all water under the bridge now, and although Redd had promised to dismiss Vanilla, he hadn't. She was an asset to any hustler's arsenal, and it was because of her he even had the Cali bud connect. In all actuality, he hadn't really needed any product from Serious. Dealing with him would've just been more convenient, and less risky than getting the pounds sent through the mail from the West Coast. The quality, however, made it all worth it, and thanks to Vanilla's contacts, Redd was able to move the bud at an alarming rate. It was those same contacts, he planned on utilizing after learning Jon-Jon was still alive.

The country kingpin had somehow managed to survive, and because of Vanilla, Redd now knew he was recuperating at his baby mother's crib in Charlotte. Exactly where in Charlotte he didn't know just yet, but she promised to have the exact coordinates in the next week. Having been bamboozled once by Jon-Jon's affiliates, Vanilla was eager to prove her loyalty, and also enact some revenge in the process. There was also the fact that Redd had her dickmatized and believing they were about to be the next Bonnie and Clyde. Unfortunately, even with the way things were coming together so nicely, he still faced two dilemmas.

The first dilemma was figuring out a way to break the news to Monae he wouldn't be going back to New York with her in a few days like he promised. The reason was simple. For the first time in his life, Redd felt like he was eating on a scale a nigga of his caliber deserved. He had bigger plans though, plans that required a different grade of narcotics. Heroin, to be specific, which brought him to his second issue: a supplier.

As crazy as it sounded, Redd was hoping to convince Serious to sell him some dope. He had a sit down with him scheduled for later in the day, and although he wasn't expecting it to go well, Monae was the one who concerned him most. On cue, she strolled through the patio doors carrying a pitcher of iced tea and a glass.

"Ain't you hot, babe," she asked as she walked over to where he sat, and poured him a drink.

Red shrugged. "I'm aight, just out here thinking," he said, taking a swig. He smacked his lips. "Thank you, babe. This shit good as hell."

"You welcome," Monae replied, appreciating his gratitude. She walked around the picnic table and plopped down next to him. "So what were you thinking about?" She questioned as she refilled his glass. "Going back to New York?"

There it was, the perfect opportunity for Redd to tell her of his change of heart. "I was actually thinking about you," he said, telling a half truth. "Just wondering when you gone take me off this pussy restriction."

Monae rolled her eyes. "Is that all you think about? It hasn't even been that long."

"Long enough," Redd said, lustfully eyeing her up and down. Just the sight of her sitting there in a wifebeater, red boy shorts, and a pair of Versace slides, caused his dick to stand at attention. "Stand up, and let me see how that ass looks," he said, testing his luck. "That's the least you can do for a nigga since I can't get none."

Monae chuckled, "Yeah, I'll give you that," she said rising to her feet. Snatching the blunt from between his lips, she took a deep drag as she did a tantalizing twirl, giving him an exceptional view of her fat ass. "Satisfied?" She snapped, going to sit.

"Hell no, I ain't satisfied," Redd shot back, pulling her onto his lap.

Without hesitation, he kissed her. Much to his delight, Monae offered no resistance. In fact, she straddled him, and began grinding on his dick as their tongues danced. After minutes of nonstop foreplay, she bit his lip as she tried to catch her breath.

"Damn boy, you got my pussy tingling right now," she moaned against his mouth.

"And what you think you doing to me?" Redd said.

To illustrate his point, he lifted her just enough so he could slide her hand over his dick. "Stop playing ma, let's go inside. You know a nigga miss that. Don't do me like that," he begged with the puppy dog face.

Monae bit her lip, contemplating whether to give in. Just when it looked like she might, Redd's phone rang.

"You can't be serious," he huffed in frustration, glancing at the screen. The number belonged to his little brother, Brian, the only person in his family who he gave a fuck about. After playing phone tag for the last few days, Redd couldn't afford to miss the call, specifically, since he was trying to persuade Brian into coming to Raleigh to assist with the Jon-Jon issue.

Reluctantly, he told Monae, "I gotta take this call babe; its super important. Can you please just give me five minutes?"

Monae snorted with disgust as she raised up off his lap with the quickness. "Then you wonder why you not getting pussy now," she spat. "Always putting everything and everyone before us. You'll learn one day. Hopefully, it won't be too late by then."

The call with his brother actually lasted longer than he expected. By the time Redd hung up he was smiling from ear to ear. Brian had agreed to come to N.C. in the next week to help him handle Jon-Jon. Redd had been hoping he would've agreed to come sooner. At the same time, he wasn't at all disappointed being he wouldn't really need Brian until he got the address from Vanilla. That was the good news. The bad news, if it could even be defined as such, related to an entirely different matter. Actually, it pertained to the reason he was in North Carolina to begin with.

A few days after he arrived in Raleigh, he'd asked his brother to keep tabs on the dude he shot.

His name was Loso, and Redd wanted to know his whereabouts, just in case he decided to come back to N.Y. Unfortunately, in all the time since then, Brian neglected to come up with any intel. It wasn't really bad news considering Redd wasn't planning on going back to New York anytime soon. He just liked to be one step ahead of the opposition.

None of that mattered to Redd now. He was too excited about seeing his brother in another week to let the Loso news, or lack thereof, spoil his mood. The only thing left to do now was inform Monae of his plans. He found her in the kitchen, pulling garlic knots out of the oven. She averted her gaze the second she spotted him, as if she couldn't stand the sight of him. Instead of fueling her attitude with one of his slick comments, Redd played it cool.

"You need me to do anything?" He inquired, setting the pitcher of iced tea on the counter.

"Actually, I do," Monae snapped. She pointed to several dishes of food sitting on the stove. "How about you take those to the table."

Redd did as he was told and was happy to do it because he was starving. Moments later, he and Monae sat down to eat.

Midway through the meal, the sound of a cellphone ringing interrupted what so far, was turning out to be a decent evening. As usual, the food was banging, and Redd was looking forward to filling Monae with something after he filled his belly. The fucking phone though...

Redd glanced around trying to determine where the ringing was coming from.

"It ain't mine," Monae offered, motioning to her cell on the kitchen counter.

"It gotta be mine then," Redd said, realizing he must've left his phone outside. He got up to retrieve it only to have Monae lay a hand on his shoulder.

She smiled sweetly, "Eat your food babe, I got it," she volunteered.

Redd sat back down, thinking nothing of it as he watched her disappear through the patio doors. He felt like jumping for joy, because he just knew Monae was giving him some buns before the night ended.

At least those were his thoughts until she returned with a stink look on her face.

Without a word, she showed him who the missed call was from. Vanilla.

Monae shook her head in disgust. "You not even smart enough to put this bitch under a different name. It's like you want me to see this shit. I thought you told me you deaded this bitch. What happened?"

Redd remained silent, knowing what was coming next. *Why did I let this girl get my phone,* he wondered.

"So, you lied to me again," Monae said, mushing him. "Not only about cutting this bitch off, but about the other night when you told me you were going out to make a sale. According to these texts, you ended up at her house." Monae mimicked the text messages. "'*Thank you for coming through, Daddy. I love when you put me to bed with that monster dick.*'" Pausing, she continued to scroll. "Listen to this one, she gushed, feigning excitement: '*Damn daddy, I can't wait until its just you and me.*'"

With a look of pure disgust Monae slammed the phone down next to his plate with such force the screen cracked.

"That's what you telling this bitch? It's gone be you and her huh? Well, guess what Redd? She can have your ass because I'm done with you. Finished!" She dusted her hands off for emphasis, then went to walk off. Abruptly she pivoted and swept the plate of food into his lap. "Fucking loser!" She yelled in his face.

Redd jumped up as the heat from the mashed potatoes seeped through his briefs, burning his inner thigh. The mushing and screaming he could take. What could he say? He'd been caught red-handed again. Pushing hot food into his lap, though. That was straight disrespectful, and there was nothing that ignited Redd's temper quicker than disrespect.

In a flash, Redd lunged, grabbing Monae by the throat.

"Bitch, is you out of your fucking mind?" He barked, driving her backwards until she collided with the wall. The lion had been released from his cage and before he could stop himself, he swung with a closed fist, trying to knock her head off.

Monae weaved the blow at the last second, feeling the whoosh of air as his fist missed her face by inches. "Fuck you," she screamed raking her nails down his face. If Redd thought she was about to take another ass whipping, he had another thing coming.

He yelped in pain as his hand shot to his face, and he swung blindly with the other. . Monae ducked and ran for the stairs, with Redd on her heels. Just as she reached the top of the steps he swatted her legs, sending her tumbling to the carpet. She scrambled to get back up, only to be pushed back down.

Before she could resist further, Redd straddled her, pinning her arms down with his knees. "I swear to god, Redd, if you don't get the fuck of me!" Monae yelled.

"Shut the fuck up! You ain't gone do shit," Redd taunted before sinking his teeth into her neck. Monae gasped from the pain. "I know what your problem is," Redd said sitting back up. "You ain't had no dick in a little while."

Reaching back, he grabbed a handful of boy shorts and tore them from her body. He slid down her body before she could protest, and planted his face between her legs, not surprised to see her kitty was soaking wet. He endured the slaps to the top of his head as he passionately tongue kissed her clit. Just as he expected Monae eventually went from thrashing and swinging to humping and singing.

Grabbing the back of his head, she mashed Redd's face against her slit. "Suck that pussy, motherfucker," she demanded, winding her hips to the rhythm of his tongue. And that's exactly what Redd did. Sucked her pussy, licked her pussy, and even hummed on it, until she exploded all over his mouth. Then he carried Monae into the bedroom, bent her over, and fucked her rough like he knew she loved.

# CHAPTER 22

Redd awoke to the sound of someone relentlessly ringing the doorbell, while simultaneously pounding on the door. Besides him, Monae lay fast asleep. The intense fuck session that followed the dinner debacle had put them both to bed.. Redd glanced at the clock on the nightstand. The digits read 7:44, and suddenly it dawned on him who was at the door. A peek out the window where he spotted the pearl white 760i parked in the driveway confirmed his suspicions.

Plopping down on the edge of the bed, he hastily slid into some red Nike sweats, a white tee, and a pair of white AirMax 95's. On his way out the bedroom he spotted the 16-shot 9mm Taurus sitting on the dresser, and thought about taking it with him. He decided not to, as more banging and bell ringing erupted.

"Hold on, I'm coming!" Redd shouted as he descended the stairs.

He undid the locks and pulled the door open to find Serious standing there, his hand poised in the air ready to commence with more banging. Dressed in red basketball shorts, a black Under Armour body shirt, and red Lebron's, he looked like he'd just come from the gym. His bodyguard Franks, standing next to him, donned similar attire. At 6' 6" weighing at least 300lbs., he dwarfed the 5"8" Serious, who was slim with an athletic build. The striking contrast were just two of the differences regarding their physical stature. While Serious was naturally handsome, with unblemished brown skin, chinky brown eyes, and a head full of waves, complimented by a sharp line up, Franks was a monstrosity. Aside from being black as night with beady black eyes, his face was blanketed by an assortment of scars, including an especially grotesque looking slash that started at his right temple and ended at the edge of his mouth. A similar gash stretched across his neck. On top of all that, Franks had the nerve to be rocking a mohawk. Sweet glistened from the face of both men, and Redd didn't know if it stemmed from the summer heat or the heat from their glares.

Scowling, Serious tapped his watch. "I see you have problem with time management. I told you I would be here at 7:30; I been ringing the bell for the last ten minutes."

"My fault bro, I must've lost track of time," Redd admitted trying to give him dap.

Serious left him hanging. "I'm not your bro," he snapped, walking inside. "Let's make this quick, I got more important shit to handle. Only reason I'm even talking to you is because of my sister. Where she at anyway?"

"She's upstairs," Redd answered, following him into the living room. "You want something to drink? Water? Soda?"

"I'll take a water," Serious replied as he plopped down on the sofa.

Franks remained standing, posting up behind him. "Let me get a water too," he demanded.

Redd retrieved the request from the kitchen and returned to find Serious thumbing through a DuPont Registry that had been sitting on the coffee table. Redd handed him a bottle of Fiji, and tossed the other one to Franks, before taking a seat across from Serious.

"You into cars?" he asked him, trying to find something they had in common.

Serious shrugged indifferently. "Somewhat," he muttered, obviously not interested in chit chat. He tossed the DuPont back on the coffee table, took a swig of water, then sat the bottle next to the magazine. "So, what up?" He questioned, scooting to the edge of his seat. "You told me you wanted to talk about something real important. Let's hear it."

Redd took a deep breath, trying to think of the right words. "So, I know you don't fuck with me like that," he began, only for Serious to immediately hold up his hand like a crossing guard.

"Wait! Stop!" He ordered. "Let's get one thing straight from the jump: I don't like you, and as I said before, only reason we're even having this conversation is because Monae fuck with you. I don't! So please let's skip all the bullshit and you tell me what you want."

Redd felt like spitting in his face, and he was kicking himself in the ass for leaving his pistol upstairs. He didn't know how much more of the disrespect he could take.

He took another deep breath to calm himself before speaking, "I respect what you saying, and I appreciate you taking the time out to come holla at me. I was hoping we could get some paper together. I got about forty-thousand I'm trying to spend on some dope."

Serious frowned, confused. "Monae told me y'all were going back to New York in a few days. What happened?"

Redd shrugged. "I mean, that was the plan, but I was thinking about staying out here, and trying to get a little more paper before I bounced."

Serious stared at him like he was crazy. "Nigga, I know you not for real?" He shook his head with disgust when Redd nodded. "I knew you wasn't too smart the first time I saw you," he remarked. "Here it is you got beef with one of the most dangerous hittas in the city, and you sitting here talking about buying some work like Jon-Jon just gone allow you to get money under his nose." He shook his head at Redd's audacity. "Let me tell you exactly the type of individuals you got drama with, so you understand what's at stake. Last year the city of Raleigh had, let's say, a total of fifty homicides. Jon-Jon and his team we're responsible for about fifteen of them. This is not someone you want to play with. When you popped him, you should've killed him. Even then, it still would've been damn near impossible for you to eat out here, especially on the dope tip. That's my lane."

Serious paused to take a drink, and Redd tried to contain the anger bubbling inside of him like hot grits. "That one-hundred-thousand you booked Jon-Jon for ain't shit," Serious continued, as he screwed the cap back on the bottle. "He got double that on your head and believe me when I say niggas is real hungry for that. Must be out yo rabbit ass mind if you think I'm putting any work in ya hands. It's not even because of Jon-Jon either. He bleed just like everybody else and he definitely gotta answer up for violating my sister. Right now, though, the biggest reason I don't want to fuck with you, is you." Redd looked perplexed. "Ya energy is off, and you got that grimey look in your eyes," Serious explained. "I peeped it that first time I saw you on Rikers Island that day. Even before Monae came on the visiting floor, you was out there flirting with some bitch that ain't worth the pussy she sit on. You know what that told me?"

"What's that?" Redd mumbled.

Serious snorted with contempt, surprised he didn't already know the answer. "Not only is you disrespectful, but you also don't value loyalty. I know my sis, she wife material. And the way you show your appreciation for her taking time out of her day to come check you in jail, is by trying to bag some next bitch, pretty much in her face."

Redd recalled the incident vividly. "I was a young nigga back then. I didn't know any better."

"And you still don't," Serious shot back. "I'm willing to bet all the cash I got on me." He paused to retrieve a brick of money from an inside pocket on his shorts, then sat it on the coffee table. "If I'm wrong, I'll even give you something for your forty racks too. I know for a fact, though, Monae doesn't know about your planning to stay out here. Tell me I'm wrong, and its yours," he said pushing the money towards him.

Redd sat there speechless. Serious shook his head scornfully at him. "See what I'm saying? Here it is, she put herself on the line for you by even bringing you out here, and you still can't keep it real with her. Now you expect me to fuck with you so you can snake me later on down the line?" He shook his head vigorously. "I refuse to let that happen."

Snatching the money up, he stood to leave. "I suggest you tell her about your plans too before I do. You got 24 hours."

"Tell me what?" Monae blurted out, strolling into the living room in a silk robe and slippers. After nodding in greeting to Franks, she briefly glared at Redd, before going to give her brother a hug. "I didn't even know you were coming over. You hungry? I got some leftover... "

"Sis, I'm good," Serious interrupted. "I was on my way out the door anyway. How you doing though?"

"I'm fine," Monae replied. "Tell me what though?" She repeated glancing back and forth from Serious to Redd.

Eventually, Redd sighed in annoyance, knowing if he didn't say something, Serious would. "Listen babe," he started. "I know the plan was to go back to NY in a few days, but I was thinking we could stay out here for a little longer."

"What?" Monae exploded, her eyes widening in shock. "Are you out your fucking mind, Redd? These dudes just tried to kill us, and you talking about you want to stay out here? I'm done. I'm so done with you," she yelled going to walk off.

Serious grabbed her by the arm before she could get far. "Hold up sis," he said pulling her towards him. He tilted her head sideways inspecting her neck. Soon his eyes came to rest on Redd, and if looks could kill... "What the fuck is that?" Serious barked, pointing to the bruises on her throat.

Redd shrugged as if he was just as oblivious.

Serious turned to Monae. "Sis, what happened to your neck?"

Monae gestured towards Redd. "Ask him."

Serious bit his lip in anger as he began walking towards him. "You been putting your hands on my sister," he stated menacingly as he undid his watch.

Instinctively, Redd stood up. He spun ready to rush upstairs for his gun, only to discover Franks had somehow maneuvered behind him, blocking his path. "Oh, so you niggas gone jump me now huh?"

Franks laughed out loud. "Jump you? Ain't nobody gone jump you, but you definitely about to get yo ass whupped though."

It was all Redd needed to hear. He reverted his attention back to Serious, and as soon as he got within arm's reach, Redd popped on him. The two of them exchanged blows, knocking over lamps and other appliances as the brawl quickly spilled from the living room into the foyer area between the front door and staircase. Hands crossed over her chest, Monae watched the fight in silence from the bottom step. Let her tell it, Redd deserved to get his ass beat. She was glad when Serious dropped him to his knees with a vicious uppercut. Instead of immediately finishing him off, he stepped back, bouncing on his toes like a boxer.

"Get ya bitch ass up," Serious taunted. "You like hitting on females, hit on me."

Redd staggered to his feet, blood dropping from his mouth. Stumbling from side to side, he purposely tried to give the impression he was dizzy. The moment Serious started to advance, he rushed him. Slamming into his midsection, he propelled him backwards, until they crashed into the wall. Both of them fell to the floor, continuing to throw punches, but it was Serious who eventually came out on top, literally. He straddled Redd in much the same manner Redd had straddled Monae earlier and tried to punch his face through the floor. Redd tried to weave and block the blows, but it was no use. He felt himself losing consciousness as the onslaught of blows caused his head to repeatedly crash into the tiled floor. If it wasn't for Monae intervening, Redd might've been even worse off.

"Alright bro, that's enough," she shouted, pulling him off Redd.

Breathing hard, hands still balled into fist, Serious stood over Redd tempted to stomp his head in. Instead, he issued a deadly warning. "Put your hands on my sister again, and I put that on my dead seed, imma murder you."

# CHAPTER 23

**G**etting shot wasn't worse the part, even though it had caused Jon-Jon to lose close to 30 pounds. He could always gain the weight back; the colostomy bag, however, disgusted him beyond words. He stared at the contraption in the mirror, furious with himself for having allowed someone to get the drop on him – an out of towner at that. He'd seen Redd reaching for something earlier in the dice game, and instead of listening to his gut, he brushed it off, foolishly reasoning Redd wouldn't have the balls to violate if only because he was outnumbered. Furthermore, Jon-Jon just assumed Serious had informed him of his stature the night they were all at the strip club. Whatever the case, Redd had indeed violated terribly, and if it was the last thing he ever did, Jon-Jon planned on getting his revenge.

The conclusion brought him only a tinge satisfaction as he flipped off the light and exited the bathroom. Downstairs in the living room, he gingerly plopped down on the sofa across from the woman who was about to help him plot the demise of not only Redd, but even more importantly, Serious. Her name was Chelsea, and she was his older cousin.

At 54 years of age, Chelsea was still a very attractive woman, and besides the crow's feet and bags under her eyes, her age was barely detectable. Her most distinguishing feature, however, was the badge on her hip, identifying her as a senior agent for the F.B.I.

For years, Jon-Jon had been utilizing Chelsea as his secret weapon, and although most would consider that as snitching, he didn't give a fuck. The Mexican cartels had been using the authorities to erase their enemies for years, and nobody called them rats. Jon-Jon wouldn't have cared either way. He lived by his own set of rules, not some fictitious code of the street that no one stuck to anyway. For proof that it was all an illusion, one need not look further than the most notorious gangstas of the past decade. In every single one of their cases, it was usually someone close to them that ended up taking the stand and sealing their fate. The few that did stick to the no-snitching philosophy were fools in Jon-Jon's opinion. Let him tell it, only a fool would refuse to rat on the same individuals who might in all probability rat on them if the tables were turned. It didn't make any sense, and Jon-Jon had vowed when he first began dabbling in the streets, to never trust anyone. This mindset was the main reason he'd survived so long in a game where treachery and betrayal reigned supreme. Of course, Chelsea deserved some of the credit too. Simply put, Jon-Jon was the worst kind of criminal. The type to blow your brains out himself, or have it done, or sic Chelsea on you if all else failed.

"So, what do you have for me?" He asked, unconsciously tightening his robe to hide the shit bag. Grabbing a can of Ensure from the side table, he took a generous sip, watching as Chelsea shuffled through a stack of pictures, she'd just pulled from a manilla envelope. When she found the one she was looking for, she clapped her hands ready to begin.

"So, I was able to gather some footage from several CCTV cameras throughout the city of the dude you told me about named Redd. The nickname is actually just an acronym for his government name, Reginald Eton Davenport."

Jon-Jon almost spit out a mouthful of Ensure as he burst out laughing. "What type of name is that?"

Chelsea smirked and shrugged. "Same thing I said when I first read it." She splayed several photos of Redd on the coffee table between them, twisting them so they faced him. "These ones we got from the cameras at the strip club where you told me you first saw him. After that, everything else was easy thanks to the facial recognition software we have at our disposal. We don't even need your name, or fingerprints anymore. If you were ever in the service, been arrested, taken a photo for a job or license, your entire history pops up. Everything from your work history, to your rap sheet, down to if you've ever purchased a gun."

She pulled a sheaf of papers from an attaché case next to the sofa and held them up. "This is Mr. Davenport's rap sheet, and I could've easily showed it to you on a tablet, but its best to take precautions considering how everything can be tracked nowadays." She spread the xerox copies over the pictures of Redd.

"Knowing you, I figured you'd probably want to keep these anyway. As you can see, he has a lengthy record, and I already know how you do, but I wanted you to have the full scope of who you're dealing with."

Jon-Jon nodded in appreciation, as he leaned forward to examine the documents. What they revealed to him, was Redd liked to play with pistols. He had two arrests for possession of a firearm, another for attempted murder, and one for drug possession. There were also a few assaults, trespassing and domestic violence charges, all of which ended with Redd pleading to a lesser offense, or receiving a fine.

"What happened with the gun charges?" Jon-Jon inquired, eager to see if Redd was a snitch.

Chelsea retrieved some paperwork from her briefcase and began silently reading. After a minute or so she replied, "Well, it looks like Mr. Davenport got lucky on both occasions. He pleaded guilty to a bullshit misdemeanor for the first gun because it was inoperable." She used her finger to scroll down the paper, talking as she read. "As for the second case, he was in some type of group home at the time, and the charges eventually got thrown out. Apparently, the search warrant didn't give them permission to search the room where the gun was located. Only reason he got arrested was because someone told on him."

"Forget about the gun charges, it's the drug beef that holds the most value," Chelsea explained.

Jon-Jon was confused. "How so? It says those charges got dismissed too."

"They did," Chelsea confirmed. "However, another thing us cops have access to is something called a 'known associates' dossier.' Basically, its comprised of all the people you're known to associate with, or in this case, caught a charge with. You asked me to look for a female that might be close to Redd, and I think I just might've found who you're looking for."

She rifled through some papers, quickly located the right one, and laid it on the table. It was a picture.

"That right there is Monae Simpson, and I'm guessing she was, or still is, Redd's girlfriend. Back when he caught the drug charge, she was actually in the cab when police pulled it over and found three ounces of coke under the seat. Obviously, they'd just come from having purchased the drugs and although Mr. Davenport was initially charged with possession, Monae ended up claiming the drugs were hers. She pleaded guilty and since it was her first time in trouble with the law, she got five years felony probation. Actually, she's still on probation now, which means if you wanted, I could call her probation officer and..."

Jon-Jon waved her off as he picked up the picture of Monae, staring at it in disbelief. He tried to disguise the look of recognition that crossed his face, but Chelsea had been trained at reading body language.

"Looks like you know her," she remarked.

Jon-Jon nodded. "I do. I actually used to have a crush on her back in the day," he confessed.

"Really," Chelsea said, somewhat amused. "What happened?"

Jon-Jon shrugged nonchalantly, mentally filtering through memories of Monae as he spoke. "I don't think she was feeling me. Even if she was, she was fucking with the Roy dude at the time. Last thing I heard, she had moved to New York, and –"

"I know you not talking about the same Roy you killed," Chelsea cut in with an astonished look. "That was her boyfriend? Does she even know it was you?"

"Nobody knows it was me but you," Jon-Jon answered, unable to take his eyes off Monae. Even in a mugshot, she was still beautiful. What had made her start fucking with a clown like Redd, he wondered? The Monae he remembered had been too smart and headstrong to deal with a dude of his caliber. And obviously, Redd didn't respect Monae at all. Considering how he'd been all over the stripper bitch, Vanilla, it was hard to tell he even had a girl.

*Oh well*, Jon-Jon thought laying the flick back on the table. Fucking with Redd was about to turn into one of Monae's biggest mistakes.

"You alright?" Chelsea inquired, seeing the dazed look in his eyes. "You over there looking like a lost puppy."

Jon-Jon chuckled. "I'm good, trust me" he assured her. "Just thinking about how crazy life is sometimes. I smoked her man, Roy, and now years later, her man Redd tried to smoke me. Ain't that some weird shit"

"Definitely," Chelsea agreed, glancing at her watch "But let's finish this up because I have an important meeting to get to in less than an hour. So, let me just tell you what I know, or actually what I don't know at this moment. Unfortunately, I can't tell you the whereabouts of either Redd, or Monae. Maybe they went back to New York," she suggested.

"They didn't," Redd said without going any further.

Not one to ask too many questions, Chelsea continued, "Okay, so if they're still out here, I can put a flag on them, and whenever they come into contact with any CCTV cameras or traffic and toll cams, I'll get notified. Once I get the location, I should be able to track them from there. Afterwards, I could easily obtain a search warrant..." Suddenly she stopped in mid-sentence. "Why are you shaking your head like that's not what you want?"

Jon-Jon emptied the can of Ensure, and sat it back on the side table. "If you get an address, I'll take it from there. You just take care of Serious. What's the status on him anyway?"

Chelsea shrugged with indifference. "If that's how you want it, fine by me. You know what I always tell you though, don't get caught," she warned. "Now as far as Mr. Jones is concerned, he's about done. Turns out he was already being investigated for drug trafficking among other things. With what you've given me, the gun and drug sales, he's pretty much finished. I'm talking about a R.I.C.O. case with him facing life in prison, if not the death penalty. That will be up to the prosecutor. All I'm waiting for is the green light from you, and I can have the agents already assigned to the case file an arrest warrant... yada, yada, yada.

"Now, are we done here because I have to get going,"

"Yeah, we done," Jon-Jon replied. Satisfied with the progress report, he left Chelsea stuffing files into her briefcase and headed back upstairs.

In the master bedroom, Jon-Jon pulled a black duffel bag out from under the bed containing a little over half a million in cash. He separated a stack from one of the bundles, zipped the bag closed, and pushed it back to its previous location.

Back downstairs, he tossed the money on the coffee table. Although him and Chelsea were family, business was business. She wasn't assisting him and supplying him with intel for free.

Chelsea rifled through the bills like a seasoned bank teller and frowned. "This is short, cousin. What's up?"

Jon-Jon grinned sheepishly. "Shit been kinda slow ever since..." He gestured to the colostomy bag. "I'll make up for it next time," he lied.

"You better!" Chelsea snapped as she got to her feet. "It's bad enough you got me risking my job, and freedom. Not to mention, you had me travel all the way out here to Charlotte. Five thousand just isn't going to cut it. The agreement was ten. It's aight though, I know you're a man of your word." She zipped up her jacket and grabbed her purse and briefcase. "Now come give me a hug," she demanded. "I love you and take care of yourself in these streets. Tell ma I send my love. How is she?"

"She's good, but she'll be even happier to hear I talked to you," Jon-Jon remarked as he walked her to the door. "Just make sure you keep me posted on both situations."

"You know I will," Chelsea reassured him, before walking out the door.

Back in the living room, Jon-Jon retrieved the spare cell phone from under the coffee table. After replaying some of the conversation he'd just had with Chelsea to ensure it was recorded, he stashed the phone in a hidden safe located under a floorboard in the kitchen. Just like Redd, Monae, and Serious, Jon-Jon considered Chelsea a liability. If she was feeding him intel for cash, no telling what other illicit activities she was involved in. In the event she got collared later on down the line and decided to cooperate, the recordings of their numerous meetings would come in handy. Even if she somehow managed to keep from getting snared, Jon-Jon knew eventually he would have to murder Chelsea. She had too much dirt on him, and family or not, he would never feel totally safe until she was dead.

Grinning wickedly, he pulled out his personal cellphone from the pocket of his robe and dialed a number to put in motion plans to murder both Monae, and Redd. Unbeknownst to Chelsea, he knew just how to find them.

# CHAPTER 24

The Forest Housing projects in the Bronx was another one of the city's more unsavory neighborhoods, notorious for crime and violence. Even at one in the morning, it wasn't surprising to see an abundance of drug activity taking place in the courtyard. The setup resembled check out aisles in the supermarket, only in this instance, instead of cashiers, there were two workers serving two separate lines of fiends. From his position across the street where he sat in the driver's seat of a stolen Honda with tints, Menace had been surveying the operation for the past hour. It was a sloppy arrangement in his opinion, but he viewed that as a benefit considering the events to come in the next week or so. Tonight, however, was simply a fact-finding mission. After observing in silence for a few more minutes, he felt satisfied enough to move forward with the next phase of the plan. He turned off the radio and twisted in his seat ready to address the other two occupants in the car with him, both of whom came with baggage.

Schoolboy was the biggest potential liability because he'd yet to demonstrate his willingness to use violence as a means for financial gain or survival. He was a natural born hustler, no question about that, but it didn't take a rocket scientist to sell drugs. One needed to be cut from a different type of cloth and possess a particular arsenal of traits to be a part of M.B.A.M. Menace wasn't sure Schoolboy fit the bill. Tonight would be the first of many tests to determine what value, if any, he brought to the table. Rosez on the other hand, who sat in the passenger seat texting, had proven valuable on too many occasions to count. The problem was Menace didn't know if he could still trust her after their last altercation. One of the only reasons she was even present was because of her performance when Raw and his cohorts tried to ambush Guntalk and Crisis. Menace hoped she would once again prove her worth in the upcoming endeavor.

"Aight, let's get down to business," he announced, waiting until all eyes were on him before continuing. "This is the situation, and before y'all start asking a million questions, let me finish first. I got some info there's a bud spot in the building right there." He pointed in the direction, and Rosez, and Schoolboy glanced at the location he was referring to. "Supposedly, they got everything from dimes and dubs to eighths and ounces," Menace revealed. "They're also using the crib as a stash spot for pounds of bud, bricks of coke, and money. In another week y'all going up in there to snatch everything." He paused to let the statement sink in, and to also watch their reaction. Not surprisingly, Rosez smiled deviously at the prospect of getting paid. Schoolboy looked a bit nervous though.

Menace took note of that. "As far as security is concerned, it's basically nonexistent," he informed them. "There's two dudes in the spot at all times and they're gripped up. Other than that, it's quiet."

"No security?" Schoolboy asked in disbelief.

"None," Menace confirmed. "And when you think about it, that makes perfect sense. More security only draws attention to the spot." Schoolboy nodded, seeing the logic. "This is the plan," Menace explained. "Tonight, y'all just going in there to cop some bud and verify what I was told. I need to know everything from how many rooms there are, down to if the workers are moving sloppy or organized. Are they toting hammers in plain sight? I need to be able to see the entire set up in my head, so record some video with your cellphone if possible. If you can't, don't stress it. Just keep your eyes open for anything out of place. Y'all gonna be coming back and forth to cop all week so you don't have to find out everything tonight. Whatever you do, just be smart about it," he emphasized, fixing his gaze on Schoolboy. "This gone be your first time really fucking with the gang, and like I told you before, what you do from here on out is going to determine whether I make you a part of my family or not."

Rosez sucked her teeth, annoyed. "Menace, I don't even know why you got this nigga here. This dude is a straight winky dink, he not ready for this lifestyle."

"I been ready," Schoolboy shot back. He didn't sound at all convincing, but Menace still decided to give him a shot. It wasn't like they were robbing the spot that night anyway. Worse came to worse, Schoolboy could be used as an expendable pawn for something in the future.

After issuing more instructions and precautions to take, Menace gave him the apartment number of the spot and sent him on his way. He waited until Schoolboy entered the building then turned his attention to Rosez.

This was the first occasion since the cutting incident that Menace had spent an extended amount of time in the presence of Rosez, and for a moment they found themselves at a loss of words. They stared at each other for almost a full minute before Menace broke the silence.

"I owe you a big apology," he said gazing into her eyes so she could see his sincerity. "Not only are you one of the most official women I know, you're an asset to this family. I should've gave you that bread. You earned it, and I played myself. Now I need to know if I can still trust you, or is this going to come between us," he said gesturing to thin scar on her forehead. Thankfully, it only required only ten stitches to close. If it wasn't for her dreads getting in the way, her injuries could've been much worse.

Rosez turned to stare out the window, as she felt herself becoming overwhelmed with emotions. "I don't even know what to say at this point," she muttered. "I still can't believe you cut me."

"Rosez, you cut me first," Menace reminded her.

"But you slapped me, Menace. Twice! What the fuck did you expect me to do?"

"Hold it down," Menace replied without hesitation. "You disrespected me and my mom's Rosez, so you should've known what was coming."

Rosez was already shaking her head with contempt. "Hold it down huh," she repeated, sarcasm lacing her tone. "Picture somebody putting they hands on me, and

I just hold it down. You must really think I'm soft. Well, Rosez ain't never been soft. Big, tall, short or small, you put your hands on me and it's going down."

Menace couldn't believe how fast the conversation had went left. Before it escalated, he nudged her chin until they we're once again eye to eye.

"Listen to me, Rosez, you already know a nigga got crazy love for you, but you played yourself. I played myself too, and for that I apologize," he added. "Your mouth is reckless though. How many times have I respectfully asked you to stop talking all crazy to me. To be honest, I can't even say I'm all that surprised this happened. Do I regret it? Of course I do. Nonetheless, what's done is done. We can do one of two things. Either put this behind us and continue to get money like we been doing, or you can go about your business. That's not what I want, but there has to be a certain level of respect between us. You have to accept the fact that it's my way or the highway, simple as that. At the end of the day, I'd rather let you go then keep going through situations like this."

Pausing, he gave her time to contemplate a decision. "So, what you wanna do?"

Rosez answered instantly. "Whatever you need or want me to do, Menace. "I'm still not feeling you forcing Schoolboy on me. Just look at his name. Let me just use one of my flower girls," she pleaded.

Once again, Menace denied her request. "Son gotta get his hands dirty. Tell you what though, let me see how he performs tonight, and we'll go from there. Fair enough?"

Rosez reluctantly nodded. "Yeah that's fair."

"Of course, its fair," Menace shot back chuckling. "Now take ya pretty ass upstairs and go handle business so we can eat. You got me?"

Finally, Rosez cracked a smile. "Yeah, I got you," she replied as she eased out of the Honda.

Menace watched her cross the street, her fat ass jiggling like jello, and suddenly it dawned on him, no matter what happened from here on out, he would never be able to trust Rosez like he once had. It was one of the main reasons he'd sent Schoolboy on the scouting mission with her. As manipulative and captivating as Rosez could be, Menace needed somebody not affiliated with M.B.A.M to keep an eye on her. Going forward, he also realized he would now have to figure out what role, if any, Rosez was going to play in the "takeover".

Sighing with distress over the dilemma, Menace began rolling a blunt. It was starting to seem like every day another issue popped up requiring his attention. Rudeboy still remained priority number one, but just like Raj warned, the Jamaican was proving a lot smarter than he looked. Not only had there been no sightings of him since the incident, inquiries into his background had so far revealed nothing tying him to Soundview besides his drug operation. There were rumors he had a baby mother living in the hood, but Menace hadn't been able to verify anything. He practically knew everyone from "The View" so he definitely would've known if Rudeboy had a baby moms residing there. With no leads to follow, he'd been forced to sit back, and hope and pray, Rudeboy or any of his henchman didn't catch him slipping, which is exactly what would've happened if it wasn't for Lotto. The irony regarding the timing of the kidnapping wasn't lost on Menace as he sparked the spliff and took a long drag. Soon, the potent strand of weed called "black diamond" had him reminiscing on the incident that might've very well been the reason he was still breathing.

# CHAPTER 25

I told you, you should've killed me," Lotto repeated once the Range pulled off. The smug expression he wore did little to disguise the fury radiating off him like steam from a freshly baked biscuit. "Put your gun on the floor and do it slow. Real slow," he ordered through clenched teeth. "If I even think you about to try some funny shit..." He cocked the hammer on the .44 Bulldog he held, allowing it to say what his mouth hadn't.

Never in a million yeas did Menace expect to once again be in Lotto's circumference. He felt like a complete fool for underestimating him once. He wasn't about to make the same mistake twice. Using two fingers, he hooked the .357 by its trigger guard, and slowly pulled it from his front hoodie pocket.

"How did you find me?" He inquired, laying the pistol on the floor.

Lowering his own gun, Lotto fixed him with a cold calculating stare as he rotated the cigar in his other hand between his fingers. "You don't even know who I am, do you?" He quizzed.

Menace shrugged, "Not really."

Lotto snorted in disgust. "So, you mean to tell me you violated an individual you know nothing about?" He gazed at Menace expectantly waiting for an answer. When it didn't it come, he shook his head perturbed. "That's the problem with you young cats. You do shit without thinking or doing your homework. I could kill you right now, and to think you only got a measly punk ass ten-grand. Is that a fair exchange for your life?"

It was in that instant, Menace noticed Lotto was dressed like he was going to a funeral. Everything from his gators to his shark skin suit was black.

"Is that what you plan on doing, you taking me somewhere to kill me?" He asked.

"I haven't decided yet," Lotto answered. "Tell you what though, you keep running ya mouth, and imma leave ya ass on the side of the road, and not so you can hitchhike home, either. Catch my drift? This ain't no damn question, and answer session unless I'm the one asking the questions. Otherwise, it's me talking, and you listening. Only reason you even alive is because I'm still trying to figure out if you stupid, or you just got a lot of heart. Either way, you owe me, and until I'm paid in full with interest, you belong to me. You understand what the fuck I'm saying?"

"I understand," Menace replied, seeing no reason to provoke him.

"Where we going, daddy?" The driver suddenly asked.

Menace still couldn't believe he'd allowed a woman to get the drop on him. A sexy one at that, he noticed after she halted at a red light, and spun in her seat. She was an older white chick, probably in her early forties with auburn colored hair, and freckles. She looked to be of foreign descent, and it was obvious now she'd been disguising her voice when she accosted him. Her most notable feature were her crystal blue eyes, which briefly lingered on Menace before gravitating to Lotto.

"Where we going?" She repeated.

"Mia, just drive for now," Lotto instructed before taking a pull from his cigar. He exhaled the fumes upward as he began talking. "One of my biggest flaws has always been giving people too many chances. Maybe it's because I'm getting old, and I'm not as prone to blow nigga's head off as I was in my younger years. Whatever the reason, it seems one of my decisions has come back to bite me in the ass. I'm sure it will eventually be the death of me, but we all have to go someday.

"For now, I'm content with hitting the nigga in his pockets where it hurts most. I could easily get him pushed off the face of the earth, it's just more fun for me this way."

*What the fuck is this dude talking about, and what does it have to do with me*, Menace wondered, watching Lotto take another drag off his cigar. After exhaling, he chomped down on the stogie, as his hand slid into the inner folds of his suit jacket. He removed a standard sized envelope and tossed it on the seat between them.

"Take a look at that," he ordered, smoke curling from his mouth.

Reluctantly, Menace picked up the envelope and flipped the flap back. A collection of at least ten pictures greeted him.

He pulled the first one out, and immediately felt his blood run cold. Staring back at him was a picture of his mother, Maleka. From the graffiti on the wall behind her, he could tell it had been taken in the elevator in their building. Seeing the distraught look on his face, Lotto laughed demonically.

"Got your attention now don't I, motherfucka!" He barked.

Menace was too stunned to respond. The realization that someone had been close enough to his mother to kill her if they wanted, left him speechless. Unfortunately, it only got worse. The next flick he removed was of his sister, Lauren, sitting outside talking on her phone, unaware of the peril lurking not even ten feet away. In an instant, the shock Menace felt transformed into an indescribable rage. He turned to Lotto with a snarl on his lips, only to be met by the barrel of his revolver.

"I'm really hoping you stupid enough to do or just say something that will make me feel good about blowing ya fucking head off," Lotto spat. "Now either get on with it, or finish looking at the pictures, and give me my shit back."

It took every ounce of strength Menace could summon to keep from lunging and trying to disarm Lotto. Finally, he tore his gaze away, reverting it back to the pictures. The rest were of every single M.B.A.M member. Lotto had obviously done his homework, and although he would only admit it to himself, Menace knew he was out of his league. Struggling to maintain his composure, he inserted the illustrations back into the envelope, and handed them over.

Lotto snatched them from his grasp and slid them back into the interior pocket of his suit. "I know you mad," he remarked, resting the Bulldog on his thigh. "You feel violated right? Well, now you know how I felt when I was minding my own business, and you took it upon yourself to violate me.

"I didn't know who you were," Menace muttered.

"Well now you do," Lotto shot back. He took one last pull from his cigar, then dumped it into the Starbucks cup sitting in the center console. "Those pictures were to show you not only are my resources extensive, but I'm playing by my own set of rules. As much as I don't want to have your people harmed, if you don't do exactly as I say, I'll murder every one of them while you watch, and not lose a minute's sleep over it." The intensity of his words left no doubt as to their authenticity.

"Now I was telling you something earlier," Lotto explained. "You probably thought I was some senile motherfucka talking out my ass. Well I'm not, and two things you're going to quickly learn about me is I don't make idle threats, and I don't talk because I have lips. Now pay attention to what I'm about to say because I'm not going to repeat myself, and if you miss something or fuck this up, it's going to cost you. You know anybody that lives in Forest Projects?" He asked after allowing the threat to sink in.

"Naw I don't," Menace muttered still simmering.

"Well, you're about to, so listen closely," Lotto instructed.

For the next ten minutes, he proceeded to describe in vivid detail an apartment located in Forest that was being utilized as a weed spot but was really a front for a stash spot. He neglected to divulge anything in regards to the owner of the crib, except to say the man had betrayed him.

"I want you to hit that spot, and take everything by any means," Lotto demanded. "Whatever drugs you find is yours. The money – every single penny of it – goes to me, *comprende*?"

Menace nodded in agreement, feeling like a straight puppet. Twenty minutes later they pulled up beside P.S. 69, the elementary school up the block from Soundview.

"You owe me," Lotto reiterated. "And this is how I want my payback. You do this right, and I might change your life. You fuck it up, and you won't have a life." He handed Menace a piece of paper with a number scribbled on it. "Make sure you keep me posted. This has to get handled within the next few weeks so get on it," he ordered.

Once again, Menace nodded. What other choice did he really have?

Satisfied they were on the same page, Lotto jerked his head towards the door. "Now get the fuck outta my ride," he ordered.

Stuffing the sliver of paper in his pocket, Menace did as he was told. On cue, Mia, who was already at the rear of the vehicle, pulled the back door open. Once outside of the Range, Menace hesitantly reached for his revolver, waiting until Lotto nodded in approval before taking possession of it. Just as he stuffed the gun in his front hoodie pocket, and went to walk off, Lotto called him back.

He scooted over to the window. "One more thing," he said with a smirk. "Next time, keep your hands to yourself."

"Huh?" Menace said, confused. He didn't even notice Mia sneak up behind him. He damn sure felt the gunbutt though that left him sitting haphazardly on the curb in a daze.

Now, as he sat in the Honda replaying everything, he found himself becoming engulfed with fury all over again. One way or another, he was going to murder Lotto for threatening his family. The sight of Schoolboy emerging from the projects derailed any further ruminations. He hopped in the car, and immediately began rambling, provoking Menace to tell him to shut the fuck up. Rosez arrived minutes later and only after they were a block away from the scene, did he ask for the details.

"Them niggas is definitely slipping," Schoolboy exclaimed.

"Facts," Rosez confirmed, tossing two eighths into Menace's lap. "And you already know I got one of them niggas that work in there all on my body," she bragged. "Exchanged numbers and everything. Even got some video for you to check out too."

Menace nodded in satisfaction. The words were music to his ears. He was eager to complete the robbery, if only so he could reconnect with Lotto. Once that happened… he grinned evilly, thinking about what he had in store for the old head.

# CHAPTER 26

For what seemed like the tenth time in the past ten minutes, Lauren surveyed the crowded clinic waiting room from her seat in the back row. Once again, she was tempted to sprint through the front doors. Medical facilities made her feel yucky, and she hated them with a passion. What she hated even more were her growing suspicions that her mother had been lying about the identity of her Pops ever since she was old enough to comprehend what the word signified. The topic had been the cause of a heated argument the night before, when Lauren finally revealed the main reason, she didn't believe Lunatic was her father. His name wasn't on her birth certificate, and according to Maleka, he'd been present during her birth. So why wouldn't he have signed, especially since he signed Naseem's birth certificate? It just didn't make any sense to Lauren, and after years of getting the runaround, she finally found the courage to tell Maleka she was fed up with her uncooperative attitude whenever the topic of her father arose.

"What are you trying to hide?" She eventually screamed.

"I'm not trying to hide anything," Maleka tried to reassure her. Lauren, however, hadn't been convinced by her mother's words or tears, and for the first time ever, she went to bed that night without kissing her goodnight.

Despite her lingering attitude, she still accompanied Maleka to her doctor's appointment that morning because regardless of anything, she was still her mother. Gigi had also come to show support, and Lauren was glad because that meant she wouldn't have to talk her mother while they waited. She glanced to her left to find both women laughing at only God knew what and went back to reading the GamePro magazine on her phone. There were a number of interesting articles enclosed, but Lauren was finding it hard to concentrate with the sound of babies crying, and people groaning in pain all around her. Sighing in frustration, she turned off the phone and closed her eyes in an attempt to blot out the scene. It wasn't long before thoughts of her father invaded her conscience, provoking snapshots to flash through her mind of the relationship she wished she could have with him.

Being that she'd grown up believing Lunatic was her father, that's the face she saw in all the portrayals. The first image was of the two of them at a picnic, laughing and catching up on each other's lives. In an instant the picture switched to them at an amusement park, front cart of a roller coaster, screaming their lungs out as it descended. The impressions continued to erupt, until Lauren couldn't take it anymore. She was seriously starting to believe her mind was the only place she would ever partake in any of these experiences.

She didn't even realize she was crying until she felt the teardrop plop onto the back of her hand.

Instantly, she opened her eyes, relieved to see nobody was paying her any mind. Discreetly, she wiped her face with her sleeve at the same time the intercom crackled to life.

"Maleka Royal, please report to the front desk," the receptionist announced.

Maleka rose to her feet. "That's me, sis; keep your fingers crossed," she told Gigi.

"Girl, ain't nothing wrong with you," Gigi reassured her as they embraced.

"I sure hope so," Maleka said, turning to Lauren. She pulled her from the chair for a hug. "I love you."

"I love you too, ma," Lauren replied.

It was as her mother walked off that she noticed Maleka was definitely losing weight. Before Lauren could dwell on it, Gigi scooted over a seat, and draped an arm over her shoulder.

"What's going on with you and your mother?" She whispered. "And before you even think about fixing ya mouth to say nothing, just remember I helped raise you, which means I know you well enough to know when something ain't right."

Lauren didn't need any further prodding. She wanted to talk to somebody anyway, and Gigi was the next best person to her mother. "It's my father," she said softly.

"Again?" Gigi said in disbelief.

"What happened this time? matter fact, let's go outside," she suggested, eager to smoke.

The fresh air immediately made Lauren feel better. Overhead, the five-train rumbled by on the elevated platform, sounding like thunder. Once it passed, she quickly explained the cause of her distress. When she finished, Gigi shook her in confusion.

"What did your mother have to say about all of this?" She asked, exhaling a cloud of smoke. "I'm sure there has to be a good explanation for him not signing."

"She said it's a clerical error," Lauren replied sarcastically. "Like, let's be real aunty, a clerical error on a signature. That doesn't even make sense."

"You're right, it doesn't," Gigi agreed. "Then again, I don't think your mother would just blatantly lie to you. And I'm not saying that just because she's my best friend either."

"So, what do you think I should do?" Lauren asked, feeling helpless.

Gigi took a slow drag off her cigarette as she contemplated her words. "Listen to me baby girl, I'm going to tell you something, and I really want you to understand what I'm saying. There's more than one way to milk a cow. These days, there isn't much you can't find out through the internet. Then you have all these D.N.A. companies that can basically tell you your entire family tree."

"But they said my father is dead," Lauren reminded her.

"And like I said, you can find out almost anything through the internet," Gigi repeated. "And that's all I'm going to say about that. This subject is a little too personal for my input. I love you though, and you already know I'm here for you."

"I love you too, aunty," Lauren replied feeling a little better.

Back inside the clinic, they continued talking until Maleka reemerged. She didn't look or sound too happy. "Let's go," she immediately snapped.

Snatching up her purse and coat, she headed for the door with Gigi and Lauren following. Not until they were a block away from the clinic did Maleka reveal, she would need to come back for more testing the next day.

# CHAPTER 27

From the interior of his black Lexus truck parked across the street, Rudeboy watched the trio exit the clinic, and begin walking up Southern Boulevard. He felt the anger rise in him like yeast, prompting him to grip the handle of the Draco sitting in his lap. The gun was an AK-47 style firearm with a shortened barrel, and no shoulder stock.

"Dirty fucking bitch," Rudeboy muttered, shooting daggers at Maleka's back. As soon as they reached the corner, he shifted into drive and began following them.

"What's up, we gone smoke all three of them or what?" Raw asked from the passenger seat. "Just give me the word, and I'll do all of them right now," he sneered, reaching for the door handle.

"Just cool yaself, bredren," Rudeboy urged as he eased to a halt at a red light.

Quiet as kept, Rudeboy was immensely disappointed with Raw for having squandered the chance to murder both Crisis, and Guntalk. The opportunity to groundhog Menace had also briefly presented itself from what he heard. Yet still, the only casualties were men from his team. Rudeboy wasn't taking any more chances. If he decided to kill Maleka and company, he would be the one doing it. It would be the perfect way to get back at Menace, and the more Rudeboy considered it, the more he liked it. Still, something made him hesitate.

Sensing his reluctance, Raw studied him as the light turned green, and they cruised ahead. "Bredren, you look kinda tense, ya alright?" He asked.

"I'm good," Rudeboy lied. He hated to lie to his closest comrade, but not even he knew of the back story between him and Maleka. Very people knew, and the ones that did considered it ancient history. To Rudeboy though, there was nothing ancient about how he felt for Maleka. Unfortunately, the feeling wasn't mutual, and he wasn't sure they'd ever been. When he recalled how Maleka had used him, only to cast him aside every time Lunatic was released from prison, he squeezed the steering wheel as if trying to strangle it. Adding insult to injury, Lunatic's son was now trying to dethrone him. How ironic Rudeboy thought, coming to a conclusion. Despite how he felt about Maleka, she along with her companions would all have to die for the sins of Menace. The trio were on the left side of the street, standing at a pizzeria window, waiting for their orders. Knowing their next destination was the subway station two blocks ahead, Rudeboy swerved around the car in front of him, to intercept them. The fact that he was about to take a major risk by attempting to murder them in broad day meant nothing to him. All he cared about was inflicting the most damage on Menace. Killing his mother, sister, and Gigi would crush his soul. Then while he was vulnerable, and overcome with grief, Rudeboy would crush him.

With the plot solidified, he scanned the street in search of a good parking spot, while he disclosed his plan to Raw. "Let me do it," he pleaded, eager to atone for his last mishap.

Rudeboy was already shaking his head before he could finish. "I got this," he stated as he pulled into the gas station directly across the street from the Hunts Point underground subway station. It was the perfect spot being that the Cross Bronx Expressway was only feet away. After the murders, he could easily disappear into traffic. Rudeboy was already imagining the chaos that was sure to ensue once the gunshots erupted, which would make escaping that much easier. After maneuvering the Lexus around to the side of the gas station, he grabbed a shopping bag from the back seat, and stuffed the Draco inside. "Be ready," he instructed Raw before exiting the whip.

Dressed in shorts and tank top to accommodate the 100-degree weather, he blended in effortlessly with the throng of people standing at the curb waiting to cross. Once the cars came to a halt, he jogged to the other side, bypassing the island where the entrance to the train station was located. Adjacent to the subway, maybe 20 or 30 feet away to his left, was the corner where Southern Boulevard ended. Maleka and crew would be coming from that direction in order to reach the train. Sitting the bag down between his legs, Rudeboy retrieved his cellphone and pretended to be having a conversation while he waited. His eyes missed little as he scanned any and everything in sight. Ten minutes later he spotted Maleka and company strolling toward the subway. Rudeboy felt a familiar calm sweep over him, as he picked up the shopping bag and began trailing them.

With his long, determined strides, it didn't take long for him to close the distance between them until he was close enough behind them to hear their chatter. Up ahead, a swarm of people emerged from the subway station, adding to the substantial amount of pedestrians milling to and fro. Weaving through the crowd, Rudeboy inched closer. And closer. He inserted his cell back into his pocket, then lifted the bag waist high, and pretended to be rummaging around inside for something as his hand curled around the handle of the Draco. He didn't even plan on pulling it out of the bag. Everything seemed to be going in slow motion, as he watched Maleka, Gigi, and Lauren approach the steps leading down into the station. Abruptly he stepped to the side as another wave of people exited the subway, several of whom were eager to catch the bus that had just pulled up across the street. One of them bumped into Rudeboy, knocking him back a step.

"Watch where the fuck you going," the man barked.

Rudeboy glanced in his direction, but the dude had already disappeared in the crowd. Chuckling to himself, he spun back around to find Maleka staring at him. Her eyes traveled from his face to the shopping bag where she noticed the outline of the gun. Instantly it registered what was about happen. Grinning wickedly, Rudeboy raised the bag about to open fire, when suddenly two uniformed officers appeared at the top of the subway steps. They were the only reason Maleka, and company would live to see another day.

Furious, Rudeboy took off jogging towards the Lexus.

# CHAPTER 28

Redd was tired of laying low. Tired of losing money, and tired of hearing Monae tell him how stupid he was for deciding to stay in Raleigh. She was scheduled to return to New York the next day, and although Redd understood by not going back with her, he was basically kissing their relationship goodbye, he didn't give a fuck, especially after Monae had allowed Serious to put hands on him. Redd still wore a few bumps and bruises from the altercation, and for him they were just a reminder that in time, Serious too would need to be dealt with.

In the meantime, Redd planned on proving him and Monae wrong by not only staying in Raleigh, but thriving after he eliminated Jon-Jon. True to her word, Vanilla had come through with his Charlotte address, and the only issue holding Redd up now was his brother, Brian. Eight days after vowing to report to Raleigh, he was still in the Bronx, handling what he said was a major issue regarding his own team. As mad as Redd wanted to be, he couldn't even fault his baby brother. If anything, his loyalty for his squad made Redd respect him even more. It still left him in a jam though. Without at least one person to hold him down, he wasn't about to go on a kamikaze mission trying to kill Jon-Jon by himself. There was no telling how many goons he had with him. Redd was certainly frustrated with having to wait, but he was even more annoyed over all the money he was missing while he waited. His phone had been ringing off the hook for the past few days, but on the advice of Monae, he hadn't been answering.

Today, nothing was going to stop him from getting to that chicken. He'd spent the last half hour touching base with some of his best clientele, all of whom were eager to get their hands on some of his Cali bud. After scheduling times to meet with his 3 biggest spenders, he plugged his phone into the charger, and headed downstairs. He found Monae in the kitchen cooking breakfast, decked out in her usual wife beater, and pink boy shorts. The smell of turkey bacon greeted Redd as he walked up behind her, and kissed her neck. "Morning babe." "Good morning," Monae replied as she turned around to kiss him. Based on their affectionate interactions it was impossible to tell they'd been at each others throat for the past 2 weeks. However, with both of their plans solidified, they'd pledged to make the best of their last moments together. For Redd, that meant getting as much pussy as possible. Monae on the other hand saw it as another opportunity to continue trying to convince Redd to come back to New York with her. Based off of that alone, Redd already knew Monae wasn't going to be too pleased about him going out later to handle business. He disclosed his plans as they sat eating a breakfast consisting of grits, scrambled eggs, homemade biscuits, and turkey bacon. Redd was sure going to miss her cooking.

Much to his surprise, Monae didn't even trip when he revealed his agenda for the day. "I figured it would only be a matter of time before you got back to it," she replied. "Of course, I wish you would just wait, but what can I say? I just want you to be safe in these streets, Redd. I know I'm probably never going to see you again after I leave," she said, her voice cracking.

"Of course, you will," Redd assured her, laying his fork down. He scooted his chair next to hers, cupped her face, and spoke from his heart. "I know I done put you through a lot of senseless bullshit, and I'll regret that forever. If I could go back in time, I swear I would change everything. I would've supported your dreams like you supported mine for all these years. I would've even pushed you more to follow those dreams. I guess I'm just selfish, babe. I mean I know I'm being selfish by choosing to stay out here, but we both know the truth is, I'm no good for you, and you're too good for me."

"I still love you though," Monae said with tears trickling from her eyes.

"And I love you too," Redd responded. "But in your heart you know this is what's best for both of us. He swiped at the wet spots on her face. "Stop crying babe, please? We promised to make the best out of these last days together. Can we just do that?"

Monae nodded as she leaned over for a kiss. Not surprisingly, the kissing led to a passionate lovemaking session right there on the dining room floor.

Hours later, Redd sat on the edge of the bed getting dressed while he watched the NBA highlights on ESPN from the previous night games. Once again, his beloved Knicks had lost. To the mediocre Orlando magic at that.

"Bunch of fucking bums!" Redd yelled at the TV. "They need to fire that damn coach, that's what they need to do."

"Who you talking to, babe?" Monae asked as she entered the room fresh out the shower.

"These damn sportscasters," Redd answered, shaking his head in disgust. "You know how I feel about my Knicks. You know how I feel about you too, don't you?" He added, pulling her between his legs. He planted his face into her damp stomach, inhaling the strawberry scent on her skin as he cuffed her yeeks.

Monae bit her lip lustfully as she undid her towel and let it fall. "Show me," she demanded.

Redd sighed in frustration, releasing her. "I can't right now, babe," he said glancing at his watch. "I'm already running late. I'm supposed to meet this dude at three, and its already a quarter to three. This nigga be spending paper, and I don't want to keep him waiting." He looked up from tying his black Foamposites. "You mad at me?" He asked, expecting her to have an attitude.

Once again, Monae surprised him. Smiling, she lovingly rubbed his head. "I'm not mad at you, babe, you handled ya business earlier. I guess I'll just have to wait until you get back. Unless you gone let me come with you," she added.

Redd's first instinct was to say no. Then he thought about how in another 24 hours Monae would be gone. *Why not*, he thought.

"Aight, you gotta hurry up and get dressed," he told her. He slapped her on the ass as she took off for the closet.

# CHAPTER 29

Half an hour later, Redd sat in the car sending a text to his peoples letting them know he was on his way. Shortly thereafter, Monae exited the house. As Redd watched her strut towards the whip, it once again dawned on him he was making a huge mistake by not going back to New York with her. In his heart he knew he would never find such a loyal, intelligent, trustworthy, down-ass chick like Monae. Not to mention, she was gorgeous as fuck. Even in a basic outfit consisting of jeans, a white and lime green Kause Karma V-neck, and a pair of black Kobe's, she looked good enough to eat. At the exact moment she hopped in the car, Redd was thinking about all the nasty things he was going to do to her when they got back home.

"Why you looking at me like that?" Monae questioned, attaching her seatbelt.

Redd licked his lips. "You know why," he answered as he pulled out of the driveway. "You a bad bitch and all the money in the world ain't worth losing you over, that's why."

Monae flipped the visor down. "Well, you still have the rest of the day to change your mind," she reminded him in between applying a coat of lip gloss. "And I'm hoping you do because, yeah, you done put a bitch through some shit, but these last few days have been beautiful. They reminded me of the reason I fell in love with you. I know if we really tried, we could make this work, don't you?"

"I do," Redd agreed, placing a hand on her thigh. "These streets is my drug though, babe. At the same time, I wanna do right by you. I'm just not no nine-to-five type of a nigga."

"So, start your own business," Monae suggested as she pushed the visor back in place, then deposited the tube of lip gloss back into her purse. She placed her hand over Redd's. "Babe, there's a million ways to make money legally these days, and you already know imma hold you down with whatever. Together we could accomplish so much. Just think about how successful you would be if you took that same energy you put into hustling and applied it to a legitimate business."

"Like what?" Redd asked as he got on the highway. "A barbershop? A record label? Come on ma, everybody doing that type of shit."

"So do something different!" Monae countered. "You've never been a follower, and that's one of the things I loved about you from the start. All you have to do is find something you like doing, then figure out a way to make money off of it. Babe, it's not as hard as you think. Do you really want to be playing in these streets forever? You got over a hundred-grand right now, and that's more than enough money to do something productive with, and still have something left over."

The more she talked, the deeper her words penetrated Redd's conscience. He definitely wasn't trying to be one of those losers still selling drugs at forty, and he certainly didn't want to go back to jail, or die in the streets, both of which were strong possibilities if he remained in Raleigh. Previously, the idea had seemed so worthwhile. Pondering over it now, though, Redd realized how idiotic it was to think killing Jon-Jon would be as easy as he'd led himself to believe. He had a team, as well as connections. All Redd had was Vanilla and some guns, which he knew weren't nearly enough to unseat Jon-Jon. On top of all that, he didn't want to lose Monae. That more than anything is what made Redd come to a sudden conclusion.

Noticing his exit ahead, Redd hit the signal to merge into the right lane. "Tell you what," he told Monae. "Right now I don't know about starting my own business. I don't even know what I'm interested in besides this street shit." Monae was already starting to shake her head in disappointment. "I know what you're interested in though," Redd continued. "If you promise to put your all into it, I'll give you half the bread I got so you can start your own clothing line. The rest we'll use to get on our feet when we get back to New York."

Instantly, Monae's eyes widened in disbelief. "What did you just say?" She asked, wanting to make sure she heard right. When he repeated himself, she unlatched her seatbelt, and damn near lunged into his lap. "I love you," she repeated over and over, as she cried tears of joy.

For the remainder of the ride, she gushed about her plans and ideas, most of which she'd been harboring since high school. Although she hadn't thought of a name for the line just yet, she did have sketches on her phone of jeans, leggings, t-shirts, and a host of other apparel. Her designs were beyond unique and stylish which wasn't at all astonishing to Redd, considering those were two of the traits that defined Monae.

As he listened to his lady passionately talk about starting her own brand, Redd pictured it all in his head. Everything from how she wanted to decorate her flagship store, to the marketing and advertising ploys she planned on implementing through social media. Redd didn't know much about business, but even he could see her ideas made sense. Whether they succeeded or not didn't even matter to him. He was just happy to be helping his woman turn her dreams into reality. He figured it was the least he could do after causing her to squander something she could never get back: time.

The time was a quarter after four when they reached their destination, and Monae was still radiating with excitement, but not to the point where she forgot about the danger they were in by being back in the city. She paused from texting Kameesha the good news, as she scanned the area, while Redd circled the block twice. Seeing nothing suspicious, he parked but left the engine running as he donned a pair of black leather gloves and checked one pistol before stuffing it into his waist. The second gun – a chrome .45 – he slid in his pocket, then grabbed the knapsack off the backseat. Situated, he turned to Monae.

"You coming inside with me or what?"

"You know I am," Monae answered without hesitation.

Grinning, Redd leaned over for a kiss. Seconds later, he and Monae exited the car and walked toward his client's house.

Redd and Monae were about ten feet from the front door when it was opened by a slim, brown-skinned dude wearing shorts, no shirt, and slippers. His face instantly lit up with a smile as he extended his fist for dap.

"Redd, what's up with you?" He greeted. "Glad to see you finally made it, I was starting to think you weren't coming."

Redd bumped fists with him. "Keyser, when have I ever stood you up? You know I would never do that to you. I'm definitely in a hurry though, so let's take care of this business, so I can be on my way."

Keyser nodded in understanding, sidestepping so they could enter. Redd took hold on Monae's hand and walked inside. The smell of fried chicken immediately filled his nose. As if reading his mind, Keyser said, "My lady doing her thing, I got a plate for both of you if y'all hungry," he offered.

"Naw we good, we just ate, but thanks anyway," Redd said, as they came to a door at the end of the hallway. Keyser unlocked it with a set of keys he removed from his pocket, and they followed him downstairs to a lavishly furnished man cave. Several arcade games lined the wall, forming a semicircle of sorts around a multitude of lounge chairs that faced a 70-inch flat screen. There was also a pool table at the back of the room, and a mini bar.

Redd had seen the area before, so he was over being impressed. Monae on the other hand, was already texting Kameesha about the luxuries.

"So this is that new shit I was telling you about," Redd said, unzipping his book bag. He pulled out two Ziplock bags filled with bud, and handed them to Keyser, who immediately mashed one against his nose.

Instantly, Keyser scrunched his face with pleasure. "This smells like some real pain. What's the name of it?"

"Purple sour," Redd revealed. "I just got that yesterday and you the first one to get ya hands on it."

Keyser nodded with satisfaction. "Yeah, I'm about to hurt the streets with this shit. Let me get you that bread so you can be on your way, and I can do my thing." He left the room, and returned minutes later, holding a brick of cash in each hand. "Nine thousand, and not a penny short," he confirmed, dropping the money on the pool table.

Redd began counting the money, while Monae texted Kameesha about how disrespectful Keyser was being. Twice already she'd caught him staring at her, licking his lips. He was blatant with his disrespect, and for a second, Monae considered telling Redd. She quickly decided against it, knowing with his temper it would take one word from her to have him going crazy. That was the last thing Monae wanted. She was eager for the transaction to be over so they could just leave.

Finally, after what seemed like a long time, Redd finished the count. He handed Monae the money, then turned back to Keyser with his hand extended.

"As always, it's been a pleasure doing business with you. You always come correct, and to show my gratitude, imma bless you with something extra next time," Redd lied.

194

"Yeah man, you already know that's gone be greatly appreciated," Keyser replied, leading them back upstairs. "I should be ready to holla in another week or so, maybe less. I already know niggas is about to go crazy for this new shit."

"You got my number, just hit me," Redd told him as they reached the front door. He hesitated on the stoop, surveying the area, and only after seeing it was safe, did he allow Monae to exit.

Monae headed straight for the car as Redd turned back to holla at Keyser. Just as she made it to the sidewalk, she noticed a pizza delivery man heading in their direction. He was of average height, with Hispanic features and a chubby build. Dressed in a red and white striped shirt, with black pants, there was nothing alarming about his appearance. Yet still, Monae felt goosebumps erupt all over her arms. She sensed something wasn't right but couldn't put her finger on exactly what it was. Glancing back at Redd, she silently urged him to hurry.

Monae turned back to look at the pizza man, and that's when it suddenly dawned on her. Keyser had mentioned his girl was cooking, so why then, would a pizza delivery be going to their house? That didn't make any sense, and the moment Monae realized it, she saw the pizza man reaching inside the insulated bag he was carrying. When his hand reemerged, there was a pistol in it.

"Redd!" Monae screamed in horror, as gunfire erupted.

*Boom! Boom! Boom!*

The first volley of bullets crashed into the wall where Redd would've been standing, were it not for

Monae's warning. He tried to run back in the house, only to crash face-first into the door Keyser slammed in his face. Redd didn't even have time to be shocked. He dove to the ground, as more slugs collided with the wall, then the pavement around him, sending chunks of asphalt whirling through the air like confetti.

Scrambling to his feet, Redd reached for the gun in his pocket. Just as he tugged it free, and spun to fire, one of the bullets ripped through his bicep, causing the pistol to clatter to the ground. The pain was unlike anything Redd had ever experienced. It felt like a bunch of scalding nails had been shoved into his flesh, and it was only because of the adrenaline he didn't scream.

Stumbling from the force of the bullet, Redd almost toppled headfirst into the gravel lining the driveway. Somehow, he managed to keep his balance as he sprinted around the side of the house with bullets whizzing past his head.

*Boom! Boom! Boom!*

With the grace of an Olympic jumper, he hurdled the fence at the back of the property. A quick left brought him to the open garage of the adjoining house, and he dashed inside, taking refuge behind a beige minivan. Momentarily forgetting about the wound in his arm, he reached for the gun in his waist, and instantly, a wave of severe pain bolted through his upper body. Redd bit his lip to keep from screaming as he glanced down to see blood dripping from his fingers, forming a small puddle on the floor. With his left hand, he lifted his shirt to check for the other gun, only to discover it was gone. It must've slipped down his leg when he was running, he assumed. One of his sneakers was also missing, he noticed. Breathing hard, he looked around for a weapon among the array of equipment lining the wall. What ultimately snagged his attention was the open door leading into the house. Redd hoped no one would come waltzing out.

Seconds turned into more seconds, and still he waited, crouched down behind the back bumper. Finally, he could no longer stand the suspense. Cradling his wounded arm, he crept towards the garage entrance. The moment he made it to the threshold...

*Boom! Boom! Boom! Boom!*

Although they sounded distant, the gunshots sent him scurrying back behind the car. He waited another full minute, counting off the seconds in his head, before repeating the process. This time no shots sounded when he made it to the opening. Cautiously, he backtracked until he found himself standing in Keyser's backyard. There was no doubt in Redd's mind he'd been set up. He didn't have time to dwell on it though, with the sounds of sirens in the distance. Nor was he about to try and locate his sneaker, or guns. Hobbling onward, he reached the front of the house.

The sight that greeted him would forever be seared into his memory.

Monae, sprawled on her back in the grass, feet away from Keyser's front door, her face covered in blood. Redd just knew she was dead. The sirens grew louder, and he looked up from her body to find a significant amount of neighbors watching him. Lowering his head, he sprinted to the car. Seconds later, he was jetting away from the scene.

# CHAPTER 30

One of the main reasons Rosez no longer stripped was because not even on a good night, could the rush she got from a customer making it rain on her, compete with the thrill she got from engaging in a life of crime. She felt that familiar sense of exhilaration now as she sauntered towards the Forest projects. She was in her element, doing what she did best, and not even the chilly night air could cause her step to falter, or dislodge the sinister grin off her lips. Pausing in the middle of the streets, she allowed several cars to zoom by before scampering to the sidewalk. The moment her foot hit the pavement, the comments and catcalls erupted from the group of dudes posted by the entrance. Rosez was unfazed by the vulgarity spewing from their mouth. After years of working in a strip club, there wasn't much she hadn't heard.

Ignoring them, she kept it pushing up the winding pathway that led to the building. She felt the heat from their stares on her back, and just to entice them, hunched up her jacket giving them a view of her fat ass. Even in a form-fitting sweatsuit, and some black

Yeezy's she was a sight for sore eyes. Chuckling at her own antics, she pulled the building door open and stepped into the dimly-lit lobby which, at two in the morning, was empty. After having visited the weed spot every day for the past week, she anticipated the elevator taking forever to arrive. Much to her delight, the doors slid open the instant she jabbed the button. Taking that as a good sign, she boarded, and pressed the number five.

As is the case with most project elevators, the interior of this one was littered with garbage, and rank with the stench of piss. Scrunching her nose at the foul odor, Rosez shook her head in disgust over the fact that it was more than likely some of the tenants violating the very appliance they used daily. It made absolutely no sense, but Rosez was too immune to such things to waste time dwelling on it. Instead, as the elevator ascended, she allowed her thoughts to gravitate to Menace.

Although she would never admit it to him, or anyone for that matter, Rosez couldn't deny to herself the notion she was in love with him. She couldn't even remember the last time she used the "L" word, reason being ever since she was little, it was always the ones who claimed to love her most that ended up hurting her the worst. Her father had profusely professed his love each night as he raped her from the age of 7 until she turned 14. And to think, his job as a cop was to serve and protect.

Her mother claimed to love her too but took the side of her husband when Rosez finally found the courage to confide in her about the abuse. On the verge of committing suicide, she ran away from home only to fall into the hands of a pimp from Soundview named Tone.

Along with schooling her to almost every aspect of the streets, Tone demonstrated his love by putting a foot in her ass whenever the occasion suited him. Two years later, at the age of sixteen, in a move psychiatrist would classify as a defining moment of her life, Rosez slit his throat one night as he sat eating dinner. The stable of four hoes he left behind would become her first Flower Girls. Even now, all these years later, despite their continued loyalty, Rosez couldn't even define what she felt for them as love.

Menace, though, had ignited something in her she'd never felt for any man. Not knowing how to efficiently express those emotions, she said slick shit in hopes he might somehow equate that with the attention and affection she sought. Unfortunately, her mouth always ended up being her worst enemy. That and her temper. The cutting incident was proof of that, and because of it, Menace no longer trusted her. He didn't come right out and say it, but Rosez had sensed him trying to figure out if their relationship was worth salvaging whenever they were in each other's presence. Tonight, she planned on proving to him it was indeed worth preserving. She was also hoping her actions would be enough to stop him from entertaining that bum bitch Isis.

Rosez had seen the two of them talking on a prior occasion, and according to Guntalk, Menace had been pursuing Isis moments before he got kidnapped. That he would lower his standards by even fraternizing with such an average looking broad offended Rosez. Then again, considering her own background, who was she to judge? During her two-year stint as one of Tone's hoes, she'd slept with hundreds of men. How would Menace look at her if he knew, Rosez wondered. She didn't even want to guess; she just wanted his love. The thought that she might be able to get that and so much more after tonight, persuaded her to smile as she withdrew chrome .380's from each of her jacket pockets. The pistols gleamed like a freshly waxed car, and after checking them to ensure there was a bullet in the chamber, she slid them back in her pockets.

Next, she inspected the NorthFace fanny pack attached to the small of her back, confirming the bulge and straps were obscured by her T-shirt. She completed the examination just as the elevator jolted to a stop, emitting a groan as if it were seconds away from malfunctioning. As soon as the hatch retracted, Rosez scurried into the hallway. Just as quickly, she turned and wedged a glass bottle between the doors to prevent the elevator from descending.

An eerie silence blanketed the hallway and for a few seconds Rosez stood in place, straining to hear anything out of the ordinary. She might've been reckless and impulsive with her mouth, but when it came to putting in work, she was cautious and vigilant. Even more so now since the majority of lights in the corridor were inoperable. The few that did work, rapidly blinked on and off like a disco ball, prompting shadows to appear then vanish in a split second. Rosez couldn't deny the unsettling feeling swarming her as she began walking. Suddenly, she jumped back as two huge rats darted out from behind the bags. One of the rodents skittered over the top of her sneakers, and just as she started to scream, she slapped a hand over her mouth, stifling the eruption. If there was one thing Rosez hated more than anything, it was rats, literally, and figuratively.

After taking a deep breath to compose herself, she continued on down the hall. Soon, she could feel the excitement mounting with each step. The sensation was similar to what a crackhead experienced right before they copped their next hit. Rosez was so amped by the time she arrived at the designated door, her pussy was moist, and her nipples were hard. Without hesitation, she pushed the square doorbell, then stepped back so she could be observed through the peephole. Seconds later, the symphony of locks disengaging echoed through the narrow hallway. The door swung open, and standing there in a wifebeater, white *Uptowns*, and a pair of skinny jeans that looked more like spandex, was the one person Rosez looked forward to violating the most. His name was Dome, and one look at his massive sized head explained the nickname. Disrespectful was the word that described everything else about him.

Ever since visiting the spot that first night and shooting down his advances, Dome had started going out of his way to be verbally abusive every time Rosez came through after that.

Tonight was no different. Spreading his arms across the threshold to block her passage, he grinned mischievously. "Let me ask you a question: what's it gonna cost to sample that mouth of yours?" He chuckled. "With those lips you got, I already know ya head game sick."

Unfazed, Rosez laughed in his face. "You can't afford me; step ya game up," she shot back. "Matter fact, with those juicy, bubble lips you got, you probably give better dome than me. That's probably how you got your name," she added as she barged past.

Dome didn't like that one bit. The door slammed shut and judging from the thud of his fast-approaching footsteps, Rosez knew there was about to be an issue. She chided herself for not remaining quiet, not out of fear, but because, she couldn't afford to entertain any senseless drama, which is exactly what Dome seemed to want. He jumped in front of her, with his face all screwed up in fury.

"What the fuck you just say to me, bitch?"

Another thing Rosez hated was to be called a bitch. She slid both hands into her pocket, as she once again allowed her mouth to instigate the situation. "Nigga, you heard what I said loud and clear...." Her words suddenly lodged in her throat as a foul smell invaded her nose. "Dude, is that your breath smelling like dog shit?" She spat, covering her nose.

"Naw, that's your rotten ass pussy," Dome replied.

Chuckling, Rosez took a step back. "The same pussy you was damn near drooling over the first time you saw me, huh?" She reminded him.

"Shorty, ain't nobody sweating you. You a basic bitch," Dome stated. "You ain't no different than any of these other broads running around with ya fake ass trying to look like Cardi B and Nicki Minaj."

Rosez turned slightly and gave her yeeks a hard slap causing them to jiggle. "Little boy, you wish my shit was fake. Now get the fuck outta my way before

I get mad!" The truth was she was already annoyed with the petty back and forth.

Dome, however, was too stupid to realize it. He actually had the nerve to grab her by the arm when she tried to walk past.

"Bitch, don't fucking walk away from me when I'm talking to you," he barked.

Rosez glanced from his hand to his face. "Imma ask you just once to take ya hands off me," she warned, her finger curling around a trigger.

"Or what?" Dome challenged getting in her grill.

Rosez turned her face. "Jamal!" She yelled. "You better come get ya peoples."

Jamal was the other worker in the spot, the one Rosez chose over Dome. She knew he was there because they'd spoken not even ten minutes earlier. Based on the intimate conversations they'd been having all week, he was expecting her for business and personal reasons.

Jamal rushed over while Dome was still talking shit, and immediately intervened. "Bruh, what the fuck is you doing? You bugging'," he said, attempting to pry his hands off Rosez.

"I knew you was gone take this bitch side," Dome said, refusing to let go.

"I'm not taking no one side," Jamal replied. "You obviously forgot where you at. We both know if Flawless hear about this, it's a wrap for you."

"Flawless!" Dome spat, scowling. "Man, fuck Flawless. That nigga can suck my dick. Y'all the ones scared of that nigga, not me."

Although his words sounded tough, Rosez noticed at the mention of Flawless, he released her arm. She stalked past him into the living room, where she spotted Schoolboy seated at a table in the corner of the room. Their eyes met at the same time Dome breezed past purposely bumping into her.

Before Rosez could respond, Jamal draped an arm around her shoulder and began leading her down the hallway towards the lone bedroom in the apartment. "Don't pay that nigga no mind, he just mad I got you and he didn't."

Rosez leaned into him grinning devilishly. "Trust me baby, he's the last thing I'm worried about."

Jamal was super thirsty, and like most men, he thought with his dick. As soon as the bedroom door closed, he pounced on Rosez, pinning her to the wall as he fondled her ass and titties, while sucking on her neck. *At least his breath didn't smell like Dome's,* Rosez thought, surveying the room over his shoulder. There wasn't much to see besides the mattress laying in the middle of the floor, a flat screen, and a stereo system sitting atop a dresser in the corner. There were no windows, but there was a closet, and Rosez suspected behind its doors lay the object of her desire. The only thing left to do now was get Jamal to confirm it.

After a few more minutes of foreplay, she suddenly shoved him backwards onto the bare mattress. Smiling seductively, she undid the draw string on her sweats. "You got condoms?"

"Hell yeah," Jamal exclaimed, scooting over to the dresser. He retrieved a sleeve of rubbers from the bottom drawer and held them up allowing them to unfurl. "Got a whole lot of condoms," he chuckled.

Rosez snatched them out his hand and pretended to study them. "You sure you can fit these?" She asked skeptically.

Jamal snorted in mock disgust. "It's only one way to find out, right?" He lunged for Rosez, but she took a step back.

"We definitely gone find out," she assured him. "First, let's take care of business, then I might let you eat this pussy." She folded her arms across her chest defiantly, and Jamal knew it would it be a waste trying to compromise.

He slapped the mattress in frustration. "Damn ma, how you gonna do me like that? Got my dick all hard..." He grabbed his tool through his jeans to illustrate his point.

Rosez sucked her teeth in annoyance. "You still talking," she snapped. "The quicker we handle business, the quicker we can get back to doing us." She pulled a folded wad of money from her pocket and tossed it in his lap. "You told me five bands for two pounds of some gas, right? Well, it's all there, count it!"

The money let Jamal know just how serious she was. Even more so after he counted it only to discover it was five-thousand dollars and not a dollar short.

Impressed, he rose to his feet. "I'm not gone lie, I thought you was bullshitting when you told me you wanted to cop some weight," he confessed. "Now I gotta show you I'm a man of my word."

"Well, show me," Rosez demanded as she watched him walk to the closet, fully expecting him to fling open the door, and reveal a safe. Instead, he opened it, and removed a plate sized digital scale.

Rosez was confused. If the goods weren't in the closet, then where, she wondered. She got the answer seconds later, when Jamal unhinged the flat screen, unveiling a safe embedded in the wall behind it. After carefully sitting the TV on the floor, he locked eyes with Rosez.

"Turn ya sexy ass around," he instructed. Giggling innocently, Rosez complied. Four beeps sounded as Jamal punched in the code, followed by a loud click. "Aight, you good," he announced.

Rosez pivoted and felt her pussy start to tingle as she stared at the contents of the safe. Bricks of neatly stacked cash on the right, and at least 10 pounds of bud to the left. Mesmerized, she walked up on Jamal, and laid a hand on his shoulder.

"Is that all your money?" She asked like she was astonished.

"Why ask why when you know?" He answered arrogantly. "Don't I got the code to the safe?"

Rosez could tell he was lying. She assumed the money belonged to the Flawless dude, whoever he was. Nonetheless, she smiled as if in awe when Jamal handed her the two pounds. He tossed the money in the safe and was about to close it when Rosez stopped him.

"Hold up, you sure this ain't no regular bud?" She asked pressing one of the pounds against her nose. "How come I don't smell shit?"

Jamal shook his head, amused. "Are you serious?"

"Hell yeah, I'm serious," Rosez snapped. "And I wanna weigh this shit too. We'll do that later though," she said as she pulled his hand off the safe and placed it on her ass. Just liked she expected, Jamal cuffed her other yeeks with his left hand.

"It's hermitically sealed, that's why you don't smell anything, and you would know that if – "

Before he could finish his sentence, Rosez dropped the pound to the floor, and kissed him. As their tongue tangoed, she massaged his dick through his jeans while guiding him towards the mattress. She pushed him on top of it and took a step back. Provocatively biting her lip, she kicked off her sneakers, then wiggled out of her bottoms.

"Come eat this pussy," she demanded, standing there in a purple thong.

Without hesitation, Jamal went to work. He might've been stupid for allowing himself to be so easily manipulated, but he certainly knew how to eat the box. It wasn't long before Rosez felt the rumblings of an orgasm brewing. Biting her lip to contain a scream, she rotated her hips as Jamal dragged his tongue up and down her clit like a squeegee.

"Eat that pussy," she ordered, mashing his face deeper into her wetness. Jamal twirled his tongue over her button faster, and Rosez threw her head back in ecstasy embracing the waves of pleasure rippling through her. Arching her back, she grabbed a handful of his hair, orgasming all over his mouth. It was one of the best nuts she'd ever experienced.

Unfortunately, the euphoric feeling quickly faded, only to be replaced by utter disgust at the sight of Jamal still lapping at her pussy like a dog. He was a weak nigga, and that was another thing Rosez hated. What type of dude ate a girl's pussy without removing her jacket anyway? A thirsty one, she concluded reaching into her pockets. Jamal suddenly glanced up with a grin on his glistening lips, probably expecting to be commended on a job well done. Instead, Rosez clocked him in his temple with the butt of the gun. Without so much as a groan, he fell sideways onto the mattress, unconscious.

With an evil smirk, Rosez stepped back to admire her work. "Sucka ass nigga," she muttered. "You really thought you was about to get some pussy, huh? Now look at you!"

Chuckling, she quickly dressed and got to work. Using several zip ties she retrieved from the NorthFace fanny pack, she bound Jamal's hands and feet, before slapping a strip of silver duct tape across his mouth. Without missing a beat, she slipped his cellphone into her pocket, then walked to the safe while pulling an additional Nike knapsack from the fanny pack. Scooping up the pounds off the floor, she threw them inside before depositing the rest of the weed from the safe. The money went in next, and Rosez couldn't resist sniffing a stack with satisfaction. She thumbed through the bundle hypnotized, and for the briefest of moments considered taking it for herself. There had to be at least $75,000 in the bag, and the one stack she held would more than make up for her cut from the Lotto robbery. As tempting as it sounded, she decided against it. She might've, indeed, been a grimey bitch, but not to the people she fucked with.

Reluctantly, she tossed the money into the knapsack then threw it on her back. The safe was now completely empty, and Rosez took a deep breath allowing the pounding of her heart to subside as she scanned the room for anything incriminating. Seeing nothing, she pulled both guns from her pocket. It was now time for some payback.

Rosez crept into the living room with one hand behind her back, and a demonic smile on her face. Much to her surprise, Schoolboy was nowhere to be found. Dome, however, sat perched on the edge of the sofa, next to a dark-skinned dude with waves, who hadn't been there when Rosez arrived. Both of them were so transfixed by the video game they were playing, they didn't even notice her until it was too late.

The stranger was the first to sense her presence, and by then, Rosez was standing directly behind him. Startled, he jumped up, dropping the Xbox controller, and before he could say one word, Rosez shot him in the leg. It was only to disable him, she had something special for Dome.

Much to his credit, Dome didn't freeze up. On the contrary, the crack of the pistol propelled him into action faster than it would a track star. Arms outstretched, he lunged from the sofa in the direction of the gun sitting on the table feet away. Rosez grabbed a handful of his T-shirt, yanking him backwards. As he struggled to free himself, she swung with all her might and crashed the butt of the gun into his head, taking the fight right out of him. He fell back on the sofa, and she smashed him in the mouth, sending bits of teeth flying down his throat.

"Call me a bitch now," she yelled, bashing him in the face over and over. For the next few minutes, she beat him until her entire hand was covered in blood. So brutal was the assault, the dark-skinned dude who she shot first was no longer screaming or writhing in pain. He was so paralyzed with fear, he must've forgotten his own injuries. It was one thing to see someone getting beaten to a pulp but watching a female do it was even more shocking. Rosez was tempted to murder both of them. Fortunately, she was in a good mood due to the success of the robbery.

Out of breath, she spit out the razor she always kept in her mouth, and slashed Dome across his face once, then twice. "Now you got something to remember me by," she muttered.

Content with the retribution she'd administered, she fled the apartment. Thanks to the bottle she lodged in the elevator door, she was able to immediately board. She poked the button for the lobby, leaving behind a bloody knuckle print, as she thought about how easy the robbery had been. Pussy was and would always be a man's greatest weakness, and Rosez planned on exploiting it until she couldn't. She couldn't wait to recount the details for Menace, and maybe – just maybe – she might tell him how she really felt about him. She was already thinking of the words that would best convey her feelings when the elevator reached the ground floor.

The doors slid back and Rosez stepped out eager to meet Crisis in the getaway car. She couldn't wait to tell him how Schoolboy left her for dead. Never in a million years did she expect to be ambushed by a dude in a ski mask, pointing a big ass revolver. Gasping in shock, Rosez took a step back. The gunmen took a step forward. Thumbing back the hammer, he snickered in amusement.

"Did you really think it would be that easy? Now drop that bag, turn around, and don't even think about reaching for that hammer in ya pocket."

*How the fuck he know I got a gun*, Rosez wondered. With no time to think about it, she shrugged off the knapsack onto the floor, and did an about face.

"Now get back in the elevator. We going back upstairs," he said, jamming the gun into her spine.

"Oh, hell no!" Rosez exclaimed, planting her feet. "You gone have to shoot me right here!"

"Well, you gone die in this dirty-ass lobby," he said through clenched teeth.

Rosez closed her eyes as she felt the barrel poke her in the back of the head. Would it hurt? Would she even feel it, she wondered, bracing herself. The answer arrived suddenly in the form of a squeaking sound followed by the roar of four gunshots.

*Boom! Boom! Boom! Boom!*

Shocked to be still standing, Rosez spun around to find Schoolboy standing halfway out the staircase door. Her eyes went from the gun in his hand to the holes in homeboy's head, and she grinned appreciatively. From the dumbfounded look on his face, this was obviously his first body. It couldn't have come at a better time, Rosez thought as she turned and grabbed the bag of money.

Schoolboy still hadn't moved. She snatched him by the wrist, pulling him out the building.

# CHAPTER 31

Menace was beyond furious. Three days after the robbery in Forest, and the anger coursing through him felt like a roller coaster as he watched Lotto's white Range Rover cruise towards him. Not only was he an hour late, but twice that day he'd scheduled a rendezvous only to cancel after Menace arrived at the location. To make matters worse, it was pouring rain and his clothes were soaked. Swiping at the downpour of water cascading down his face like a waterfall, Menace took several breaths in an effort to calm himself. Never in his life had he felt more like a sucka. Gritting his teeth, he once again vowed to groundhog Lotto the first chance he got.

He'd been on the verge of having Crisis follow from a distance the first two times Lotto summoned him, but not knowing what to expect from the old head, he vetoed the idea at the last minute. He knew it would only be matter of time before Lotto or his bodyguard, Mia, slipped up and revealed some vital tidbit that would lead to their downfall. In the meantime, as hard as it seemed, Menace knew he would just have to remain patient.

Lotto took one look at him when he hopped in and burst out laughing. Today he was decked out in brown slacks, a cream cardigan, and brown Gucci loafers. "You look like a wet dog! Where the heck is your umbrella?" He chuckled.

"It broke," Menace muttered, finding nothing funny.

Lotto wagged a finger at him. "See, that's why you gotta stop with all this petty crime shit. You need a car, only broke motherfuckas walk."

Menace could no longer hold his tongue. "Broke or not, if you would've showed up the first two times I wouldn't have needed an umbrella or a car. Obviously, you not a man of your word like you said," he spat.

Instantly Mia slid the gun from her shoulder holster and glanced back at Lotto with a questioning look.

He waved her off. "It's alright, Mia, don't pay this joker no mind. He obviously doesn't know any better. If he did, he would never insult my integrity by implying I'm anything less than an honorable individual." In the blink of an eye Lotto's expression transformed to a murderous glare. "You're right we were supposed to meet up two times prior to this but I don't trust you. I had to make sure you didn't have anybody following you. Just so you know, I would've killed you and whoever you had following." He let his words sink in. "By the way, don't think for one second I owe you an explanation. You owe me!" He barked. "Now gimme my money so I can be on my way. And to think I had something lined up for you," he muttered, shaking his head. "Seeing as how you want to give me this attitude, I've changed my mind. Let's see how long you last being a stick-up kid before somebody makes you a statistic."

Menace handed him the bag of money. "Ain't nobody gone do shit to me; my shit go off too," he spat.

Lotto chuckled as he pulled out a stack of bills. "Oh, like how it went off on Rudeboy, huh? "Didn't think I knew about that, did you," he remarked rifling through the rest of cash. Pleased with the contents, he yanked the draw strings tight, then sat the bag on the floor between his legs. "The majority of you young cats think with your emotions instead of your brains. Here you are telling me your shit go off like that really means something. How the fuck you plan on doing something to somebody you can't even see coming? Look at how easy it was for me to find you. Granted, I'm a lot more connected than most, but what happens next time you violate someone of my caliber?" He paused, waiting for a sarcastic retort. Menace, though, was still trying to figure out he knew about Rudeboy. "Exactly my point, you not gone be able to do shit," Lotto snapped. "Now if you don't mind, I'd appreciate it if you exited my vehicle. Our business is concluded. Mia pull over," he instructed. "They say ignorance is contagious and I don't want none of that shit infecting me. It's obvious he not trying to get no real money anyway."

Even though Menace was curious to know what he meant, his pride prevented him from asking. Mia eased to the curb and popped the locks.

Lotto gazed at Menace with pity. "And to think, I was really about to give you a shot."

"You can still give it to me!" Menace blurted out.

Lotto looked at him like he was crazy. "Why should I when it's clear you have no control over your mouth or yourself for that matter. Didn't anybody ever tell you lack of self-control is the number one reason why people have AIDS, are addicted to drugs, and are serving Life in either jail or the cemetery? So, tell me again, why should I fuck with you? Be honest… if you were me, would you fuck with you?"

"Honestly, if I were you, I would definitely fuck with me," he answered. "And if you do choose to fuck with me, I guarantee you won't regret it. My team is strong, I'm strong, and yeah, I got flaws but who doesn't. Whatever you find me lacking in teach me, I'm willing to learn."

"But are you willing to listen?" Lotto shot back as he put flame to the tip of a cigar. "Because if you're not, then it doesn't even make sense continuing this conversation. I didn't survive for this long in the game by being reckless, you understand what I'm saying?"

Menace nodded. "I definitely understand."

"Do you really?" Lotto inquired, staring into his eyes. "Because I'm telling you right now, ain't no more chances after this. You cross me and its lights out."

He fell silent as he gazed thoughtfully at Menace. "What you think, Mia?" He finally said. "You think he deserves a shot?"

Mia shrugged. "There's only one way to find out. I mean, he did take care of the situation in Forest."

"No, the girl with the dreads handled that," Lotto corrected.

"But at my command," Menace countered.

"You told me to get it done, and I did. That's gotta count for something." He didn't even attempt to exhaust time wondering how Lotto knew about Rosez committing the robbery.

Silence filled the air in between the swish of windshield wipers going back and forth, as Lotto studied Menace. "Give it to me, Mia," he suddenly demanded.

Without hesitation, Mia flicked the headlights on and off, then turned the radio to a specific station, before beeping the horn twice. Just as Menace was trying to figure out what she was doing, a secret compartment clicked open on the passenger side dashboard, deep enough to engulf Mia's arm when she reached inside. When her hand reemerged, she was holding a thick package wrapped in a black plastic bag. She promptly handed it back to Lotto, who laid it on the seat between him and Menace, but kept his hand on top of it.

"Once you open this bag and see what's inside, you own it, you understand? Are you willing to take that risk?" He inquired.

Too curious to do otherwise, Menace let his actions speak for him. He opened the bag and removed what felt like ten decks of cards wrapped in saran wrap.

Lotto immediately snatched the square block from him and held it in the air. "Do you know what this is?"

Menace looked at him as if to say, *are you serious?* "It's coke, right?"

"Wrong," Lotto replied. "What you're looking at is a quarter brick of the purest dope you'll probably find on the East coast, and I'm not exaggerating in the least. You could put a seven or eight on it, meaning you could make that many more quarter bricks just from this one and it would still be potent enough to have fiends coming back in droves. As long as you cut it right, this shit will sell itself."

On cue, Mia retrieved another parcel from the secret enclosure, and passed it back. "This right here is 100 grams of fentanyl," Lotto revealed, sitting the bag on the seat. "This is one of the chemicals you can use to cut the dope, and you don't need a whole lot of it either."

The jargon was unfamiliar to Menace. Heroin was as foreign to him as Chinese arithmetic. He wasn't about to tell Lotto that, though, especially since he knew just the person to school him to everything he needed to know. Rosez was a drug connoisseur, and he was positive she would know exactly what to do with 250 grams of dope, which meant only one question remained.

"How much you want back for this?" Menace asked taking possession of the work.

"Fifteen thousand," Lotto replied without hesitation. "And trust me, that's more than fair. There's a lot more where it came from too. You want the coke, I got that too. The dope is where the real money is at though."

Menace mulled over the numbers in his head, trying to figure out what type of profit he stood to gain if what Lotto said was true about making seven more quarter bricks from the one.

Eventually, he voiced his decision. "Give me two weeks!"

Lotto looked at him skeptically. "Are you sure? Because I could start you off with something smaller..."

"I'm sure," Menace said cutting him off. He deposited the dope back into the bag, cementing the transaction. "I'll have ya money in two weeks, and next time I'll pay up front. I don't like consignment."

Lotto smiled approvingly. "Neither do I," he said, offering his hand. "Let's shake on it."

Menace gripped his palm, and without even realizing it, changed the entire trajectory of his life with one decision. In the drug game there's nothing more important than a solid connect. Menace was now plugged in with one of the biggest in the country.

It actually took Menace only six days to get rid of all the heroin. The quality was as stellar as Lotto said it would be, but just so it was even more potent, Menace only cut it three times instead of seven or eight times like he suggested. What that meant was, using the fentanyl, and another chemical called *quinine*, he made three more quarter bricks from the original one, giving him a total of 1000 grams. All thanks to Rosez. Just like Menace suspected, she knew all there was to know about dope.

That very first night after receiving the work from Lotto, Rosez gave him a crash course on everything from how much fentanyl and quinine to use when cutting the dope, to the proper sized spoon needed to measure the perfect amount for each $10 bag. She also stressed the importance of always using mask and gloves when mixing the narcotic. According to her, the heroin (but more specifically the fentanyl) was so powerful, a person could get high or even die from simply inhaling the fumes or allowing it to seep through their pores. The dope could also spoil if it wasn't stored in a location with a cool temperature, she warned. Where Rosez learned so much about heroin, Menace didn't know. Nor did he care. All that mattered to him was because of her he could now attest to the hustlers' adage: there was no money like dope money.

Instead of selling weight, Menace had broken down every gram into dimes, and stamped each bag with the name, Russian Roulette. His M.B.A.M squad did the rest. As is the norm with good dope, word of the potent product seemed to spread overnight. Sales had increased daily, until before Menace knew it, all the work was gone. His profit after expenses was a little more than $80,000 – $60,000 of which he'd given to Lotto just that morning. In return, Lotto blessed him with 2 kilos of coke, and half a brick of dope. Menace was now in position to take his hustle to the next level, and he already knew exactly how to do it. For now, he was going to keep the dope for him and his team, and wholesale the cocaine to the individuals assembled before him in the living room of Rosez's apartment.

Menace surveyed their faces. Besides himself, Crisis, Rosez, and Guntalk, there were five individuals present, three of whom were from the projects neighboring Soundview. There was Two-Five from Castlehill, Wayne from Monroe, and Makevelli from Bronxdale.

Also in attendance were the twins, Rell and Rod. Two days prior, Menace had finally gotten the chance to have a sit down with them, and he know understood their agenda mirrored his. Simply put, they just wanted to eat, and be able to feed their team in the process. Menace was going to make it possible for them do both for one simple reason. By controlling the twins access to drugs, in essence, he would be controlling them. It didn't hurt either that they'd pledged to assist in killing Rudeboy, as well as participate in "Blazer Day".

Menace still didn't trust either of the brothers, and he'd already concluded killing them would be his first and only option if he got the notion they were up to no good. Hopefully it wouldn't come to that, he thought as he raised his hands to get everyone's attention.

When all eyes were on him, he commenced with his spiel. "I want to start by saying you're welcome, being that you'll all be thanking me in a minute."

Light laughter erupted, before the room went silent again.

"Seriously though," Menace continued, "I appreciate y'all coming through on such short notice, and I already know for niggas like us, time is literally money. So, let me get down to business. We all know why we're here, and I know all of you well. Not only have we done good business in the past, even more important, I respect you as men, which is the main reason I've decided to break bread with you." He gestured to the brick of coke sitting in the middle of the coffee table. "As you can see, I've managed to get my hands on something we can all get rich off, and believe me when I say, it's more where that came from. In other words, I can handle whatever you got the money to pay for."

"What the numbers look like?" Wayne asked. He was a slim light-skinned dude with freckles, known more for being a serious hustler than a gangsta. Considering the team of young wolves on his payroll, he didn't need to be super tough.

"Prices is more than fair," Menace told him. "But they're non-negotiable, which means imma take it as a sign of disrespect if at any time one of you tries to haggle with me to go lower. We all know right now, grams is going for anywhere from $35 to $40. I'm letting mine go for $30 a gram, and 25 bands for the whole pie."

"That's more than fair, that's straight love!" Wayne said. Everyone else nodded in agreement.

"And before you ask, the quality is Grade A," Menace continued. "Because of that, I'm not getting out the bed for nothing less than one-hundred grams. We not doing no chatting on the phone. Before y'all leave imma give everybody a new number. When you ready to holla, text that number, and you'll receive a time and location where to meet. If you don't get a text back, that obviously means I'm not on deck at the moment. Other than that, this shit ain't rocket science. As I said, the work is fire, but just this one time, imma give y'all a play as a sort of incentive to cop so you can see for yourself what the flavor is like. You can do one of two things: either take one-hundred grams on consignment today and give me back thirty-five hundred, or give me twenty-five hundred right now for the one-hundred. Everything after that is what I said: thirty a gram, and twenty-five bands for the whole brick. Always cash on deck."

On cue, Rosez began pulling apart pre-weighed and cut, 100-gram blocks from the brick on the table. Menace waited until she handed one apiece to Two-Five, Makevelli, and then Wayne before continuing.

"Today is Tuesday. If you decide to take the work on consignment, I'll give you until next Tuesday to get me my bread, then I'm coming to look for you." Although a good-natured smile accompanied his statement, nobody doubted he was as serious as a heart attack.

Two-Five dug in his pocket and came out with a knot of cash. "I got the twenty-five hundred right here," he announced. Standing at about 5'7", he was dark-skinned with a brush cut, and a lazy eye. Being that they'd previously done a short bid together, Menace had a more meaningful rapport with him. He smiled approvingly, as Two-Five counted out twenty-five blue faces, then laid them on the table.

Not one to be outdone, Makevelli retrieved a brick of currency from his pocket and held it up. "There go five-bands right here," he stated. His 300-lb plus frame was the only difference in his resemblance to the late, great rapper, Tupac Shakur, hence the nickname. His pockets however, were just as heavy as his stature. "You already know how I do, if it's as fire as you say, I'll be back tomorrow for the whole thing," he promised.

"Oh, it's definitely fire," Menace told him with a satisfied grin. He didn't mind doing consignment, but there was nothing better than money on the wood.

Rosez quickly collected and counted all the money, and seeing it was all there, she nodded at Two-Five, before handing Makevelli another 100-gram block. The duo departed shortly after.

Wayne also copped 100 grams, his interest, though, lay elsewhere. "What's up with that dog food?" He inquired, as Menace walked him to the door 20 minutes later. "Everybody know you eating heavy off that Russian Roulette stamp. What I gotta do to get my hands on some of that?"

Menace didn't like his tone, or the fact it felt like Wayne was subtlety trying to press him. "Did I mention anything about any dog food?" he snapped.

Wayne sighed, already seeing where it was headed. "Naw, you didn't, but..."

"So it ain't nothing to talk about," Menace interrupted.

Wayne smiled disarmingly, but his demeanor radiated anger at being brushed off. "Aight big bro, ain't no need to catch an attitude. I was just asking," he commented, offering his fist for dap.

Menace returned the gesture before letting him out the door. He made a mental note to deal with Wayne cautiously going forward. He'd seen something in his eyes he didn't like, a mix of greed and envy. Shaking his head in amusement, Menace returned to the living room to address the twins. Then again, there really wasn't much else to talk about. The particulars of their agreement had been solidified in the sit-down days earlier, and the terms were simple. For the purpose of not having to compete with each other, Menace had agreed to let the twins control the entire crack flow in "The View", while he did his thing on the dope tip. In addition, being that they were from the hood, they would be the only ones allowed to get all their work on consignment. After a few more minutes of meaningless banter, Menace gave them 200 grams to jumpstart their operation and sent them on their way, just as the rest of the MBAM squad began arriving.

Menace had summoned them so he could finally reveal some of the takeover scheme he'd disclosed to Crisis weeks earlier. Once everybody was present, he wasted no time getting down to business. In a calm tone, he explained some of the details of the new system being implemented.

There would be two workers for every 12-hour shift. One to collect the money, the other to dispense the drugs from the stairwell on the ground floor. No longer were they going to further disrespect the tenants by subjecting them to the sight of junkies congregating in the lobby. Rosez would be in charge of distributing the bundles to the workers, as well as picking up the money and dropping off more work when necessary. Frillz, who they'd just bailed out the day before, would handle security, and at 6'4" weighing a solid 280lbs, nobody was surprised. His duties would entail overseeing the rooftop lookouts and protecting the stash houses.

A stunned silence filled the room when Menace concluded his speech. There was nothing elaborate about the blueprint, however, each member understood the seriousness of what they were a part of. Not to mention all the money they stood to gain if all went as planned. Nobody doubted it would, especially Menace.

Just to make sure everybody was on the same page, he spent the next half-hour answering questions, before dismissing everyone except for Crisis. Being that it would now be his duty to manage the entire Soundview operation, Menace wanted to go over exactly what was required of him so there were no misunderstandings. They utilized another hour to discuss among other things, shift scheduling, penalties for disobeying protocol, and of course, Rudeboy. Even though they were practically running things in "The View" now, the Jamaican was never far from their thoughts. He was obviously trying to rock them to sleep, and Menace reiterated the importance of remaining vigilant. He figured it would only be a matter of time before they caught up to Rudeboy, especially now that Gigi was giving them unrestricted access to the footage from all the cameras throughout the hood. They were the only three people who knew about the arrangement, and Menace stressed the importance of keeping it that way. Satisfied they were clear on everything, both friends agreed to meet up early the next morning.

"Yeah Mo, it looks like you the one that really came up off that Lotto jux," Crisis joked as they walked to the front door.

Menace chuckled but shook his head in disagreement. "We came up," he corrected. "You might've bagged Aminah, but this is our plug, our operation. You my brother, and no amount of money can ever come between what we got. Don't ever forget that."

Crisis bounced, and Menace retreated to the bedroom where he found Rosez fresh out the shower, twisting up a blunt. It was a quarter to three in the morning, and he already knew how the night was going to end. The upcoming sexual tryst, however, was the last thing on his mind, as he stood under the shower minutes later. Rudeboy was the first, and him still being on the lam frustrated Menace more than he was willing to admit. He was now ready to swallow his pride and take Lotto up on his offer to assist in murdering Rudeboy. At the end of the day, it really didn't matter who killed him as long as it got done. He would call Lotto in the morning to put things in motion.

The conclusion brought Menace a semblance of comfort as he hopped out the shower and began inspecting himself in the mirror. As expected, everything about his physique, from his abs and chest to his thighs and calves were on point. That he took such immaculate care of his body was one of things Rosez said she loved about him. She'd been acting strange lately, as if there was something she wanted to get off her chest. Maybe she would disclose her inner musings before the night ended, Menace thought as he exited the bathroom.

He entered the bedroom to find Rosez dolled up in nothing but a red G-string and heels, twirling and twerking on the pole in the corner of her room to the sounds of a Lil Durk banga. Rosez was in love with the Chiraq rapper who was her favorite artist. As sexy as she looked dancing to his music, it was the pile of money neatly stacked on the dresser from the earlier transactions that stole his attention. Without even tallying it up to ensure it was indeed ten bands, Menace counted out $5000, walked over to Rosez, and made it rain on her. He'd already given her two pounds for herself from the Forest heist, but he felt it was only right he bless her with some cash too.

"That was to show you with my actions how much I appreciate you," he told her, after muting the music. "You my bitch for real, and once again, you've proved why you're a major asset to this family. Now we about to take off something crazy, and real talk, I couldn't have done it without you."

Receiving that type of recognition from Menace meant more to Rosez than the money he'd just given her. Blushing, she leaped into his arms, wrapping both legs around his waist. "I love you," she gushed, in between planting kisses all over his face.

"Love you more," Menace replied, cuffing her yeeks. Although he was sincere with his declaration, he didn't mean it in the profound way she did. Rosez on the other hand took his words to heart. She slid down his body real sexy like, landing on her knees in front of him, and in one motion tore the towel from his waist. Without hesitation she reintroduced her soft lips to his dick.

After a minute of nonstop sucking and gagging, she paused to look at him, while continuing to slowly stroke his dick.

"I adore you, Menace. You like a god to me, nigga, and don't ever again for one second think I don't respect ya gangsta. When I say I love you, I mean that with everything in me. I would die for you no questions asked, so you must know I'm ready to live for you, and only you," Rosez declared. "Just remember, though, that bitch ain't gone never suck ya dick like me."

"What bitch?" Menace muttered as she went back to work.

The things Rosez did with her mouth made his toes curl. Moments later, she came up for air. "You know what bitch I'm talking about, Dirty Diane's daughter. Ugly-ass bitch," she spat in disgust. She dragged her tongue ring in a circular motion around the head of his dick knowing it drove him crazy. "Play with me if you want, Menace, like this dick don't belong to me," she said in between licks and slurps.

"Shut the fuck up with all that noise," Menace said intertwining his fingers in her dreads. He grabbed a handful, and with a tug of her head, inserted his cock back into her mouth. "Always running ya mouth," he mumbled. "Concentrate on what you doing, 'cause if you bite my shit imma be mad."

He chuckled out loud at his own words, knowing Rosez would never make a mistake and bite his dick. Her head game was way too serious for that. Be that as it may, it was the image of Isis that caused him to groan with pleasure. Menace hadn't even been thinking of her until Rosez said something. And now, he couldn't stop thinking of her. No wonder he erupted so fast.

# CHAPTER 32

A meeting of a very different kind was taking place in the Forest projects, apartment 5E, that contrasted drastically from the one hosted by Menace in "The View". When this pow wow ended, someone, or maybe even several people would be dead, and all 10 individuals present knew it, including Flawless, the man running the show.

Standing at close to 7-feet tall, he was muscular with a bald head, and a midnight black complexion. Gold framed Cartier specks gave him the look of an intellectual but as the saying goes, looks can be deceiving. Flawless was, indeed, intelligent, however, everybody present knew he was also a straight psycho. The rage oozed off him like steam as he paced back and forth with a black Sig Sauer .45 dangling from his right hand. Just as terrifying was his 200-plus pound Rottweiler named Macho, freely roaming around the room. With a sharp whistle, Flawless summoned the beast to his side as he surveyed the crowd. The deranged expression on his face coerced everyone to avert their gaze when his stare fell on them, but they still felt his rage.

After spending one week in the Cayman Islands with a lady friend, Flawless returned to the city that morning to the news his spot had been robbed for close to a hundred-grand in drugs and cash. To make matters worse, his brother, Fire, had been murdered by the robbers, and left to die in the filthy lobby like a worthless dog. He'd only been in the country for about 6 months after coming from Jamaica, and now he was dead. The anguish coupled with his fury had Flawless about ready to explode. What was he supposed to tell his 80-year-old mother back in Jamaica, he wondered miserably. Shaking his head with grief, he took one last pull from the cigarette he was smoking and dropped it to the floor, thoroughly crushing it with a stomp and twist of his black leather Gucci hard bottoms.

"Somebody better start talking and soon," he barked, causing Macho to growl menacingly. "For starters, how the fuck anybody even know about this being a stash crib to begin with? Only people that supposed to know is y'all, which means, one of you niggas was bumping ya gums to the wrong motherfucka. Either that, or you helped set this shit up."

Abruptly, Flawless halted in front of a dude named Funny Mike. He was known for being the comedian out the bunch, and even though he hadn't been present during the robbery, Flawless was just looking for any reason to knock someone's head off. "Was it you?" He snarled, his finger tightening around the trigger.

Head down, Funny Mike vigorously shook his head. "I put that on my kids it wasn't me, Flaw. Some shit just ain't meant to be talked about."

"Good answer," Flawless replied. "I believe you too. You a funny little nigga, but you ain't a stupid one." His eyes suddenly slid to the brownskin cat sitting next to Funny Mike. "What about you, Fierce? You be fucking all the bitches in the hood, maybe the pussy was so good you pillow talked to the wrong chick. We've all done it before, even me. Tell me the truth and you good," he lied, trying to bait him.

Fierce was already shaking his head. "Ain't no pussy in the world good enough to give me loose lips, especially about anything concerning you. At the end of the day, ain't shit more important to me than this paper. I wouldn't jeopardize that for nothing."

"Is that right?" Flawless remarked, sarcasm dripping from his tone. "What about the time you went to go drop that package off, and you had some broad in the car after I specifically told you to go by yourself? You don't call that jeopardizing my money? If you did it once who's to say you wouldn't do it again?"

"I couldn't help that though," Fierce answered nervously. "The lady in the car was my aunt. She was pregnant, and – "

"You were taking her to the hospital, right?" Flawless finished for him. "That's what you told me, but you still went against my instructions, right or wrong?"

"Yeah, you right," Fierce muttered reluctantly.

"Of course, I'm right," Flawless barked, satisfied he'd made his point.

He went to walk off, then without warning, pivoted and shot Fierce in the face, sending him toppling from the crate he was sitting on. It happened so fast, by the time it registered what just occurred, a pool of blood was already spreading like a halo around the young boy's head. Equally disturbing, was the way Macho rushed forward, and began greedily lapping at the liquid before a swift kick to his hind parts from Flawless sent him scampering off with a yelp.

Grinning like a madman, Flawless took a moment to make eye contact with everyone, taking immense pleasure from the fear written on their faces. Soon, his vision came to rest on Vicious, the top shooter on the team.

"I ain't tell nobody shit," Vicious offered before he could be asked.

And so it went, everybody denying responsibility for the robbery. Quiet as kept, Flawless already knew the person responsible. His name was Lotto, and at one point, the man had been like a father to him. Then, in a move most would call grimey, Flawless robbed him for close to a million in drugs and cash, almost a year earlier. He then used the drugs to cement his position in Forest.

Any doubt Lotto was the one responsible for the jux disappeared with the text Flawless received from him that morning: *"Anytime, or any place I want you touched, I can snap my fingers and its done. You of all people should know that. Maybe next time, I'll end you for good instead of playing with ya paper. Hope you enjoyed your vacation in the Caymans, it just might be your last."*

Flawless knew better than to take his words for granted. What concerned him most, though, and the main reason he was so incensed was because somebody had obviously informed Lotto of his vacation. He assumed that same person had also supplied the intel needed to breach his lab. The snake had to be someone in the room, and Flawless wasn't going to stop the madness until he found out who.

"One of you motherfuckas ran your mouth," Flawless barked. "There ain't no ifs, ands, or buts about it. How else would they...." Suddenly he stopped speaking as his eyes landed on Flacco, the only Spanish dude in the crew. "It was you, wasn't it?" Flawless roared, striding towards him.

Flacco's eyes widened in terror as he jumped up and started backpedaling. "Naw Flaw, I swear to god it wasn't me..."

Before he could utter another word, Flawless rammed the gun in his mouth, breaking his two front teeth.

Flawless pushed Flacco back until his head hit the wall with a loud thud. "All your spic motherfuckas is racist. You probably been plotting on me since day one," he babbled, spittle flying from his mouth.

Flacco attempted to speak, but with a gun jammed in his mouth, only gibberish escaped. Tears slid down his face, but elicited no sympathy from Flawless, who had flashed back to some of his stints on Rikers Island in the late nineties.

Back then, the race wars between the Spanish and Black prisoners had been at its height. Any Black man confined to Rikers at the time, could more than likely attest to the oppression they'd been subjected to at the hands of two Spanish gangs called the Latin kings, and the Netas. The worst clashes took place in a sector called H.D.M., nicknamed House of Dangerous Men because it housed the most violent, and uncontrollable prisoners. This was the environment Flawless found himself thrust into at the age of 19 after being arrested for attempted murder. It was under these brutal conditions the true monster in him had been awakened. Flawless knew Flacco probably hadn't even been alive. Nevertheless, the experience had left a bad taste in his mouth when it came Spanish dudes. Let him tell it, they were all racist, and two-faced. The only reason he didn't smoke Flacco right then and there was because he just happened to be one of his best workers. Based on that, he would live to see another day.

Yanking the pistol from his mouth, Flawless relocated to the center of the room. Dome almost shit his pants when his gaze landed on him.

"So, tell me what happened again Dome," he demanded, coming to stand in front of him. He wiped the barrel containing spit and blood onto Dome's T-shirt, but Dome paid it no mind. He could always get a new shirt. The same couldn't be said for his life.

"It's like I told you," he said trying not to stutter. "Dudes just came in here and backed us down. It was like five of them, all wearing ski masks. When I reached for the grip, bitch ass nigga cut me, then started gun-butting me." As if to emphasize his point, he gingerly touched his face, a canvas of stitches, bumps, and bruises.

Suddenly Flawless trotted over to Jamal, whose head was down. Positioning the .45 under his chin, he lifted until their eyes met. "Is that what happened?" He asked. "Tell me the truth, and you have my word, you'll walk outta here alive."

It was in that moment, Jamal realized somehow Flawless knew the true story. The way he said tell me the truth, sounded more like a warning. Swallowing hard, Jamal glanced at Dome, issuing a silent apology. "Naw, that's not how it happened," he confessed, triggering a ripple of shocked gasps.

Everybody but Flawless seemed surprised. "Of course, that's not how it happened," he barked. "And to be honest, I was looking forward to slumping ya stupid ass. Oh well," he mumbled, shaking his head in disappointment, as he walked over to the TV.

He began tinkering with the DVD player, and Dome felt his heart trying to jump out of his chest. He suspected what was coming next and wondered how he could've been so stupid not to think Flawless would have a camera secretly installed somewhere. The conclusion made his mouth go dry. He glanced at Jamal, but Jamal refused to look at him, as did everyone else. They were too busy watching and listening to him spew disrespect at Flawless. Dome knew he was going to die. There was no need to even watch the recording. His eyes gravitated to the gun Flawless held, and the way it hung loosely as if his grip wasn't that tight. *Why not go out with a fight,* he reasoned. The moment the idea popped into his head, he knew he couldn't wait any longer. In an instant, his despair morphed into rage, propelling him into action.

Without warning, he lunged from the chair, and for a split second, it seemed he might be able to snatch the gun. All of a sudden, a streak of movement flashed through his peripheral right before something hard slammed into his body. Teeth sank into his face, accompanied by a blow to his temple, and the next thing Dome knew, everything went black.

When Dome regained consciousness, he found himself secured so tightly to the radiator, he could hardly breathe. Nor could he talk due to the sock stuffed in his mouth. He could feel though, and the pain reverberating through his face was unbearable. Macho, the culprit behind half his cheek missing, sat at his feet growling, blood dripping from his fangs.

"Let this be a lesson to all of you. Even when I'm not watching, I'm watching," Flawless warned, beckoning Jamal to his side. "You should really be the one about to die for letting that bitch do you like that. That motherfucka lied though," he spat, pointing to Dome. "I can't stand a liar, but there still has to be some consequences for you. You gotta take care of this busta."

He pulled another gun from his waist, and handed it to Jamal as he ushered him forward. "Don't think too hard about it, just pull the trigger," he coached. "This nigga ain't ya friend, and if the shoe was on the other foot, trust me, he wouldn't hesitate to murk you."

Jamal took a deep breath as he looked at Dome. The fright on his face crushed him. Despite what Flawless said, he did consider him a friend. They'd grown up together, and it hurt deeply that he was being forced to kill him. What choice did he have though? It was either Dome's life or his. Hand shaking, he raised the gun, gulped hard, and pulled the trigger twice. Boc! Boc!

# CHAPTER 33

There was absolutely no one in the world besides his wife, Sasha, that Serious cared for as much as his sister, Monae. The sight of her laying comatose in a hospital bed, the recipient of multiple gunshot wounds, caused him more pain than any physical ailment ever could. With tears in his eyes, he once again took inventory of the numerous devices attached to her body. There was an IV drip feeding her fluids, a ventilator helping her breathe, and an assortment of other mysterious tubes inserted into her. All of them attesting to the fact that Monae was on death's doorstep. The doctors said it was a miracle she was even alive. Serious, however, didn't believe in miracles, or luck for that matter. The Monae he knew was a fighter, and even in her damaged state, he knew she was fighting for her life.

"Keep fighting, sis," he urged, taking hold of her limp hand. "Don't let that sucka nigga win."

He was referring to Redd, and the fact that her injuries had been indirectly sustained at his hands only intensified his grief. Not only had Redd left Monae to die in the street like she was worthless, but he also then fled the city afterwards. Serious had already been by the house, and all of his belongings were gone. *Why didn't you listen to me*??? He wanted to scream. Then again, how could he even judge her for fucking with Redd? If there was anybody who understood the power of love, it was him.

His wife, Sasha, a former stripper was proof of that. Ironically, Monae had never liked her for whatever reason. Serious wondered what she'd seen in Redd to make her fall so head over heels in love with him. What was so special about him that she chose to overlook his foul nature? Sighing with anguish, he walked to the window and gazed down on the traffic below. He wasn't even going to waste time concocting up schemes of revenge for Redd. It went without saying if he ever stepped foot back in Raleigh, and Serious found out about it, he was a dead man.

In the meantime, there were more pressing matters beckoning his attention. Monae was obviously the first. The second was Jon-Jon, the orchestrator behind the hit that almost claimed her life. From the texts she'd been sending Kameesha, Serious knew both Monae and Redd had been at Keyser's house moments before the shooting. Unbeknown to them, Keyser was Jon-Jon's first cousin. For his part in the assassination attempt he'd already paid with his life. Jon-Jon on the other hand was going to be a much more formidable opponent. His resources throughout the state and abroad, combined with his financial means, meant he could lay low for a long time, while still running his drug empire. Serious already had his men raiding all of Jon-Jon's known drug dens, murdering anyone unfortunate enough to be inside. At the same time, he was preparing for a war he didn't foresee ending until either him or Jon-Jon was dead. The conclusion only caused Serious to sigh in distress as he returned to the seat by Monae's bedside. It had been his home for the past few days, and if it wasn't for Kameesha, he probably wouldn't have eaten, or even changed his clothes.

Kameesha was a godsend, but Serious already knew her character from their past history. She too had been a permanent fixture in Monae's room up until twenty minutes ago when she left to go home and shower. When she returned, only then did Serious plan on leaving for a few hours so he could connect with his team and strategize on ways to rouse Jon-Jon from hiding. Afterwards, he intended on coming straight back to the hospital.

Despite what the nurses said about his presence having no effect on Monae's recovery, Serious begged to differ. A while back he'd watched a documentary based on people who eventually awoke from comas. The majority claimed to have heard what was going on around them, although they'd been unable to respond. Further scientific research also proved in some cases, the vibratory waves generated from someone's speech aided in the body's recovery. As farfetched as it might've seemed, Serious could verify the theory from his own experience. His gunshot wounds hadn't put him in a coma, but they'd been severe enough to require several surgeries. After each one, He could vividly recall the feeling of love and good energy radiating from the abundance of friends and family crowding the room.

Now, he hoped and prayed, Monae felt his aura. Once again, he couldn't help but entertain thoughts of murdering Redd. After a while, he realized the only way to keep from being consumed by inclinations of revenge was to focus on something pleasant, like the day he laid eyes on Monae for the first time.

It was on a Monday, the Browns brought Monae home. Serious knew that for certain because he was on the track team back then, and it was as he ran home from practice (which was on Mondays) that he encountered Monae getting out of their minivan. She would make the fourth foster child under their care, and from that first day he sensed she was different. Different in the sense, that yeah, she was a normal looking 12-year-old, her solemn demeanor however, was that of an adult. Serious knew from his own hectic childhood, trauma had a way of forcing kids to grow up faster than most. He'd suspected this was the case with Monae. She barely spoke besides what was necessary during those first few months, but he would catch her intently watching him, or one of the other foster kids. Whenever he tried to engage her in conversation, she would just stare at him with a blank expression.

Eventually, he gave up trying to connect with her. He remained cordial because the Browns wouldn't have tolerated anything else. They couldn't force him to get familiar with her though. He was only 13 at the time but already his life had been molded by a series of traumatic events, starting with the death of his mother, who died of a heart attack when he was 11. He'd never known his father, and with no other family willing to take custody of him, he was thrust into the foster care system. By the time he came to stay with the Browns, he'd already been with one other family. The foster mother at that home was a Christian woman so devoted to church, one would think her incapable of the physical abuse she administered for the smallest of infractions. Things like leaving the toilet seat up or forgetting to do his chores. It was only after Serious arrived at school one day with welts crisscrossing his skin like railroad tracks, that he was removed from the home.

The Browns took him in two months later, and despite them subjecting him to unconditional love from the start, he was still finding it hard to open up by the time Monae arrived. He was anti-social anyway so for him she simply didn't exist. At least not until the day he saw her getting bullied at school by three white boys. Someone not knowing any better would've assumed she was his girl based on the way he defended her. Although the boys ended up beating his ass, and Monae's too when she jumped in, the seeds that would eventually form their bond were planted that day. It would take another year for them to fully blossom, and when they did, it happened in the most unexpected of ways.

One night, Serious was on the porch doing homework when Monae ventured outside, and without a word sat down beside him. When he glanced in her direction, she was staring off into the distance, obviously in deep thought. Unconcerned, Serious went back to work. Overall, he was a good student, but math was his worst subject. He was in the process of trying to make sense of a rather difficult equation, when out of the blue, Monae asked if he needed help. Without waiting for a reply, she then proceeded to break down the solution with such ease. Serious was a little embarrassed he hadn't figured it out himself.

Monae returned the next night, and the night after that, until he began to look forward to her company. What he liked most about Monae was she was just as comfortable with silence as he was. Nonetheless, in time their conversations took on a more personal note.

Serious was sad to discover one of things they had in common was the death of a parent. Monae's father had been killed by police in a raid on their house gone wrong. Unable to cope with the grief, her mother turned to alcohol. This in turn bred the mental and physical abuse she subjected Monae to, ultimately leading to child protective services removing her and her two sisters from the home. Serious felt, and saw her despair when she divulged the info, and it drew him to her even more. He began to see Monae as a reflection of him, in the sense that both of their lives had been transformed by a single devastating incident, then calloused by others. Even back then, Serious knew nothing would be the same between him and Monae after that night of disclosure. There was nothing sexual about their relationship, just a clear comprehension on both their parts of trauma, and tragedy. This understanding made them extremely close, and with each passing year their bond became more profound.

In high school, Monae began dating Kameesha's older brother Roy, and almost immediately, she introduced Serious to him. He would be the one to introduce Serious to the streets, and later bestow on him his nickname, due to the fact that he rarely if ever smiled. Similar to a father schooling his son, Roy taught him everything there was to know about the drug game. Monae was right there learning with him too, but she chose to stay in school while Serious dived head-first into the streets. Then, just like that, tragedy struck when Roy was found murdered.

Once again, Serious found himself cast into a familiar abyss of anguish, and pain. Not as intense as when his mother passed, but there nonetheless as a constant reminder that whoever he loved or got close to could be snatched from him in the blink of an eye. To combat the heartache, Serious vowed to never let anyone get too close to him. Eventually, he would fail to keep this oath with several individuals. Back then though his demeanor had been cold as ice. Ironically it was Jon-Jon, also a member of Roy's crew, that wound up fingering the culprits he claimed were responsible for Roy's demise. They would become the first two homicides Serious committed, and afterwards, the money began to flow, along with the blood of anybody who opposed him.

And through it all, Monae remained by his side, never folding, not even when she was arrested for conspiracy to commit murder. According to the cops, she set up her then boyfriend to get killed. The accusations were true, and the victim had been one of several on a growing list of enemies Serious was making. Thanks to Monae, he became one less opp to worry about. Serious bailed her out, and the charges would eventually get dropped due to a lack of evidence. However, the ordeal demonstrated just how official Monae was. Now because of an unofficial sucka – two to be exact – she was on the verge of losing her life.

Shaking his head in disgust, Serious angrily swiped the tears from his eyes, before walking out the room.

# CHAPTER 34

After a two-week long robbing spree, Redd was finally back in NYC. Unfortunately, his accomplice, the stripper Vanilla, was dead. Redd had picked her up after retrieving his belongings in the wake of the shooting at Keyser's house. Their subsequent travels had taken them through Virginia, Washington, and Baltimore with Vanilla finding a strip club to dance at in every location. The customers she persuaded into coming back to her motel room under a pay-to-play guise, all fell victim to Redd's penchant for armed robbery. Things were going lovely until an incident in B-More caused them to fall out.

Vanilla didn't mind fucking chicks together with Redd, the key word being *together*. When she woke up one night to find him sexing the stripper she'd brought home, she went ballistic. During the ensuing argument, she began issuing veiled threats about maybe not keeping her mouth shut if they were ever apprehended. She was angry, and her words were probably harmless. Redd, however refused to take any chances. He put a bullet in her head as she slept, then set the motel room on fire to destroy any evidence linking him to the scene.

One would never suspect him of committing such a gruesome act only hours earlier, based on the huge smile creasing his lips as he emerged from the Port Authority bus terminal in Lower Manhattan. Vanilla wasn't even a figment in his thoughts as he stood in the middle of the sidewalk taking in the sights like a tourist. The bustling crowds, and competing car horns all created a symphony of activity, in stark contrast to the sedate atmosphere of Raleigh. Even the air in NY smelled different. The aroma of hot dogs and roasting peanuts reminded Redd he hadn't eaten all day. He spotted a food truck on the corner selling Mexican food and remedied his grumbling stomach with a beef and bean burrito.

As he ate, he strolled through Times Square gathering his thoughts. Vanilla might've been far from his ruminations, but Monae remained a constant presence. Her face, the sound of her voice, the sex, and cooking all evoked memories that had been tormenting him ever since leaving N.C. Getting a full night's sleep since then had been virtually impossible. Although he'd been relatively certain Monae was dead, the guilt still ate at him like termites for not, at least, taking her to the hospital. Only moments before they'd been discussing plans for a new life, and then in the blink of an eye, disaster struck. The sight of Monae's bloody face was an image Redd would never forget. Even with his eyes open, he could still see her lifeless body. Oh, how bad he wished he could turn back time, he thought.

Draining the rest of his grape soda, Redd tossed the empty can into a trash receptacle as he entered the

Times Square subway station. Armor wearing, AR-15-toting officers affiliated with Homeland Security were everywhere, and Redd wondered if they could tell from the heft of his book bag that it was filled with guns and drugs. He chided himself for not taking a cab, but after being pulled over and arrested on a prior occasion, he'd been reluctant to risk a repeat. . He breathed a sigh of relief when he made it to the downstairs platform without being accosted. Moments later, the Five train rumbled into the station, and he boarded, placing his book bag on the empty seat beside him.

Thoughts of Monae continued to frequent his conscious, but it was Loso who he found his attention thoroughly consumed by. Now that he was back in NY, Redd knew the nigga needed to be handled asap. He was still kicking his self in the ass for not killing Loso when he had the chance, which had been his every intention when he shot him twice in the upper body area. Fortunately, for Loso, an ambulance just happened to be right around the corner. Ironically, the beef stemmed from a dice game, and on that occasion, it was Loso who refused to pay after losing, prompting Redd to clap him.

The train halted at another station, ejecting, and accepting passengers, before jetting off again, and Redd continued to contemplate the issue. Loso definitely couldn't be taken lightly. Not only was he an amateur boxer, his gun game was just as official. Redd figured it wouldn't be that hard to track him down being he was so well known in Castlehill, where they were both from. Maybe his brother Brian could assist, if not with some newly-discovered info, then with the actual murder when it came time for that. Whatever the case, Redd was looking forward to seeing Brian more than anything. Everybody else in his family including his moms and pops were vultures. Always looking for a handout, but never willing to reciprocate. Redd wasn't giving them the chance to ask for shit this time around. Instead of going home, he planned on staying with a little hood rat, at least until he put Loso to bed. Afterwards, he figured he could either return to Castle Hill, and set up shop on the weed tip, or fuck with whatever Brian had going on. Every time they spoke, he bragged about all the money he was touching, and judging from all the pics on his Instagram page of him in designer threads and heavy jewels, he wasn't lying. Redd was curious to see exactly what and who his younger brother was involved with. Either way he didn't plan on staying in NY for long. There was nothing like out-of-town money, and the instant he got word of an opportunity to bounce, he was gone.

In the meantime, his objectives were simple. First, find and finish Loso. Second, stack some more paper, and third, try to keep from putting a nigga's brains on the curb.

Frustrated with the trains slow progress, Redd got off at the next stop, and called an Uber to take him the rest of the way. During the drive, he sent Brian a text letting him know he was back in town. Next, he texted the redbone whose crib he was headed to, informing her he was in route. Her name was Sassy, and Redd had met her almost a year earlier while shopping downtown Brooklyn.

Coincidentally, Monae had been with him that day, and it was after she stepped in the dressing room to try on an outfit, that Sassy approached him. Without a word, she pushed a piece of paper with her number scribbled on it into his hand, then walked away. She was bold, and sexy – two traits Redd found irresistible. A few nights later he discovered she was also a bonafied freak. The only issue was her three bad-ass sons, ranging in age from 5 to 9. Redd wasn't trying to be their daddy, or anybody's for that matter, and it had almost been a deal breaker. The superb sex, though, had made him put off kicking Sassy to the curb. Now he was glad he hadn't.

Sassy went crazy the moment she heard his voice when he called during the bus ride into NY. Of course, he could come through! Her kids were staying with their grandparents for the summer, and if he needed a place to crash for a little while, he could stay with her, she said. Her words were music to Redd's ears, but he hadn't expected anything different. Sassy was a little thot who loved to smoke and fuck, and she knew Redd would be able, and willing to satisfy both cravings.

Redd was thinking of her crazy head game when the cab pulled up in front of her building. He stepped out into the sunshine, at 2:47pm on a Saturday, the weather was nothing short of spectacular. For a moment, he stood there at the curb taking in all the eye candy prancing about in biker shorts and daisy dukes. Eventually, his eyes came to rest on the dudes posted up in front the building, most of whom were wearing red to signify their affiliation. They were one of the main reasons Redd hated coming to Webster. Not only were the projects right up there in the top-five most dangerous housing developments in the Bronx, there was also a heavy gang presence throughout the entire neighborhood. Even with two pistols on his hip, and a bookbag filled with more, Redd still felt uneasy.

Sassy was standing amongst the goons dressed in flip flops, and a multicolored sundress. Her hair was styled into a single braid that reached the middle of her back, however, her most noticeable feature were the piercings in her lip, nose, tongue, and cheek. Of course, there were others that couldn't be seen until she was naked. Overall, Sassy wasn't a super bad bitch, but she was definitely a cutie. At the sight of Redd, she screamed with excitement as she ran towards him and leapt into his arms. She tried to kiss him, but he turned his head at the last moment causing her lips to collide with his cheek.

"Oh, it's like that," Sassy said, gently biting his earlobe.

Redd lowered her to the ground. "Come on ma, you already know I'm not with all that kissy kissy shit. What's up with your peoples though, why they staring so hard?" He inquired looking over her shoulder.

Sassy chuckled as she took his hand and began leading him towards the building. "I know you not scared with them thangs I felt on your waist," she joked. "Them niggas is harmless anyway, they just hating. You know how niggas be feeling some type of way when a dude from another hood be fucking with a chick from the hood."

Redd knew exactly what she meant, mainly because he was usually the one robbing those strangers when they came through Castle Hill. And contrary to what Sassy said, there was nothing remotely harmless about the dudes standing out front. Redd peeped the bulges on some of their waist, as well as the menacing glares they shot him as he walked inside. All it would've taken was one act of aggression, or a slick comment for the tension to ignite. Fortunately, no words were exchanged, and he made it upstairs without incident.

Sassy was all over Redd the instant they entered her three-bedroom apartment. Pushing him against the front door, she pulled both guns off his waist, laid them on the floor, then unbuckled his belt. She yanked down his jeans, then his polo briefs, dropped to her knees, and inserted his dick into her mouth.

That's how their sessions always started, with some mean head, and Sassy was a certified head monster. She spit on the dick, smacked it against her lips juicy, and swirled her tongue around the tip before injecting it back into her mouth. Redd leaned his head back on the wall, enjoying the marvelous feeling of her deep throating him, while she fondled his balls. Usually, getting his tool polished didn't make him cum. Sassy's head game was on a different level, though, and it wasn't long before he felt the all too familiar sensation of an approaching orgasm. Immediately, he jerked his hips back freeing his tool from her mouth with a plop.

"Naw, nigga, don't run!" Sassy demanded rushing forward to gobble the dick back up.

Redd, however, wanted some pussy. Seconds later, he had her bent over the sofa, digging her tight box out from the back. Her screams of delight echoed through the apartment, blending in with the sound of ass smacking against thighs.

"Yeah daddy, fuck me like that. Just like that!" Sassy moaned, throwing her ass back in a circular motion.

Without warning, Redd smacked her yeeks, causing her to squeal with glee. "You missed this dick, didn't you?" He asked as he leaned forward and twirled his tongue in her ear.

Sassy shuddered with pleasure. "I missed the fuck outta this dick! I swear I did. Oh my god, you about to make me cum," she screamed, looking back at him.

"Come all over daddies dick," Redd encouraged, hitting her with long strokes.

In one swift motion, he spun them around and sat on the arm of the couch, allowing Sassy to bounce herself into a frenzy. As she rotated her ass faster and faster, Redd repositioned his hand from around her waist to her throat. The faster she gyrated, the harder he squeezed. Tighter, and tighter until he felt her body starting to go limp. Right before she went completely unconscious, he released her.

"I'm cumming, I'm cumming," Sassy immediately yelled, as her eyes rolled back in her head.

Redd felt her juices running down his leg, in addition to the tremors rippling through her body. Now it was his turn.

He spun Sassy back around, bent her over the arm of the couch, and pulled her arms behind her. "Tell me when you about cum," she gushed as Redd put his weight on top of her and began drilling her pussy. It was so wet and tight he had to bite his lip to keep from screaming when he felt the tingling sensation working its way up his leg. He wound his hand around her ponytail and yanked her head back.

"I'm about to cum," he moaned through clenched teeth.

Sassy pushed herself backwards so that she was standing back up, then immediately fell to her knees and began mopping him off something crazy. "Cum all in my mouth! I wanna taste that nut," she said in between slurps.

It was the insanely sexy way she stared into his eyes while she sucked that sent Redd over the edge. He grabbed the back of her head, fucking her mouth as he felt his dick spitting.

"Suck all that nut out," he instructed out of breath. And being the nasty, freaky chick she was, Sassy sucked all that shit up like a vacuum. Then, she spit the nut back on his dick, slurped it back up, and swallowed it.

Drained, Redd collapsed to his knees with a smile on his face. He knew that was only round one.

# CHAPTER 35

R ound three was the one that put Redd down for the count. When he awoke, darkness blanketed the sky, and the digits on the nightstand clock glowed 8:30 on the dot. Sassy was nowhere to be found, but the sound of slippers shuffling over linoleum, combined with the mouthwatering aroma of fried fish led Redd to suspect she was in the kitchen cooking. Sassy could definitely throw down, and he was certainly looking forward to some grub after their marathon fuck session. For now, though, the food could wait.

Redd threw his leg over the side of the bed, and grabbed the half blunt out the ashtray, along with his phone. After lighting the spliff, he began scrolling through the missed calls, and text messages. There were several texts from his brother, Brian, and his last attempt at reaching out had come in the form of a call an hour earlier. The rest of the transmissions were from individuals Redd contacted in between sexing Sassy, in hopes they could provide info on Loso's whereabouts. He realized he'd been taking a risk by alerting them to the fact he was back in town, but considering all the people who didn't like Loso, it was a risk he reasoned was worth taking.

Loso was a straight grimey nigga, and the list of individuals he swindled over the years was extensive. The first two dudes just so happened to be on that list. Unfortunately, neither of them had seen Loso in months. The third dude didn't answer. The fourth had potential.

"Man, fuck that nigga, Loso. He sold me some garbage coke," the caller spat, after Redd revealed his reason for calling. His name was Concrete, but it really should've been Cotton because the nigga was softer than baby shit. Sometimes, though, soft niggas were the most dangerous being that the majority of their actions were motivated by fear. And fear was one of the greatest motivators in existence. Well aware of this fact, Redd let Concrete spew his venom, before reeling him in with an opportunity for payback.

"Tell you what, big bro," he said, when Concrete was breathing heavy with anger. "How about I *cash app* you the bread right now that Loso beat you for, and you tell me where he at."

"Redd, you can keep the bread," Concrete replied. "Real talk, it ain't even about the money, it's the principle, you feel me. I'd put some heat on that nigga myself, but son been ducking me ever since."

Redd almost laughed out loud. Loso might've been a grime ball, but he was a tough one. The type to tell you to your face you were dead, on money or whatever.

"Yeah, I already know how son be doing mad sucka shit. He did the same thing to me," Redd lied. "That's why I need you to tell me where he at so I can holla at him for the both of us."

As the last words left his mouth, Sassy walked in carrying a tray of food. Redd put a finger to his lips, motioning for her to stay quiet. Five minutes later, after some more ego stroking, he disconnected the call with the address to the new boxing gym Loso was supposedly now frequenting. According to Concrete, he had a big fight coming up in a few weeks and had been posting videos of his training sessions to his IG page. How he was back to training so soon after getting shot baffled Redd. He definitely planned on fixing that ASAP. Instead of waiting, he was heading to gym that night.

"So, you leaving already, huh?" Sassy inquired from the edge of the bed, where she sat rolling a blunt.

"Imma be back in a little while," Redd mumbled as he devoured the food. Setting his fork down, he took a swig of Pepsi, and belched loudly. "Damn ma, I'm not gone even lie, this shit is banging. Let me find out you stepped ya shit up."

Sassy cheesed hard at the compliment. "You know I had to do my thing after you did yours," she chuckled. After putting the finishing touches on the blunt, she sparked up, and took a deep pull. "So what time you coming back," she asked, exhaling.

"Why, what's up," Redd asked suspiciously. Sassy shrugged.

"Ain't nothing up, nigga. It's just a bitch ain't seen you in a while, and you just got here, and you leaving already. Nigga I want some more dick. Is that too much to ask for?"

"Same ole, Sassy," Redd chuckled, as he shoveled in the last bite of food. "Only thing on your mind is balls and blunts. Bitch, didn't you just hear me say imma be back in a little while?"

"Call me a bitch again," Sassy demanded strolling in between his legs. "The way you be saying that shit be getting my pussy wet." Blowing smoke in his face, she plugged the blunt between his lips, before setting aside the empty tray of food. As she thoroughly cleaned his hands with some damp napkins she sat on the tray, she gazed into his face with that sexy look of hers. Then she started sucking on the fingers of his right hand.

"On my kids, Redd, you the only nigga who be having my pussy on Niagara Falls," she claimed in the midst of licking. "You probably think I'm just saying that. What about now, you still think I'm fronting," she asked, dragging his hand across her slit. Her kitty was indeed wet, and it only got wetter as she used two of his fingers to stroke her clit. Back and forth. Up and down. Faster and faster, until finally she came all over his fingers. Redd licked his lips with lust, as he sat in silence, mesmerized by her degree of freakiness. And just when he thought it was over, Sassy pulled his fingers from her snatch, and sucked the cream off.

Grinning, she strolled off. "That should give you something to think about while you gone."

Redd was indeed thinking of Sassy's freak show an hour later as he sat parked in her red Dodge Charger up the block from the *HANDS R US* gym, located in the Gun Hill section of the Bronx. A glance at the nickel plated P90 Ruger in his lap made him refocus on the task at hand. The possibility of catching Loso slipping, and putting the drama to bed for good, provoked a sadistic grin to ease across his lip as he continued to watch the gym. It was positioned in the middle of the block between a Chinese store and a bodega, and at 11:13pm, there was a moderate amount of traffic going in and out of both establishments. Not to mention the handful of people loitering in the area. Redd cared about them, as much as he did Loso, and he'd already decided, if any innocent bystanders happened to get in the way, they would get the same thing he had coming. He wasn't about to let the advantage of having the element of surprise go to waste. All it took was remembering what happened to Monae, to comprehend the significance of destroying an enemy completely when the opportunity presented itself.

Redd was desperately hoping for that opportunity now.

The skittering of his cell phone on the passenger seat derailed his train of thought. A quick peek at the screen revealed it was Brian.

"Talk to me," Redd greeted, as he watched a woman enter the bodega next to the gym.

"Ahhh man, what's up with you, bruh bruh," Brian gushed with excitement. "I been trying to catch up with you ever since I got ya message earlier. Where you at? I'm trying to get up with you?"

"I'm around," Redd said vaguely. "You remember that situation I asked you to look into? Well, I'm looking into it right now – literally."

Silence ensued as Brian tried to decipher his words. When it finally registered seconds later, he laughed out loud.

"Damn bro, you be moving hella fast," he said, sounding impressed. "If you need me, I can be wherever you at with the quickness. I got the hooptie right now, what's up?"

Redd loved his energy. "Not quick enough," he said, as two dudes exited the gym. "Listen though, we definitely gonna link up tomorrow. I'll hit ya line later on, make sure you alert. You already know, I love you!"

"Love you too, bruh bruh," Brian replied.

Smiling, Redd disconnected, and tossed the phone back on the passenger seat. The hairs on his arm were at attention, but he refused to get excited just yet. The two dudes standing in front of the gym fit Loso's build, but the lack of lighting prevented Redd from clearly seeing their faces. Just in case, he turned the key in the ignition, and shifted into drive. Minutes later, another dude emerged from the gym, and Redd felt his heart begin to race with anticipation. The height and weight were about right, but the angle obscured his face. At that exact moment, the girl who entered the bodega earlier, stepped out slapping a pack of cigarettes against her palm. The clapping noise made the trio in front of the gym glance in her direction, and in the process reveal their faces.

Redd instantly noticed Loso. "Got ya ass, motherfucka," he said with delight. Loso was wearing a grey hoodie with black sweats, baby blue-colored Puma sneakers, and a book bag. He was also very alert. During the conversation with his cohorts, his head was on swivel.

Although he was parked at least half a block away, and there were tints on the windows, Redd slid down in his seat, just as his cell vibrated. The caller was

Sassy, and he decided she could wait. When he looked back up, Loso was on the move.

Redd waited until he was a block ahead before pulling away from the curb. As he cruised at a reasonable speed, he lowered the window on the passenger side. The opportunity to handle his business was about to present itself. He could feel it. Halting at a stoplight next to a black Jeep Cherokee, he impatiently drummed his fingers on the steering wheel.

Loso was still about a block away. Suddenly, as if somehow sensing danger, he stopped right there in the middle of the block in front of a 24-hour laundromat. His eyes swept the area, and he did a double take when they landed on the Charger. In a flash, he took off running.

"Fuck!" Redd roared, mashing the pedal to the floor. The Charger shot through the light almost plowing into a couple crossing the street. At the last moment, he yanked the wheel to the left, barely avoiding the collision. Now that Loso knew he was being pursued, Redd saw no reason to disguise his intentions. He drove up alongside him, aimed as best as he could (considering his own gunshot wound) and began firing. The gunfire sent people who happened to be in the vicinity, running for cover, as bullets pinged off parked cars, store fronts, and everything else except for Loso. Zigzagging as he sprinted with his head low, he was making himself a hard target to hit.

Redd didn't want to run out of bullets. Nor could he allow Loso to reach the subway station up ahead, which is where he suspected he was heading. He decided to switch tactics. Timing it perfectly, he waited until Loso was almost to the end of the block, then sped past him. Swerving around the corner, he came to a screeching halt, cutting him off. Loso immediately pivoted and tried to run in the opposite direction, but he didn't get far. Redd was too close to miss anyway. Without hesitation, he raised the Ruger, and fired. Boc! Boc! Boc! Boc!

Shots ate up Loso's back, sending him tumbling face first to the pavement. His screams of agony filled the air as Redd slammed the gear into park and hopped out. Gun outstretched, he ran towards Loso, who was struggling to turn over. A brutal kick to his midsection helped flip him onto his back and his eyes widened in horror when he saw who it was.

"No, no," he pleaded, instinctively raising his hands like a shield.

Grinning wickedly, Redd emptied the rest of the clip, transforming Loso's face into a bloody, holey mess. Satisfied Loso was indeed dead, he raced back to the Charger, and sped off.

# CHAPTER 36

Most hustlers would never in their lifetime see the insane type of dope flow like the one B.R. was witnessing. There had to be at least fifty fiends crammed into the narrow hallway of the ground floor staircase, eagerly awaiting the chance to get their hands on some "Russian Roulette".

Ever since Menace had put the dope out, the number of junkies coming through "The View" to cop had doubled every day. The only issue B.R. faced now, was whether or not he had enough product left to serve everyone present. He didn't think so, and he was a little annoyed since his shift ended in another hour. Then again, how could he even be mad after running through 8 sleeves in 11 hours?

Another group of fiends squeezed into the stairwell, and he grinned like a kid in a candy store. For the first time in his life, he was making serious money, and it felt good. There was no one else to thank but Menace. He was like a god in the eyes of B.R. and the sentiment was shared by many. Not only did he have the entire M.B.A.M squad eating heavily, he'd run Rudeboy out of Soundview. The only other person B.R. could honestly say he respected as much as he did Menace was his older brother Redd.

Once again, he checked his phone for any missed transmissions. He'd been expecting to hear from Redd all day, but for whatever reason the call had yet to come, and calls to his cell were going straight to voicemail. The only reason B.R didn't stress it was because of all the money he was making.

Retrieving four, dope-filled glassine bags from the Ziplock bag sitting in his lap, he dropped them into the outstretched hand of the junkie standing in front of him. Cheesing with glee, the man spun off, only for someone else to immediately fill his space. He handed his money to the other worker named Frillz, who counted it before revealing the number of bags to be distributed.

"Six," he announced, and B.R counted out that many, and handed them off.

The operation ran like clockwork, just like Menace had structured it to.

"Looks like we gonna need another sleeve," B.R said, peering inside the Ziplock. A sleeve, equated to ten bundles of dope, and each bundle held ten separate bags worth $10 each. B.R guessed there was no more than $300 worth of dope left.

Frillz glanced at the dwindling Ziplock, and nodded in agreement, before taking possession of a bunch of balled up bills. He scowled at the currency, then at the man who gave it to him.

"What the fuck I tell you about giving me bread like this!" Frillz barked. "Matter fact, take this shit back, and straighten it out," he ordered, throwing the money in the dude's face.

He dove to the ground to gather the money, and when he stood back up, Frillz waved him off.

"Now take ya ass to the back of the line," Frillz instructed. Muttering angrily, the man did as he was told.

Suddenly, Frillz climbed to the middle of the staircase, so he could be seen by everyone, particularly those at the back of the line. "Listen up," he barked. "I'm not going to keep telling y'all the same thing over and over again. Make sure your money ain't balled up. We don't got no time to be straightening out twenty, one-dollar bills; that's your job."

Satisfied he'd made his point, he descended, pausing next to B.R who sat on the third step from the bottom.

"So, what you wanna do, holla at Rosez for another sleeve?" We only got about..." he peeked at his watch. "Forty-five minutes left anyway, you think we'll be finished by then?"

"Definitely," B.R answered, dangling the almost empty Ziplock so he could see for himself. "I know for sure we'll be done before then, and I want all this money."

"That's a whole fact," Frillz agreed as he accepted a wad of currency from Dirty Diane. "It's only $66 fellows, can I get seven for that?" she pleaded with a hopeful grin.

Frillz flicked through the money like a bank teller, then nodded. "Give her seven," he instructed.

Ten minutes later they were out of work, and B.R hung up his cell after having just talked to Rosez. "Just be patient y'all, we'll be back on deck in a minute," Frillz announced, eliciting groans of annoyance. Nobody left though. For a bag of Russian Roulette, they would probably wait all night if need be.

All of a sudden, Frillz emptied his pockets, and handed B.R. all the money. "I'm about to run to the store for some Dutches and shit. I'll be right back," he promised.

B.R. accepted the cash as he looked at him skeptically. "You sure that's what you wanna do, bruh bruh? You already know how Menace feels about there always being two of us in the hole at all times. We only got half an hour left anyway; you mean to tell me you can't just wait? You that thirsty to smoke?"

Frillz nodded, "Hell yeah, you know I fucks with that bud hard. That shit is like my medicine. I'll be back in a minute anyway," he reiterated. Without waiting for a reply, he exited the staircase. B.R shook his head disappointed, before ordering everybody to wait outside. After the last of them departed, he dropped the money in his lap, at the same time thinking about how stupid Frillz was for leaving. Menace had caught him off post twice already, and if it happened again, B.R was willing to bet money there would be some type of physical punishment administered.

"Oh well, I tried to talk him out of it," he mumbled as he started the count. As fast as his hands allowed, he separated the different denominations, making sure to position each bill face up. It was a habit he learned from Menace years earlier, and the procedure was automatic, not to mention boring as fuck. Eventually, B.R, found his thoughts gravitating to the issue that had been overwhelming his conscious for the last few months.

Truth be told, as much as B.R loved the street life, he loved playing basketball more. The feeling of a ball leaving his fingertips, then swishing through the net, excited him in ways drug dealing couldn't. Making money felt good too, but B.R wasn't foolish enough to think the benefits outweighed the risk. If it wasn't the police he needed to be weary of, it was the jackboys, and the individuals closest to him. Then there was Rudeboy.

His currents whereabouts were unknown, and there had been no sightings of him lately. Nonetheless, only a fool would believe he was going to willingly surrender a territory generating in excess of $15,000 dollars a day. B.R was many things, but a fool wasn't one of them. He loved Menace and he didn't mind killing for him; however, he didn't want to die for or because of him. At the moment, the scales were tipped in his favor, but for how long, B.R wondered as he finished the count.

The knot totaled $937 due to shorts. Still, $937 out of $1000 was definitely good. $600 of that went to Menace, the rest to him.

B.R stuffed his cut in one pocket, and the rest of the money in his other as his thoughts continued to percolate. In his opinion, the beef between Menace and Rudeboy was stupid. They were fighting for control over drug real estate that in all actuality belonged to neither of them. The drama hadn't started over that but considering the takeover blueprint Menace had been hatching even before the Rosez incident, they would've eventually bumped heads. In the grand scheme of things what did the money, cars, clothes, and hoes really mean if in the blink of an eye it could all be snatched through an indictment or bullet? B.R. didn't find either of those endings appealing, especially since for him there were other options. Playing ball was one of them, and with each passing day the urge to follow his heart grew stronger. He knew that in order to perfect his craft, he would need to leave the streets alone. He just wished there were more people in his life to support his decision.

Earlier that day he revealed his intentions of going legit to Rosez, only to have her laugh in his face as if what he said was the silliest thing ever. B.R. viewed Rosez as a sister, but in that moment, he'd felt like she really didn't give a fuck about him. Menace, on the other hand, didn't laugh, but his response was neither inspiring nor encouraging. Crisis had been the only one to suggest he do whatever he felt was best. B.R. was desperately trying to figure out what that was before it was too late. Either fucking with M.B.A.M. – which was guaranteed money – or chasing a dream that could actually lead nowhere. Before he could ponder the issue further, the stairwell door creaked open, and in walked Menace. A grin instantly erupted onto his face at the sight of his protege.

"Love is love," he greeted, pulling a fresh sleeve of heroin from his pocket.

"Loyalty is everything," B.R. replied handing over the $600. "Damn bruh bruh, let me find out Rosez got you doing her job for her," he joked, as he took possession of the work and dumped it into the old Ziplock. He laughed a little too hard in attempt to disguise the guilt he felt for even entertaining the thought of abandoning Menace. The nigga had done more for him than his own family, and here it was they were in the midst of serious drama, and he was considering leaving just so he could play ball. What type of loyalty was that? B.R. wondered to himself.

Menace didn't seem to notice his conflicting emotions. "That bitch really starting to get on my fucking nerves with this lazy shit," he said, referring to Rosez. "It's aight, she gone learn when...."

His voice suddenly drifted as he scanned the stairwell like he couldn't see it was just the two of them. B.R. already knew what was coming.

"Where the fuck is Frillz at?" Menace barked. "Please don't tell me this dumb motherfucka left his post again."

B.R.'s silence confirmed the answer. Menace angrily clenched his teeth, causing his jaw muscles to flex.

"This nigga really think this shit is a game," he spat. "I see imma have to make an example out of this winky dink."

"Give him another shot, bruh bruh," B.R. begged. "He said he was just running to the store. He'll probably be back any minute now."

Menace silenced him with a stern glare. "What I tell you about always trying to save niggas? Frillz is a grown-ass man just like you and me, and he knows the fucking rules. What's going to happen if Rudeboy shows up? Matter fact, is you gripped or what? You better be."

B.R. lifted his shirt, exposing the butt of the Glock 20, 10mm stuffed into his waistband.

Menace nodded approvingly. "Make sure you stay on point, lil bro. Don't let this money make you forget we still at war," he warned, before bouncing.

"Damn," B.R. muttered, already feeling bad for Frillz. He knew whenever Menace caught up with him, it wouldn't be to talk. Shaking his head with pity, he cracked open the stairwell door, and summoned everyone back inside.

Soon, he was caught up in the monotonous routine of counting the money, then serving each fiend. It was a slow process, but B.R. didn't mind. Every time he looked up to the sight of more junkies crowding into the staircase, he saw dollar signs. The money had him in a trance, so much so he failed to notice the spooky silence that unexpectedly swept through the crowd. Danger was literally looming in front of him in the form of a masked gunman, and B.R. was too busy with his head down, hand in the Ziplock, to even reach for his pistol. Finally sensing something was amiss, he glanced up into the eyes of an all-too familiar face, and instantly felt an icy shiver of fear bolt up his spine. There was murder in the man's eyes, and even before he slapped the Ziplock bag out of his hand sending fiends scrambling to the floor; even before B.R. saw the gun in his hand, he knew what was coming.

# CHAPTER 37

Menace trekked out of the building with purpose in his step, and discipline on his mind. Frillz was playing a dangerous game, and it was time he be held accountable. Even more so because he'd been lying to B.R. by telling him he was going to the store, when in all reality, he was going to holla at a project smut, who had his nose wide open. Menace couldn't figure out why he was jeopardizing his safety, as well as B.R.'s, all for a broad not worth the pussy she sat on. He'd learned a long time ago not to waste time dwelling on the reasons why people did dumb shit. The only thing that mattered to him now, was showing Frillz the error of his ways. This would make his third time getting caught off post and seeing as how having his pay docked hadn't worked the first two times, Menace figured a thorough ass whopping would remedy the situation.

Menace knew where to find Frillz, because like any good boss, he kept tabs on all of his soldiers. He headed in the direction of the girl's building, stopping periodically along the way to holla at other squad members, fiends wanting credit, and a few females who were clout chasing. Menace flirted with them because he liked the attention, however, none of the chicks really interested him. They were in love with his status more than anything, and although he remained cordial, he kept the conversations brief. He was all too happy when his sister saved him from one such interaction with a hood booger named Judy.

Her name should've been Wendy Williams, with the way she gossiped about a little bit of everything going on in the hood. Not surprising, since she was the neighborhood hairdresser. Lauren didn't waste a second trying to disguise her dislike for Judy. She glanced at her with pure disgust before pulling her brother in the other direction. Menace laughed out loud. His sister was something else.

After chopping it up with her for a few minutes, he instructed her to take the money he'd just collected from B.R. to the crib. Just as he went to walk off, he spotted Isis getting out of an Uber. She was dressed casually in tight blue jeans, a "Black Girls Rock" T-shirt, and crispy black Airmax 95's. Her hair was wrapped in a scarf, and she carried a small clutch. Being that her head was down, she didn't see Menace approaching.

"I thought you said you were going to say hi," Menace reminded her when he was a few feet away.

Isis looked up at the sound of his voice, and it was immediately clear to see from her reddened eyes, she'd been crying. Still, she forced a smile onto her face, as she spoke.

"What's up, Menace, I didn't even see you."

"I see you though," Menace replied. "Why you looking so sad, is everything alright?"

Isis bit her lip, reluctant to disclose any personal info. "My grandmother is in the hospital, and it's not looking good," she eventually revealed. "The doctors are saying she could pass any day now."

Menace felt crushed like someone had just told him it was his grandmother in the hospital. He didn't even know his grandparents. Yet still, he felt for Isis. "Damn ma, I'm sorry to hear that. I can see she means a lot to you."

"She means everything," Isis said, wiping her eyes.

Menace was tempted to hug her. Instead, he decided to take a chance. "Listen Isis, I know what you said last time we spoke, but you look like you going through it right now. I'm guessing you been at the hospital all day and you probably didn't even get the chance to eat yet. How about we go catch a meal, and just chop it up. No strings attached, it's a just a meal," he added.

Isis stared into his eyes studying them for a hint of a hidden agenda. "Where did you wanna go?" she asked after a moment, satisfied with what she saw.

"How about City Island," Menace suggested, trying hard not to smile. The destination was an actual island in the Bronx, where an array of seafood restaurants was located.

Isis smiled shyly. "That's one of my favorite spots," she said, before glancing at her watch. "It's 7 o'clock now, if you promise to have me back before 11..."

"I got you," Menace agreed before she could finish. Without thinking, he draped his arm across her shoulder. Much to his surprise, Isis didn't pull away as they began walking up the block. Menace recalled what Raj said about persistence breaking down resistance and couldn't help but smile.

Unfortunately, the expression was short lived. He'd just pulled his Samsung from his back pocket with intentions of calling an Uber when suddenly a bevy of gunshots split the air. Blocka! Blocka! Blocka! Blocka!

Instinctively, Menace and Isis ducked behind a car parked at the curb. He pulled the .357 off his hip as he scanned the surroundings. Everywhere he looked, people were frozen in place or mirroring his position. Besides that, nothing suspicious jumped out at him.

Then he heard the screams.

He glanced in the direction of the gunfire, only to see a gang of people jetting from the building he just left. More shots erupted as he turned to Isis.

"Imma have to get up with you another time," he regretfully told her.

She nodded in understanding. "Be safe," she warned.

Menace took off running towards the building with thoughts of B.R. swirling through his head. He was halfway there, when the side door flew open, and a figure emerged, gun in hand. He turned slightly to survey the area, and Menace felt his heart drop. Even with a mask on, Rudeboy's physique was unmistakable. He dashed around the corner of the building, vanishing from sight. *Please don't tell me he hit B.R.,* Menace silently prayed, as he raced past the crowd already forming by the front entrance towards the side door. Yanking it open, he stepped inside.

The smell of gunpowder was heavy in the air, but it was the sight of B.R. crumpled in the corner with his head tilted at an odd angle that made his knees buckle. His bloodied face was disfigured from at least three gaping holes, including one where his left eye should've been. His right eye was open, staring at nothing.

The gruesome image would haunt Menace forever.

# CHAPTER 38

The sex could be described as nothing short of spectacular. The juiciness of the pussy, combined with how tight it was, had Flawless about ready to lose his mind as Mia rode him reverse cowgirl. The sight of her yeeks jiggling resembled a bowl of Jello, and he couldn't resist giving them a hard smack. Mia squealed loudly, loving the stinging sensation.

"Harder!" she demanded, leaning forward to grab his ankles. Flawless kneaded her yeeks like dough before delivering an even stronger whack, provoking Mia to shudder with delight. "You're going to make me cum," she said breathlessly, bouncing uncontrollably on his dick. The rest of her sentence caught in her throat when she felt the finger slip into her ass. The feeling sent her over the edge.

"Ahhhh yes, I'm cumming," she screamed throwing her head back in ecstasy. She continued riding him until Flawless flipped her onto her stomach.

"Throw that ass back," he ordered as he began relentlessly ramming her pussy with short, hard strokes. Most woman would've folded under the onslaught of pounding. Mia however wasn't the average woman. Not only was she older and more experienced, she preferred a combination of pleasure *and* pain with an emphasis on the latter. Flawless was one of the few that could deliver the duo with the level of intensity, and balance required to drive her mad, and bring her to multiple orgasms. She felt his teeth sink into her neck and groaned with contentment, as she reached between her legs and began rubbing her clit.

As Flawless felt his own nut creeping, he raised up on his forearms, drilling the kitty like he was doing pushups in it. Minutes later, him and Mia climaxed simultaneously. Breathing heavy like he'd just run a marathon, he rolled onto his back and immediately reached for the pack of Newport's on the nightstand.

"That's why you're so out of breath now," Mia chided, fanning smoke from in front of her face. "Soon, you won't be able to keep up with me. You barely can now," she chuckled.

Ignoring her, Flawless grabbed his cellphone to check for any missed communications. Now that the sex was over, he no longer had to pretend like he wasn't extremely vexed with Mia. She would soon find out why. There were several missed calls, but nothing Flawless deemed important enough to require his immediate attention. He dropped the cell atop his clothes on the floor before outing the cigarette in the ashtray. Mia went to get out of bed, and he grabbed her arm, violently yanking her back onto the mattress. Before she could say anything, he bellowed,

"Why the fuck you ain't warn me Lotto was going to hit my spot? And before you fix your pretty little mouth to say you didn't know, remember you talking to someone who was once a part of the inner circle, which means, I know he tells you everything."

With her extensive martial arts training Mia could've easily broken his wrist at any moment, but then she would've had to kill him and of what value did a dead man have? Absolutely none. So, she played her position and hung her head as if ashamed.

"I wanted to tell you, but Lotto has been acting very strange lately. Besides him, I was the only one who knew, so obviously if you found out, he would've known it was me who told you," she explained.

Flawless wasn't sure whether to believe her or not. "Lately, you've been acting strange too," he snapped. "I've been calling your phone for weeks, and you been ducking me. You mean to tell me you couldn't have somehow gotten word to me? I sent you a picture of the little dread head bitch that ran up in my spot, so you could check if any of your peoples recognized her, and you didn't even respond."

"And risk Lotto finding about it, about us?" Mia shot back. She shook her head disappointed. "You're a very smart man, Flawless, but often you allow your emotions to supersede your intelligence. I've demonstrated my loyalty to you countless times, and you still don't trust me."

Without warning, Flawless grabbed her face roughly, and turned it towards him so he could search her eyes for any hint of deception. Mia made no move to pull away.

"I've given you everything," she continued, her gaze unwavering.

"Everything but the one thing that means anything," Flawless countered. "All the money and drugs in the world don't mean shit if that old fuck is still alive."

"Just be patient," Mia pleaded. "Very soon I'm going to serve him up to you on a silver platter. I know I've been telling you that for some time, but you of all people should know killing Lotto is a lot easier said than done."

Flawless knew her words were true. Lotto wasn't just some poo putt corner hustler. He was a made man, plugged in with the cartel. Not to mention his many other alliances. Flawless still didn't give two fucks about any of that, especially since he was no longer a part of the crew. He simply wanted Lotto dead. Whatever repercussions came afterward, he would gladly deal with.

After a beat of silence he asked, "What about his peoples? Are you sure they'll deal with me once he's gone."

Mia nodded. "If we do it right, they'll deal with whoever I ask them too. I've earned their trust. Now I need you to trust me," she said caressing his face. "I need you to understand that just because I might not call you back right away, or we don't speak for a little while, what we have is still solid. I'm simply trying to put the pieces in place. When I do, there will be nothing to stop us from being together. Forever!"

Mia pushed Flawless back onto the bed, laid down beside him, and began stroking his dick as she whispered into his ear.

"Soon, we'll have more money than we know what to do with. We'll travel all around the world. Eat the best foods. There won't be anything we can't do or have. Nowhere we can't go. The world will be our playground. Do you see it?"

Flawless nodded as if in a daze. He could, indeed, see the luxurious life that awaited. Unfortunately, his reverie didn't include Mia. His plans to kill her shortly after he murdered Lotto were unchanged, and his reasoning behind the decision was simple. If Mia could betray Lotto after all he'd done for her, what would stop her from snaking him later on down the line?

As if reading his mind, Mia put her mouth on him causing the rest of his thoughts to go astray. Thirty minutes later, after another raucous fuck session, Flawless watched her scamper into the bathroom. Soon, he heard the shower come on, and by then, he was puffing on another cigarette, contemplating another dilemma.

Mia had no clue, but Flawless knew a portion of the animosity he'd directed at her stemmed from the events occurring in Forest. Not only had the robbery relieved him of a substantial amount of money and drugs, his response afterwards caused his team to begin detesting him. They feared him as well, but what good was fear if they were too scared to work for him? In addition, days after the murder of Dome and Fierce, Jamal had disappeared. He hadn't been seen since. If that wasn't enough, three of his soldiers, including Flacco, were now flat out refusing to work for him. It was Jamal, however, that Flawless found most worrisome. If he went to the cops, things could unravel quickly.

Shaking his head in frustration, he took a pull from his cigarette. Maybe Mia was right, he thought. Maybe sometimes he did allow his emotions to get the best of him. In retrospect, he now realized he'd overreacted. The robbery and subsequent murder of his younger brother had ignited such an intense, uncontrollable level of rage, he ended up violating the very individuals putting food in his mouth. Because of those actions, his empire in Forest that he'd worked so hard to build was crumbling before his eyes. Word had also reached him that several members of his team were plotting against him. How accurate the intel was, Flawless didn't know just yet. Nonetheless, he'd definitely sensed the hostility, and on a few occasions even caught some of his squad mean mugging him. The resentment and discord his violent actions had stirred up were a recipe for murder, Flawless now realized. People got killed for less every day, and to keep from becoming one of them, he knew he would have to remain extra vigilant. The conclusion didn't sit well with him, but the situation was now past the point of return.

This was one of the main reasons he was more eager than ever to kill Lotto. With an unlimited supply of narcotics, he could abandon Forest, and seek revenue streams elsewhere. The problem was he didn't trust Mia one bit. She was devious, and although she'd proven her loyalty in the past, it came at the price of crossing the man who literally saved her from a sex trafficking ring. Lotto asked for loyalty in return, and for over a decade, Mia had given it to him. Then, for a reason she still refused to disclose, she revealed the location to one of his stash houses to Flawless, then persuaded him to rob it.

On another occasion, she divulged the address to an eatery where Lotto would be hosting a luncheon for several of his close associates, so Flawless could assassinate him. Fortunately for Lotto, the restaurant where the meeting was supposed to occur, mysteriously burned down one day before the get together. Despite all of that, Flawless still didn't trust Mia. In fact, when he agreed to the current rendezvous, he'd done so with every intention of subjecting her to a thorough beating. First, for failing to alert him to the robbery plans, and second, for failing to provide any info on the dread head chick. The time had now come for him to fulfill his mission, especially since he couldn't decipher if Mia was being truthful or not.

Sliding from the bed, Flawless took one last drag, before stabbing the cancer stick out. With a wicked smile creasing his lips, he retrieved the blue steel Desert Eagle from the bedside dresser, then headed towards the bathroom. He was feet away, hand poised to grab the knob, when he heard muffled talking coming from the inside. On tiptoes, he crept a little closer, placing his ear against the door.

Even with the shower running, he could hear enough of Mia's words to keep up with her conversation. Based on how she kept interjecting the word *daddy* into her sentences, it was obvious she was talking to a man.

Flawless felt the jealousy swell up in his chest like a balloon. "Disrespectful bitch," he angrily muttered, tempted to barge in on her. Reluctantly, he decided to continue eavesdropping.

His efforts were soon rewarded when he heard Mia giggle, right before declaring, "I'll see you in a little while, daddy."

Flawless grinned deviously as the potential significance of the statement sunk in. Who was Mia going to see in a little while? *Was it another one of her fuck buddies, or was it Lotto,* he wondered. That it could possibly be the latter seemed too good to be true, Still, Flawless felt his excitement start to mount, as the shower went silent. He heard movement from inside the bathroom, and dashed back to the bed, inserting the gun back into the draw just as Mia emerged fully dressed, with a smile of her own.

"Did you miss me?" she joked, strolling to the bed.

Flawless pulled her in between his legs, possessively palming her yeeks. "Of course, I did," he replied with a sly smile. He couldn't wait to follow Mia to discover the identity of her "daddy". If it just so happened to be Lotto...

# CHAPTER 39

**W**hy *did it always seem to rain on the day of a funeral?* Menace wondered, gazing at the grey-colored sky. He was standing outside the church where the services for B.R. were being held, hoping the fresh air could diminish the intensity of his grief. Furthermore, he would much rather stand outside in the rain, than listen to some preacher who didn't even know B.R. ramble about how he was a good man, but had made some poor choices in life. It almost sounded like he was trying to justify B.R. getting killed, and to keep from spazzing on him, Menace walked out. The drizzle wasn't that bad anyway. His black Hugo Boss suit was barely even wet. Not that it would've mattered anyway. After today, he didn't plan on wearing the getup again.

He took one last pull from the blunt protectively cuffed in his hand, before plucking it into the gutter. As he watched a torrent of murky water carry it downstream, he thought about how he was going to severely miss B.R. The sentiment seemed all inclusive, evident from the 1,000-plus who'd come out to pay their final respects. The outpouring of love lifted

Menace's spirit somewhat, but also reminded him of the beautiful comrade he was never going to see again. The realization reignited his sorrow so intensely, tears instantly welled up in his eyes.

Menace made no move to stop the tears from falling. Instead, he retrieved the fifth of Hennessey from the interior pocket of his suit jacket and took a swig. The liquor burned his throat but did nothing to reduce the unrelenting pain suffocating his entire being. He took another gulp and returned the bottle to his pocket, just as a city bus rumbled to a stop directly across the street, bearing a poster on its side for Six Flags Great Adventure. The sight triggered Menace to flash back six months earlier, when he paid for two charter buses to transport close to fifty individuals from Soundview, including B.R., to the theme park.

These days, it seemed like everything he saw or heard provoked a memory of B.R. to surface. Most recently, he'd been eating at a cuchifrito restaurant in the Highbridge section of the Bronx, when the female waitress serving him asked about "his friend". She was a petite, twenty-something-year-old Dominican cutie, and it wasn't until that moment, Menace recalled the occasion when him, B.R., and a few other homies ate at the same restaurant after having visited some females in the area.

All of them had been trying to holla at the waitress, but it was B.R who she ended up giving the number to, in addition to bringing them free drinks all night. When Menace informed her of B.R.'s death, tears instantly filled her eyes. Before leaving, he gave her the address where the funeral was being held, not really expecting her to come. Amazingly, she was indeed one of the many mourners present. Menace could recall plenty of other instances, where B.R used his charm and charisma, to get them preferential treatment, in the form of free food and drinks, and entry into the V.I.P. section at a few clubs. On top of all that, he possessed a great a sense of humor, which in a brutal environment like Soundview was incalculable.

Sighing with anguish, Menace finally wiped his eyes. He couldn't remember the last time he'd cried so much or been this out control of his emotions. He felt no shame though. B.R. had been one of his closest friends, and his death hurt immensely. Even more so, whenever he thought about the fact that if he would've killed Rudeboy during the Rosez debacle, B.R. would still be alive.

The guilt continued to eat at him like termites, as he watched the traffic zoom through the nearby intersection. Now, he could only hope Lotto had some good news for him regarding Rudeboy's whereabouts. He wasn't scheduled to arrive for another half hour, and as Menace considered going back inside to wait, his sister Lauren poked her head out the front door and spotted him. Without a word, she walked over and hugged him. Menace held onto her for dear life as he silently cried. When the tears eventually subsided, he gazed into her eyes, smiling sadly.

"Thanks sis, I needed that," Menace admitted.

"We both did," Lauren said. "B.R. was like a brother to me too."

They spent another few minutes comforting each other before she breezed off to make a quick store run.

By then, Menace was composed enough to head back inside.

He arrived back in the sanctuary, relieved to see the preacher was no longer eulogizing his friend. Rosez was climbing the steps to the podium, and for once she wasn't dressed provocatively. On the contrary, she looked classy in a pair of loose-fitting black slacks, black pumps, and a cream-colored silk blouse. Her voice cracked as soon as she began speaking into the microphone.

"Ain't it crazy how you start thinking about all the stuff you wished you told somebody, after they die?"

Heads in the congregation bobbed up and down in agreement. Sniffling, Rosez dabbed at her eyes with tissue.

"I remember the last time I talked to B.R.," she muttered miserably. "We were at my place, and he was telling me how he wanted to go back to school to play ball. Anybody who's ever seen him play, knows for a fact he could've gotten a scholarship to play at any college in the country. And instead of telling him that, I laughed at him. For some reason, I just thought he was joking."

She shook her head, devastated by the recollection, before reluctantly continuing.

"I feel like a part of me died with B.R., and I keep wondering what would've happened if maybe I'd told him to follow his heart. Maybe he wouldn't have been in that building that day." Her words caught in her throat as she lowered her head, silently sobbing.

"Take your time, girl," someone in the audience chimed.

"Life is so short," Rosez went on "You have to cherish the ones you hold close. You have to love the ones that love you, and tell them you love them every chance you get," she said, staring at Menace.

Menace heard the passion in her voice, but was too consumed by his own anguish to really focus on what Rosez was saying. In all actuality, listening only intensified his grief, so he tuned out the rest of her speech.

Crisis took the stage following Rosez, and based on the expectant gazes family and friends kept directing his way, Menace knew they were anticipating him saying something next. He couldn't do it. His pain was more intense being that he'd seen B.R. in the staircase, and he knew if he started speaking, he would break down.

Crisis actually did break down seconds into his spiel. As he was being led from the stage, Menace felt his phone vibrate. A text from Lotto had just come through stating he would be arriving shortly.

Motioning for Guntalk to accompany him, he headed for the door.

Back outside, the first thing Menace noticed was the rain had ceased, and the sun was now shining. The second thing he noticed was his sister, Lauren, talking to an unfamiliar face up the block.

Immediately, Menace began walking in their direction. As he got closer, the stranger gestured for Lauren to look behind her. When she saw her brother and Guntalk approaching, she smiled nervously. Her lips parted to speak, but Menace spoke over her.

"Sis, who the fuck is this," he snapped, ice grilling dude. He was a chubby, short fellow with bleached dreads and huge ears. B.R. had big ears too, and for some reason, that's exactly who Menace thought about as he stared at the newcomer.

"Who the fuck is you?" He shot back, shifting his eyes from Menace to Guntalk, then back to Menace. To his credit, not an ounce of fear existed in them. They were actually so bloodshot, Menace assumed he was high.

"Who am I? This is who I am," he spat, reaching for his waist. Guntalk followed suit, and surprisingly so did the stranger.

"Naseem, stop!" Lauren pleaded, stepping in front of him. "This is B.R's brother, Redd," she quickly revealed.

Menace was stunned. "B.R.'s brother," he repeated skeptically.

Lauren nodded. "Yes, B.R.'s brother. Now can you please put the guns away; y'all making a scene for nothing." She gestured to the bus stop across the street where people were recording the incident with their phones.

Reluctantly, Menace slid the gun back into his waist, but left his jacket unbuttoned just in case. Redd and Guntalk did the same, and only then did Lauren step aside. Nobody spoke as Menace studied Redd. He couldn't front, the nigga did look like an older version of B.R. And now that he really thought about it, he did recall B.R. mentioning something about an older brother who was on the run. He never mentioned why, but he did say he was somewhere down South.

Menace wanted to see if Redd's story matched up. "B.R.'s brother huh? So, where you been at all this time?" he inquired.

"I just got back in town from North Carolina a few days ago," Redd confirmed. "What did you say your name was again?"

"They call me Menace."

Redd immediately began nodding in recognition. "I remember my brother telling me about you. He spoke extremely highly of you. Said he would introduce us when I got back. Then this happened," he muttered, waving in the direction of the church. "It's fucked up we have to meet under these circumstances."

Menace nodded in agreement. "That's a fact! And my fault about just now, with the hammers and all that. I'm going through a situation right now, so I guess you can say I'm a little paranoid, especially when it comes to my little sister."

"Little?" Lauren snapped with attitude. "Nigga I'm grown."

"Yeah whatever," Menace mumbled, not taking his eyes off Redd. He still couldn't believe how much he favored B.R. Before either of them could utter another word, a horn split the air. Menace already knew it was Lotto.

He extended a closed fist to Redd. "I gotta take care of something, but we definitely gone chop it up. You plan on sticking around for a little while?"

"Definitely," Redd confirmed, dapping him up. "At least until I find the nigga who did this to my brother. I got something real nice for him."

"That makes two of us," Menace remarked before stepping off with Guntalk. They spun to find a pearl white, Range Rover Sport, idling at the curb.

Menace hopped inside the Range, and nodded at Mia in the driver's seat, before offering Lotto a firm handshake. According to the old head, grown man shook hands, kids dapped fist. As usual, he was dressed to the nines in a navy-blue two-piece suit, with cream snakeskin gators, complimented by a cream fedora and matching ascot. Lotto was quite the fashionista, Menace thought chuckling. The two of them had gotten extremely close in the past few months, and truthfully, he was the closest thing to a father besides Raj.

Menace still wasn't expecting what he did next.

"I'm sorry to hear about your comrade," he said sympathetically. "You have my condolences, and this is just a little something for the family, to show my respect."

Reaching into the inner folds of his suit jacket, he removed an envelope and handed it over. "Obviously, this won't bring him back, or make up for the loss, but it's something."

Menace took the cash filled envelope, too stunned by the gesture to say anything except, "Thank you." Lotto never ceased to amaze him.

"What, you didn't think I had a heart?" he said in response to his astonished expression. "I just wish you would've allowed me to help you with Rudeboy when I first offered. Ain't no sense crying over spilt milk though. What's done is done, and I actually have some good news for you anyway. I had some of my contacts look into Rudeboy's background, and one of them found a few things that might be helpful. Unfortunately, I was rushing out of the house this morning, and forgot the file. I'll get it to you before the night is out. You have my word. Now let's get down to business because I got a flight to catch."

On cue, Mia worked her magic, and retrieved a shopping bag from the secret compartment. She handed it back to Lotto, who sat it on the seat.

"I added a little something extra being that you won't be able to reach me for the next month or so," Lotto said. "I'm going out the country to handle some very important business, and I don't want you to go dry. This should be more than enough to hold you down until I get back. I'll pick up half the money for this when I drop off that Intel tonight, copy?"

"I appreciate that," Menace said, offering his hand.

Lotto gripped it and held on. "You're turning out to be even more thorough than I expected. Keep it up, and I'm going to start plugging you in with some of my other contacts. Always remember, your network determines your net worth, and it's not what you know, but *who* you know."

Menace nodded, soaking it all up. "I just wanna say thank you again for everything. Not only for this," he said, gesturing to the drugs. "But in regards to Rudeboy, I definitely should've accepted your assistance. I just thought I would've had it handled by now."

Lotto nodded in understanding. "Don't even mention it," he said as he reached into the bag, and pulled out a book. "I'll have that info for you tonight, and hopefully it'll help. In the meantime, I want you to read this."

He handed over the book, lapsing into silence as Menace studied it.

"'The Art and Science of Respect', by James Prince," Menace read aloud. Suddenly his eyes widened with recognition. "Ain't this the dude that put Drake on?"

Lotto nodded. "That and a lot of other things people don't know about. Simply put, he's a boss, and a man of outstanding character, and if you truly want to be either of those things to the highest degree, you need to start familiarizing yourself with this type of material." He glanced at his watch. "Now, let me get going because you already got me late," he joked.

Grinning, Menace grabbed the bag, opened the door, and got out. "I'll be waiting for you to come snatch that paper, just hit me when you ready. Be safe!"

"You do the same," Lotto replied.

Menace closed the door, and the truck pulled off.

The funeral was over, and the sidewalk was now crowded. As he watched the Range cruise up the block, and halt at a red light, Maleka walked up on him.

"Who was that?" she snapped. "Matter fact, I don't even want to know. What I do wanna know is, why didn't you get up there and say something about B.R.? You think you the only one hurting. You see that didn't stop anybody else from speaking."

Menace heard his moms ranting, but his attention suddenly shifted to a black Cadillac Escalade that sped by. It was going way too fast for a residential street, which is why he couldn't take his eyes off of it. The truck pulled up alongside Lotto's Range and skidded to a halt. It didn't take a rocket scientist to figure out what was going to happen next. Menace snatched the gun off his hip, and took off running, even before he saw the barrel poke out the passenger side window of the Escalade.

In an instant, gunfire destroyed the driver's side, and back window of the Range. Somehow the Range still managed to zoom forward into traffic – right into the path of an oncoming city bus, unfortunately.

Menace was running at top speed but was still at least a half a block away. He could do nothing but watch in horror as the bus slammed into the middle of the Range, flipping it once, then again. It landed on its side, gliding into a fire hydrant, before coming to rest on the sidewalk.

The Escalade drove up, unleashing another quick burst of gunfire.

*Blocka! Blocka! Blocka! Blocka!*

It sped off and bent the next corner just as Menace made it to the intersection. Out of breath, he tucked his hammer, and approached the demolished Range Rover. Water sprouting from the decapitated hydrant caused him to slip a few times, but he finally managed to scramble up onto its side. By then, Crisis, Guntalk, and a number of other squad members were pushing through the ranks of the crowd starting to form.

"Help me pull him out!" Menace shouted to them. Crisis climbed up beside him, and after a few attempts, they pried the back door open to a gruesome sight. Mashed against the door farthest from them, lay Lotto, his entire face an unidentifiable mask of bloody flesh, mutilated by at least four gaping bullet holes. Menace knew without question no medical attention could save him. Lotto was dead.

The same couldn't be said for Mia. She groaned in pain, and a glance in her direction revealed she was being held in place by her seatbelt. Someone handed him a knife, and Menace slit the restraints, before pulling her from the wreckage with the help of Crisis and a few bystanders. They laid her on the concrete nauseated by the extent of her injuries. Shards of broken glass jutted from her face like the quills of a porcupine, and her upper body looked like it had been drenched in red paint. Combined with array of bullet holes decorating her shirt, it didn't appear likely Mia would survive either.

*TO BE CONTINUED...*

# ACKNOWLEDGMENTS

No one is deserving of more praise than you God. Thank you for giving me this gift to write. For so long I was lost, and although it took me this long to wake up, I now understand all the trials & tribulations were lessons & blessings intended to get me right here. I gotta shout out Mrs. Hamilton again because none of this would be possible without you. Literally!! Love you more than life itself.

To my beautiful mother: Its only because of your prayers that I'm still alive.

I told you one day I would make you proud. This book is just the beginning. Finally started to realize everything you used to tell me about God was real. That's when my life started to change.

To my lovely daughter Niah, aka Little ME: Love you so much. If you only knew. Not a day goes by that I'm not fighting to get to you.

Thank you, Shaun Sinclair, for the phenomenal job you did on the editing.

Kathleen, your work on the cover speaks for itself. Just another testament of your greatness. Thank you, & I look forward to what the future has in store for us.

JAH RAS... You really like my brother considering the major impact you had on my life. Love you big bro. We Back!!!

Big salute of respect & gratitude to Kindra. I told you the blueprint & you never doubted. You believed when almost everybody else didn't, then let your actions reflect. We gone be friends for life. MBAM!!!

Salute to some of the real ones behind the wall: CB...MAC11...XAVIER... INSANE (80HIGH. You a real friend).

TEK MONEY (when niggas turned they back on me, you didn't. I'm never going to forget that) ....

JIGGA (The ex-hurk. Love you for real big bro.)

SHA (Read the wall my bro.)

ZIGGY ZAH... (You saw the vision from the start.)

TRIGG (You truly understand the concept, ya network determines ya net worth. You connected me with Shef G without hesitation. Love you for that.)

MIKE MURDA (appreciate all the knowledge you dropped on me. You were one of the first to urge me to self-publish, just like you did) Check out Mike's book on Amazon... Brenda's Baby.

GANGSTA P (Miss being in ya presence. You a genuine individual. Legendary Boss Series on the way. You first up to bat. Coop City finest).

SOUTHSIDE (When everybody turned on me you didn't. Love you for that, & imma show you too)

BLAKK WALL STREET... LOVE ALL YOU NIGGAS STILL

Gotta give a big shout out to you. Yes, you, the one reading this. Thank you for taking the time out to read this book, even if you didn't purchase it. Maybe it will somehow make it into the hands of someone who will see what I did & realize they can do it too, or even something bigger & better.

Last but definitely not least, to all my fellow prisoners across the world, I leave you with this message...

REMEMBER, too, that all who succeed in life get off to a bad start & pass through many heartbreaking struggles before they "arrive". The turning point in the lives of those who succeed usually comes at the moment of some crisis through which they are introduced to their "other selves" – THINK & GROW RICH... NAPOLEON HILL

RIP STERLING... I WISH YOU WERE HERE TO WITNESS THIS BIG BRO...

# BOOK ORDER FORM

NAME ________________________________________________

ADDRESS _____________________________________________

CITY/STATE/ZIP _______________________________________

EMAIL (OPT.) _________________________________________


**Murda in My Eyes, Book 1** ($22)  QTY. _____  SUBTOTAL ________________

**Shipping** ($8 for 1–3 books; free for 4 or more)          ________________

**Total**          ________________


Checks/money orders payable to:

**Havok with the Pen Productions LLC**

Send order form and payment to:

**Havok with the Pen Productions**

**PO Box 904, Bronx, NY 10455**